Readers love AMY LANE

Running Scared

"Amy Lane has delivered a story that is both heartwarming and thrilling, with characters that linger in the reader's mind long after the final page. For fans of romantic suspense, this book is a must-read, offering a perfect balance of passion, intrigue, and emotional depth."

—Next Page Reviews

Bowling for Turkeys

"Amy Lane is my favorite storyteller. She can weave a tale that will take underdog characters through all the emotional ups and downs of life and lead those characters to be their personal best."

—Rainbow Book Reviews

Riding Shotgun

"It's a quick, fun story with lots of action and some hot sex. And a HEA that satisfies."

—Sparkling Book Reviews

By AMY LANE

An Amy Lane Christmas
Behind the Curtain
Bewitched by Bella's Brother
Bolt-hole
Bowling for Turkeys
ChrisMyths
Christmas Kitsch
Christmas with Danny Fit
Clear Water
Do-over
Food for Thought
Freckles
Gambling Men
Going Up
Hammer & Air
With Andrew Grey: Holiday Cheer
Anthology
Homebird
If I Must
Immortal
It's Not Shakespeare
Karma Kitty Christmas
Late for Christmas
Left on St. Truth-be-Well
The Locker Room
Mourning Heaven
Phonebook
Puppy, Car, and Snow
Racing for the Sun • Hiding the
Moon
Raising the Stakes
Regret Me Not

Shiny!
Shirt
Sidecar
Slow Pitch
String Boys
A Solid Core of Alpha
Swipe Left, Power Down, Look Up
Three Fates
Truth in the Dark
Turkey in the Snow
The 12 Kittens of Christmas
Under the Rushes
Weirdos
Wishing on a Blue Star Anthology

BENEATH THE STAIN
Beneath the Stain • Paint It Black

BONFIRES
Bonfires • Crocus
Sunset • Torch Songs

CANDY MAN
Candy Man • Bitter Taffy
Lollipop • Tart and Sweet

COVERT
Under Cover

Published by DREAMSPINNER PRESS
www.dreamspinnerpress.com

By Amy Lane (cont)

DREAMSPUN BEYOND
HEDGE WITCHES LONELY
HEARTS CLUB
Shortbread and Shadows
Portals and Puppy Dogs
Pentacles and Pelting Plants
Heartbeats in a Haunted House

DREAMSPUN DESIRES
THE MANNIES
The Virgin Manny
Manny Get Your Guy
Stand by Your Manny
A Fool and His Manny
SEARCH AND RESCUE
Warm Heart
Silent Heart
Safe Heart
Hidden Heart

FAMILIAR LOVE
Familiar Angel • Familiar Demon

FISH OUT OF WATER
Fish Out of Water
Red Fish, Dead Fish
A Few Good Fish
Hiding the Moon
Fish on a Bicycle • School of Fish
Fish in a Barrel • A Perfectly
Sonny Daye • Only Fish
Devil and the Deep Blue Fish

FLOPHOUSE
Shades of Henry
Constantly Cotton
Sean's Sunshine

GRANBY KNITTING
The Winter Courtship Rituals of
Fur-Bearing Critters
How to Raise an Honest Rabbit
Knitter in His Natural Habitat
Blackbird Knitting in a Bunny's Lair
Weddings, Christmas, and Such

JOHNNIES
Chase in Shadow • Dex in Blue
Ethan in Gold • Black John
Bobby Green • Super Sock Man

KEEPING PROMISE ROCK
Keeping Promise Rock
Making Promises
Living Promises • Forever Promised

LONG CON ADVENTURES
The Mastermind • The Muscle
The Driver • The Suit
The Tech • The Face Man

LUCK MECHANICS
The Rising Tide • A Salt Bitter Sea

PRINCETON ROYALS
Riding Shotgun • Running Scared

Published by DREAMSPINNER PRESS
www.dreamspinnerpress.com

Karma Kitty Christmas

Amy Lane

Published by
DREAMSPINNER PRESS

8219 Woodville Hwy #1245
Woodville, FL 32362 USA
www.dreamspinnerpress.com

Karma Kitty Christmas
© 2025 Amy Lane

Cover Art
© 2025 L.C. Chase
http://www.lcchase.com
Cover content is for illustrative purposes only and any person depicted on the cover is a model.

Trade Paperback ISBN: 9781641088787
Digital ISBN: 9781641088770
Digital eBook published November 2025
v. 1.0

To Mate, still and always. To Mary, because of course. To the kids and dogs, yup yup yup. And to Steve the cat, who while not an orange boi, is as cat as cat can cat.

Author's Note

THIS IS pure sugary goodness. Enjoy it like shortbread, my friends.

Knitting on the Porch in May

Isaac scowled with dissatisfaction at the six giant bins full of yarn. Fingering weight, bulky, wool, wool/acrylic, acrylic—he even had some gloriously colored gradients in (unfortunately) cotton. And don't forget the sumptuous alpaca skeins that he reserved for the depths of winter. Or the winter blues—it was good for both. Basic solids in pastels and primaries, exotic colorways—enough for an entire sweater for somebody *really* generously sized. Even blankets' worth of acrylic in all the rainbows.

Not to mention all the whimsical balls of scraps from the hats he'd made for students over the years. Bouncing around in their own box, the scrap balls beckoned, although Isaac had yet to think of the perfect project, so he kept making more hats in fantastic color combinations and keeping the extras.

He *yearned* to start a new project.

God, Isaac—can't you finish one lousy thing!

Isaac bristled at the sound of his late husband's voice in his head. *Oh Jesus, Todd—it's been almost two years. Can't you leave me the fuck alone?*

The venom in his own internal monologue startled him. Isaac couldn't remember ever being that angry at Todd in their lives together.

Or at least never *voicing* how angry he was at Todd in their lives together.

He shuddered at the intrusiveness of that thought. It had been popping into his head more and more over the last year and a half.

He's dead. He can't possibly care now whether or not you were happy.

Oh, but Isaac hadn't been. He tried to squelch that thought—it was *wrong* to speak ill of his dead husband, *wrong* to hold on to the pain, the… the *crushing loneliness* of the previous ten years, and use it to resent a dead man that the rest of the world seemed to revere.

So wrong. He needed an act of penance, stat. He needed to eat a bland meal (when he preferred spicy) or to ship his old, comfortable clothes to charity (when he liked to wear them around the house) or to (no!) return the quiet reserve of cargo pants and funny T-shirts he'd been buying over the last year to wear to school because the *other* teachers his age wore them, and one day—*one* day—he'd wear them too.

He couldn't bear it. He couldn't. But… but he'd been thinking about splurging on some new yarn. He'd added to his stash over the past year, but not too much. Two of the bins here, the ones with the wildest colors. He'd been able to justify it because he had more scraps—and more time to knit—since Todd had passed, and he'd managed to make a hat or hand warmers for every kid in his honors algebra class this year—and some for the kids in pre-algebra who had taken it more than once and finally passed. Usually those kids walked in with the barest of math skills, but the state didn't really fund remedial classes these days, so pre-algebra it was. Isaac felt for the sophomore, junior, or sometimes *senior* students who started out not knowing their times tables but were finally able to say they'd passed pre-algebra. On the one hand, it felt like a meager accomplishment—it certainly didn't look good on paper. But on the *other* hand, it was an *amazing* accomplishment, because they'd had to work the hardest, and he was proud of them.

But Todd had reluctantly approved of Isaac spending his yarn and his time on rewards for the smart kids. He'd been *so* disapproving of Isaac's desire to reward the underachievers for perseverance that Isaac had needed to squirrel money away to so much as give them "Congratulations" cards in the past.

This year Isaac had worked his ass off getting those hats and hand warmers done on time—he'd even had enough time and yarn for a scarf for the freshman in pre-algebra who'd gotten the highest grade. So he had *plans* for his yarn, including a sweater—a bright rainbow-hued sweater he wanted to knit or crochet for himself! One that would replace the plain blue one he'd made ten years ago and the boring cream-colored one with a few cables (More would look junky and ostentatious, Isaac. Tone it down!) that he'd finished five years ago, after Todd had threatened to withhold his yarn budget if Isaac didn't finish it.

And sweater vests. *So* many sweater vests, with adorable patterns on them. Isaac had made one—but oh the plans he had for many!

"If you'd wanted money for crap to buy your students, you should have completed those projects first! Jesus, Isaac, do I have to plan your life for you?"

"No," thought Isaac, "but fuck me if you're not micromanaging the breath out of me!"

He recoiled from another crappy memory, as well as from the cringey thought that he might have had more of his own life under his belt by now if he'd actually *said* some of those angry things in his head, behind his eyes, instead of merely thought them and swallowed them.

He might even have kept more of his hair from his faintly receding widow's peak.

It was that last bitter thought—as well as Todd's incessant hammering that Isaac needed to finish what he started before he began something else—that drove him to it.

He ignored the rainbow cardigan he'd been planning to crochet for himself, or the bin of scraps that he wanted to use for Fair Isle so he could make the "hats with the pictures" that his students so loved, and reached instead for the plain cotton tote full of brown yarn.

He'd been planning to knit a basic top-down crew-neck sweater. Yup, German neckline, which Todd hadn't appreciated but Isaac had known he'd take for granted as a feature of a "real" sweater—raglan sleeves, a subtle band of texture across the chest, and the same German hem at the bottom. Yup. That was it.

Brown.

It's a quality yarn. Alpaca and wool, with some acrylic to keep it from pilling. With some brushing and some cedar chips, this will be practical and last forever and ever and ever and ever.

Just like this bad relationship that I can't seem to shake even though you're dead.

With a sigh, he grabbed the project bag, made sure his little pouch of tools—extra circular needles, yarn needles, double-pointed needles, measuring tape, ruler, scissors, stitch markers, etc.—was in the bag as well, and stood.

It had been warm this early May day, but under the awning of his porch, with the two fans creating a breeze, his porch swing would still be cool. He could sit outside, listen to his favorite audiobook, and watch the neighborhood kids play. The family across the street had a *huge* front yard, and fierce competitions of everything from soccer to stickball to red rover often ensued after dinner. And of course there was always Luca.

Isaac swallowed and tried to tamp down on his thoughts of Luca Giordano, the grandson of Sophia and Geordie, who was currently fixing up their house to sell so they could live off the proceeds in retirement. Todd had been right about this neighborhood only appreciating as they'd lived there—residential properties with big yards and unique two-story floor plans, as well as wide sidewalks and roads, were becoming a luxury in the day and age of tiny prefabs. Sophia and Geordie could spend a good twenty years in their retirement villa after this house was flipped, and their grandson and his construction crew were doing the place up right.

And Luca was a nice guy. A nice-*looking* guy. A midsized guy with broad shoulders, blond-streaked wavy brown hair, bronzed skin, a dazzling white smile under a bold, unapologetic nose, and inky black eyes.

He's a polite young man, Isaac told himself, but that line sounded so much like Todd that Isaac was compelled to emotional honesty. *Who's at least thirty and runs his own business and looks stunning without his shirt when his jeans are hanging around his hips.*

Oh God. Isaac was going outside to knit on the porch and ogle his neighbor's grandson. He was going to hell.

Well, maybe Todd's self-righteous ass will end up in a cold, sterile heaven, and I'll be spared that at least.

That thought almost did it—almost derailed a ten-year habit of knitting on the front porch in blissful solitude, free to listen to whatever he wanted, doing a thing he loved and refused to give up, watching a happy world go by during the prettiest moments of the seasons.

Because the fact was, he'd rather go watch the neighbor's unfairly attractive grandson, covered in paint and drywall dust and carpet fibers, finish a laborer's menial job (as Todd would have referred to it) than spend the afterlife with his supposedly beloved husband, and damn if that wasn't a big truth to swallow.

In fact, it was *such* a big truth to swallow that Isaac couldn't. In the end that's what drove him to the porch, to his place of peace, with his hated brown sweater and the audiobook he'd *really* been looking forward to. He just really needed to escape his own head right now, and he couldn't afford to turn down any avenue to help him do that.

Magic Hour

Luca hated to admit it to himself, but he was anticipating Magic Hour more than usual today.

It had started when the job he and his guys had shown up for that morning had been cancelled, because the price of their materials had gone up so much that their client hadn't been able to afford the project. It had only been a mother-in-law cottage—he and his boys could have done it in a week or two—but the average Joe only had so big a cushion, and in this case, Joe decided mom-in-law could continue to live in the guest room.

Luca had met the old bat, and he had his doubts—and from one glance at Mrs. Average Joe's face as her husband had given them the news, he thought she did too. Since it was *her* mother-in-law, she should know. But hey, he was neither marriage counselor nor old-bat remover, and he and his guys were just trying to get by.

He'd let the guys go home and had driven to his trailer on the tiny warehouse lot—the "location" of his business, where he kept materials for upcoming jobs as well as the trailer office—to see if he and his office assistant (also known as his little sister, Allegra) could juggle up another job for that week.

They managed to move their next job up a week—but only a week—and he had to tell the guys he had no work for them until next Monday.

So that had sucked.

And then as he and Allegra had been settling gloomily into their lunch—a big triple portion of Chinese dumplings to share—Allegra had confessed tearfully that her shitty boyfriend had broken up with her and asked her to move her stuff in the next two days or he'd dump it on the lawn.

Because she was pregnant.

She was pregnant, alone, and wholly dependent on the income Luca was trying to provide with the company that was getting more and more frayed shoestring by the day.

Aces.

But Allegra had been scared, and their parents weren't speaking to *either* of them (judgy assholes), and he'd been all she had. So what had started as a quiet lunch where Luca could get his head on straight had turned into an angst fest during which he had to hold his sobbing sister and help her pull on her big-girl pants so they could get through the next couple of weeks of figuring out what to do.

Of course the obvious solution—temporary—was to move her into the spare room of Luca's apartment, but Luca knew that wouldn't last. Even without the baby, Allegra liked to spread out, and Luca needed *somewhere*—a yard, a den, a study, somewhere—to himself in his own home.

His last boyfriend had called him "withholding." Luca had called himself "recovering from a childhood with parents who wouldn't let me poop without checking to make sure I wasn't doing something the Bible says I shouldn't."

His last boyfriend hadn't thought that was funny, and Luca had, and that's why his last boyfriend was his last boyfriend.

So by the time Luca got to his grandparents' place to see what new horrors awaited (he'd had to replace the subflooring and drywall in both bathrooms *and* the adjoining bedrooms, and don't even get him started on the dry rot in the kitchen), he'd *really* been looking forward to Magic Hour.

His grandparents' neighbor, Mr. Browning, was a quiet man—but cute. So cute. He'd probably been quite a twinkie delight in his twenties, but now, at not yet forty, he was quietly pretty, with pale brown hair and kind eyes with the crinkles at the corners that said he smiled more than he frowned. Luca knew (because his grandmother was a terrible gossip) that the man had lost his husband not too long before they moved to the villa, so Luca had been trying to respect the man's grief, but oh, that didn't stop him from enjoying Magic Hour.

Every evening, weather permitting, Mr. Browning would come out and sit on his front porch and knit or crochet. He had a heater for cold days and a light for the fall and winter days when it was dark by six o'clock, and he would simply sit quietly, listening to something on his EarPods, and create… magic.

Luca knew knitting and crocheting because his grandmother still did it. Hell, he'd been the one who'd been responsible for moving half her yarn to storage, with the promise that he'd take her "yarn shopping" from her stores once a month. His parents had told his grandmother to throw it away, and Luca could forgive them for cutting *him* off for being gay, but he would never forgive them for the tears of hurt and devastation in his grandmother's eyes when she told him, "Bianca says I have to throw it away. Your father agrees with her, and now…."

Luca could have cheerfully killed them both.

He didn't do either craft, but when he was a kid, he used to ask his grandmother, in wonder, what she was going to do with all the pretty yarn.

"Anything, Luca," she'd reply with pride. "This yarn can be anything in the world."

Allegra puckishly referred to the yarn stash as "Schrödinger's Hats," because until you opened the box, anything was possible.

Luca knew that nice Mr. Browning and his grandmother used to plan projects all the time. Sometimes she'd buy yarn *for* him, because she said his husband had put him on a "yarn diet" (which sort of sounded like an asshole move to Luca, but hey, wasn't his relationship, right?), but they'd trade patterns and all the neighborly things that most people probably associated with cooking. As far as Luca knew, they'd traded recipes too, but what he really loved was how much his grandmother enjoyed having somebody to talk about yarn with.

He knew Mr. Browning still visited his grandmother, which made him like the man even more, and his grandma told him that they used to "yarn" on the porch together sometimes, but Luca had never seen that. What he'd seen in the last six months as he'd been working on the house to get it ready to sell had been Mr. Browning himself, a soft-handed miracle, a quiet, self-contained rainbow maker using deft movements and brightly colored fiber to make useful, beautiful things—mostly for other people—and infusing the world with a sort of silent happiness by the act of creation.

Luca really needed that quiet happiness this evening.

But the minute Mr. Browning sat down, Luca knew there was something wrong.

The man was chilling in the shade on his white-cushioned porch swing in a pair of Dockers and a button-down that looked oddly formal for a man in his late thirties. He often dressed like that, Luca knew, because those were his teaching clothes, but the effect was still… old. Stuffy. Stodgy. Which didn't match what his grandmother said about the man at all.

But it wasn't his clothes that struck Luca wrong. It was the project in his lap.

For one thing, it wasn't… bright. Luca was used to seeing him work with bright colors—solids or variegated miracles, woolly rainbows—and loving them. Stopping often to appreciate their effect against each other and smile.

But this project was… well, brown.

Not that Luca objected to brown—some people looked quite fetching in it. But this guy—that bright yarn stash seemed to be where all his excitement lay, and now it had been dampened to… well, brown. Plain brown.

It didn't sit well with Luca, although it wasn't his place to say anything. God forbid he try to change the man's yarn choice, right?

But the sixth time he watched Mr. Browning glance down at the project in his hands and then crumple his face like he was about to cry, something in Luca broke.

"Heya, Mr. Browning—can I help you with something?"

The man glanced up in surprise, swiveling his head wildly like he'd gotten caught picking his nose or something. His gaze landed on Luca, and he stopped abruptly and chuckled to himself, taking an earbud out as he did so.

"Oh my goodness, Luca. You *startled* me." He gave a quick brilliant grin. "I thought I was at school for a minute. You don't need to call me Mr. Browning, you know—my name is Isaac."

Oh wow. This was like winning the lottery or something.

Luca grinned. "Really? See, my grandma, she only talks about 'Mr. Browning'—I don't think she ever mentioned your first name!"

Isaac's laughter was really a balm to the soul. "See, *that's* weird. Grandparents are a gray area, right? First name, or is that too formal, or do you just call them 'Grandma' and 'Grandpa' because that's how the people *your* age know them?" He shook his head. "I'm sorry. I'm rambling. Anyway, yes, you can call me Isaac, but if you don't mind, I'll keep calling your grandmother Mrs. Giordano, or things will get weird."

Luca chuckled with him. "Yeah, I can definitely see that. Okay, so, uhm, Isaac." He sobered. "What seems to be the problem? I… I gotta admit, I've watched you come out here and yarn for a lot of days, and I've never seen you so unhappy."

Luca had just finished hauling most of the kitchen cabinets out of the house and loading as many as he could fit into his truck. He'd be back the next day with one of his guys, working for bennies and not much else, to load the rest and then to bring back the flooring in one of the company vans. But right now he was pretty much done for the night. With a quiet sigh, he moved toward the four-foot plank fence and leaned against it, taking in Isaac's tidy if boring yard, and the white-painted farm-style house, two stories, with at least two master suites and probably two more smaller rooms, as well as a downstairs guest bathroom. It was far too big for two men—he'd always thought that—but now, with only Mr., uhm, Isaac living there, it seemed *way* too large.

And Isaac, sitting cross-legged in his school clothes while staring glumly at the pile of *brown* in his hands, seemed even less substantial than he had all winter.

As though Isaac could see that himself, he glanced at the yarn, on what Luca's grandmother called a circular needle, and then set it down and sighed.

"I really don't want to finish this sweater," he admitted baldly.

Luca peered at the little bit of round knitting on the needle. "It doesn't hardly look like you started it," he said, hoping he hadn't cursed the man in his native tongue or something.

Isaac assessed the project again and nodded unhappily. "I know, right? I...." He grimaced. "I started it for Todd originally. And it was just *glaring* at me, nagging me, in Todd's voice. 'You cannot possibly afford more yarn, Isaac, if you don't finish the project you started!'" He grunted. "Bastard."

Luca stared at him. "Really?"

To his amazement, a low flush came up on Isaac's cheeks. "I'm sorry," he mumbled, starting to stand up. "I-I should go inside. That was terrible of me—I shouldn't say things like that."

Luca was suddenly *starving* for his company. "Why not? Do you feel them?"

Isaac nodded and then seemed appalled. "I shouldn't!" He clapped his hand over his mouth. "I shouldn't say anything bad," he muttered, almost to himself. "I should be grateful for everything he did for me, take the house, take the inheritance, and just shut my mouth and—"

"And knit ugly sweaters? No offense, Isaac, but that's like taking lemons and making liquid bullshit with them. My God, if you've got the house and the money, shouldn't you be able to knit whatever the hell you want?"

Isaac stared at him, his enormous hazel eyes stunned. And for a moment, it was as though two people were at war inside this one unassuming man—Luca could almost *see* them vying for control, and he wondered which one would win.

He was rooting for the guy who was like his grandmother and wanted to knit and crochet *all* the yarn, and who deserved at least ten boxes of Schrödinger's Hats.

When Isaac finally spoke, his voice was so quiet, Luca had to lean his head in. "I'm sorry, what?"

"Yes," Isaac whispered. Then he said it again, louder. "Yes." Then he *shouted* it. "*Yes, yes, yes*!" It was almost sexual—as was the expression of profound relief on Isaac's face. He stood abruptly and gathered his knit bag, and for a moment, Luca was truly disappointed. The conversation had been wonderful, but he felt as though he'd destroyed Magic Hour— and, well, he'd really wanted to see it happen.

Then Isaac paused. "Actually, Luca, is there anything *you'd* like me to knit? Something small and colorful? Hat, scarf, throw pillow?"

Luca grinned at him. "I'd say yes, but I'd have to answer to my grandma, and that wouldn't be pretty."

Isaac's laugh was genuine. "Oh, you're right. I'd almost forgotten— she loves to yarn for you."

"Yeah, she does," Luca said fondly. "But you know…." Suddenly the reason for *his* shitty day crashed in on him. "You know, my sister…." And this felt personal—but then he'd sort of intruded on this man's personal time, so it was only fair. "See, my sister, Allegra, told me today that she's, uhm…." He rubbed the back of his neck. "Well, it's a mess. She's pregnant, and her boyfriend kicked her out—"

"Because why?" Isaac asked, shocked.

"Because he's an asshole," Luca said, voice grim. "And that's as far as I want to look at it. Anyway… the boyfriend's an asshole, my pregnant sister is in my spare room, and—" He sighed. "—she's freaking out. And the thing is, I think she'll make an amazing mother. She'd already decided to keep the baby, but she's still freaking out. She just needs to take a breath and get her shit together. You wouldn't want to make her a baby blanket, would you? Something small, for a newborn. Something pretty that would make her see that hey, life's a little bit hard right now, but it'll get better. You know? I mean, it's a lot to ask from a blanket, but my grandma's so good at loving us with yarn—we don't want to tell her yet, but, you know…." He bit his lip, suddenly embarrassed. It had been a huge request. "I'd buy the yarn," he said, trailing off. "I'd pay you as much as you'd want."

"No," Isaac said kindly. "I don't knit for money. But I do knit for friends. Tell you what. How about I go inside and pull out some of my pattern books and colors, and you come in and help me pick something out? I've had to make three baby blankets this year—students don't always wait for the best time either—so I've got some extra skeins. How about you go wash up, and you can come in?" He looked uncertain for a moment. "I'm, uhm, heating up some beans for dinner—I can heat up enough for two, if you like."

Oh wow. *Oh wow.* This was amazing. This was fantastic. This really *was* Magic Hour. All this time Luca had been waiting until it was appropriate to make his move on Isaac Browning and Isaac Browning had just invited him to dinner! It wasn't sexual—and Luca *wouldn't* make a move, he swore he wouldn't, but….

"Yeah, Isaac," he said, appreciating the man's trim form up and down. "Yeah, I'd really like that. Thanks so much for asking. Let me finish up and wash up like you said, and I'll be over in fifteen, if that's okay. I've planned stuff with my grandma since I was a little kid—I'd love to plan a blanket."

I'd love to throw you down on a blanket and kiss your little body until you flush all over!

But he didn't say that last part. At this juncture, it would be rude.

HE HAD a spare T-shirt and cargo pants in his truck—he hated stopping by his grandparents' place after work smelling like BO and whatever funk he'd been working with that day, so he always kept a change of clothes, and, hey, the bathrooms had been the first things remodeled, and there was shower shit in there. He even had flip-flops so he didn't have to wear his boots, and while the more rational, saner part of his brain was muttering, *This isn't a date, this isn't a date, don't get your hopes up, he's a widower for God's sake*, the part of his brain that hadn't been laid in a year was like, *Hey—his husband seemed like sort of a tool anyway.*

It was an unworthy thought; he hadn't known the guy, but his grandmother had sort of prejudiced him with that "his husband put him on a yarn diet" thing. It smacked of Allegra's shitty ex-boyfriend, who used to try to put her on a food diet. Like he should have any say over what went into his sister's mouth, period!

And it *really* reminded him of his parents, who had tried to put *him* on a boy diet, because boys shouldn't want to taste other boys, or his friend Jimmy Bob's phobic ex-girlfriend, who had wanted to put Jimmy Bob on a Luca diet because she thought he would make Jimmy Bob gay.

Basically Luca had a problem with obsessive, controlling assholes, and, well, he couldn't seem to get over that look on Isaac's face when he'd said he really didn't want to finish that sweater.

The mixture of grief, relief, and vindication in his eyes, in his posture? Luca *really* wanted to get to the bottom of that.

"OH WOW! You got all spiffed up!" There was no grief, relief, or vindication in Isaac's eyes *now*, Luca noticed as he opened the door. Just a blatant appreciation that Luca rather enjoyed. "I'm sorry, I… well…."

"Our work clothes are pretty different," Luca said with a wink. "You're fine. I didn't want to track dirt and drywall dust into your house is all." He glanced around, liking the sturdy woodwork in pale colors and the cream furnishings with the gentle sage green of the rug. The whole place spoke of class and understatement and… well, it was a little bland.

Isaac followed the direction of his gaze and sighed. "It's… boring," he muttered. "So boring. Sorry. I… that's what you get when you spend more than a decade with somebody who thinks mauve is a statement."

Luca's eyebrows raised, and Isaac buried his face in his hands. "I'm sorry!" he wailed. "I swear I don't make it a habit to trash-talk my late husband. Today is an exception, I *promise*!"

Luca had to laugh. "Hey, no skin off my nose. I never met him. I guess I'm surprised because my nonna's got, like, a sixth sense for that sort of thing. I'm surprised she never gossiped."

Isaac let out a frustrated sigh. "We…. Todd and I kept things private," he said after a moment, leading Luca through to his white-tiled, white-walled, gray-countered kitchen, where a pot of fragrant bean soup was simmering, as well as—oh wow. Was that homemade bread? The smells made up for the sterility, Luca thought… or, well, hoped.

"Was that a you thing or a Todd thing?" Luca asked perceptively, and Isaac let out a whimper.

"You really don't want to hear this," he murmured. "Come on in. Is it okay if we sit at the island?" He gave a nod to the kitchen table, which while not *piled* with stuff, did have a healthy stack of mail on it. "I keep meaning to get to it, but until I get a cat to kick stuff off—" He stopped. Right there in the middle of the kitchen.

"What?" Luca asked, surprised.

"It's like a weird barrier broke in my brain," Isaac murmured, almost to himself. "Like, there I was, looking for my yarn stores, and I *made* myself pick a project Todd would like, and that... it's like that was the thing that broke the dam. *All* the things started spilling out."

"I'm sorry?" Luca said, not sorry at all. "I mean, maybe this was just the day for it, right? It's been a while since he passed, right?"

Isaac glanced at him, nodding. "Yeah, a year and a half in July. I...." He swallowed, like he was trying to swallow everything down again, and Luca had a moment of panic. No! Swallowing everything down meant working on the hated brown sweater! It meant not getting a cat—which would be a bad thing, right? It would mean....

It would mean that the somewhat bewildered man who had gazed at Luca so appreciatively wouldn't be the man who'd asked him over for bean soup and a thrilling evening picking out yarn.

"Listen," Luca said gently, glancing at the kitchen island, which had been set nicely with placemats and matching bowls, "I can see this isn't your normal day. But you're offering to do something really nice for my sister—and I realize you said something small, and I said something bigger, but I swear, I'm so grateful. If you need to trauma dump on me tonight, I promise I won't hold your bullshit against you. I may ask questions, but that's because I'm interested, okay?"

Isaac's limpid-eyed gaze was actually heartbreaking. "Interested?" he asked.

"Well, *yeah*. I know you've only seen me around here since my grandparents moved out, but truth to tell, my grandma's been talking about you guys since you moved in. She was so excited, right? Marriage equality passed, and wasn't that great, and then you guys moved in and you were *married*. She wanted me to know that it was okay. I'd just come out to my family, and my parents were assholes about it—still are. She kept telling me about you and what a nice guy you were, and you were a teacher—which still didn't make me want to go to college. But, you know, I feel like I *know* you. And…." This was embarrassing. "Watching you knit was nice. My grandma tried to teach me when I was a kid. Me and Allegra were hopeless at it. So it made me happy to watch you knit. It… it would be nice to get to know the *real* you after all this time, you think?"

Oh God. He'd said all that—he'd *actually* said all that. How embarrassing. But Isaac seemed to really be going through something tonight, and Luca felt like he needed to explain his vested interest in making sure the poor man was okay.

And it seemed to have worked.

The next look Isaac sent him was still limpid—but a little less desperate.

"Same," he said, with a crooked smile. "Mrs. Giordano kept talking about you and Allegra. She's, uhm…." His smile straightened out a little. "She's really proud of you guys."

"Well, she's my grandma. I'd say she has to be because she's family, but my parents are proof that you can still be assholes to your family."

Isaac nodded emphatically. "I know that—I see my students deal with that every day." He let out a breath. "Well, I still don't want to dump all over you about my late husband. That seems… wrong, somehow. But maybe I can take a breath and not be so… so *weird* about talking to a whole other human."

He gestured to the stools then, and Luca made himself comfortable.

"What would you like to drink?" Isaac asked over his shoulder as he went to stir the soup. "I've got milk, juice, wine?"

"Mmm… not that I don't *love* me a glass of wine sometimes," Luca said, "but I think I'll stick to juice."

"Good thought," Isaac said dryly, going to the refrigerator and then reaching into a plain cupboard for juice glasses. "I'm obviously weird enough right now."

"Oh, I didn't say *you* shouldn't have a glass of wine," Luca told him, thinking it should probably be a *requirement* for this poor guy, "but I've got to drive home and make sure Allegra's all settled in the guest bedroom."

Isaac sent him a droll glance over his shoulder as he busied himself pouring drinks. "I think I should lay off the sauce tonight. I apparently let down enough barriers as it is."

"We all have those days," Luca said, accepting the orange juice appreciatively. "I swear, if Allegra hadn't dropped the baby bomb on my lap, you'd be getting an earful about the economy and clients who bail. Although honestly this guy was totally nice about it. It wasn't his fault some bozo crashed the supply chain and now he can't build a cottage for his mother-in-law." Luca shook his head. "I understand she's a little slice of heaven too—a woman who needs her own space."

Isaac's delighted laugh was as unexpected as it was amazing. Low and happy, it sort of burbled up from his stomach and past his open mouth as he tilted his head back, and Luca wondered how he could get the man to do it more often.

"That's uhm, tactful," Isaac said, still chuckling, and then he sobered. "And generous of you to be so kind to the client. I'm sorry about the cancellation, though. It's that sort of thing that makes having a small business so challenging, I would imagine."

"Yeah," Luca admitted, a little disappointed that they were on to his shit now. Isaac's shit had been so... surprising, from such a self-contained man. "I took over the company from the guy who gave me my first job when I was in high school. Good guy, and I just kept working for him and getting certified. I...." He sighed and resisted another look-see around the quiet, bland house. "I really like doing stuff with my hands, you know? I mean, yeah, I can read a book, although audiobooks are a blessing, because they get me through the drives to the different work sites. But to make something and say, 'Hey, that's mine! I did that!'? It's one of the reasons I love watching you and Grandma do the yarn thing. It's like it's all people magic, you know? Like math made real. All that stuff I learned in geometry and trig and physics perfected, right?"

Isaac had been pulling the beans off the stove and was in the process of putting them down on the countertop between the two place settings. After the pot was in place on the hot pad, he glanced up and smiled into Luca's eyes.

"You know I teach math," he said, his voice lower now, almost dreamy. "What you just said—that's... that's *awesome*. I keep trying to set up experiments and draw analogies and examples so they can see it's not bare symbols on the page. I love that's how you see your job."

Luca's stomach gave a low thud, and his pulse started a thrumming, a sort of Bugs Bunny rhumba—*No sex for a year, hey! No sex for a year, hey!*—and he had to remind himself *again* that this wasn't a date.

That didn't mean it wasn't a… prelude of sorts, but definitely not a date.

After a long, quiet moment, Luca became embarrassingly aware that he was just… *staring* at Isaac's dreamy-eyed smile. *About math, bozo!* Then Isaac seemed to startle, as if he too was remembering where he was, and he took an awkward step back from the island.

"Here," he said quietly, "let me get the bread. I've been keeping it warm in the oven."

He pulled out a bread pan covered in foil and set it on the counter, then removed the foil, moved the bread to a cutting board, and covered it with a plain white cloth napkin instead. Luca spent a moment wondering what Isaac's kitchen would look like if he'd ever given himself a chance to decorate, and then the fresh-bread scent wafted up from under the napkin, and he almost moaned.

"God, that smells sexy," he said, and Isaac's throaty laughter brought him to himself again—but it didn't do anything to diminish his baby boner.

"I love the smells of basic foods," Isaac admitted. "Greens with balsamic and a little bit of basil or three-ingredient bread or bean soup."

"How about hamburgers or chicken sandwiches?" Luca asked suspiciously.

"*Definitely* hamburgers or chicken sandwiches," Isaac told him, eyes twinkling, "as long as there's fresh lettuce and tomato or avocado on it."

"I can see that," Luca said, and then watched appreciatively as Isaac ladled the soup into each of their bowls and sliced the bread, then handed Luca a piping-hot slice on another plain napkin.

After a shy moment of acknowledgment of the simple human ceremony of breaking bread, they both dug in, and Luca had to work hard not to moan with absolute decadence.

"Oh man," he said, after a few bites of both soup and bread, "this is *amazing*. I mean, I try to cook for myself a couple times a week, but this is *wonderful*. Thanks so much for inviting me over!"

Isaac gave him a quiet smile and took his own bite. "I guess I was feeling the need for comfort food," he admitted. "Cooked a ham last week and wanted to use the bone, so…." He shrugged.

"What'd you do with all that food?" Luca asked. "I mean, feed an army?"

"My friend Roxy and her husband are just crazy stupid busy," Isaac confessed. "They've got three kids in diapers, and Roxy's at her wits' end. I mean, she's a great teacher—the kids adore her—but she's... you know."

"Busy," Luca said, appreciating how much work that had to be.

"About every two weeks I'll cook a giant family-sized meal and then bring the bulk of it to her house. She only lives a few blocks away. We have prep together—lots of gossip happens by the copy machine, you know?"

"I did not," Luca confessed. "But now I do. So you figure out when she'll be excited about food, then?"

"Yup." Isaac shrugged. "See, when I cooked for me and Todd, it was always so... so involved. Small calorie-appropriate portions of things like braised salmon in honey sauce and risotto, or margherita chicken with lime yogurt sauce. And I'd be cooking for what felt like an hour or so, and then we'd eat, and that would be it." Isaac took a blissful bite of his soup. "I spent Sunday night cooking ham, potatoes, and green bean casserole, saved a couple portions for myself, and Roxy and her husband and kids eat for a week on the rest. It's almost the same amount of time, but it *feels* more important, you know?"

"And you'll have leftovers here too," Luca said. "Good system."

"Well, I can send some home with you," Isaac said with another one of those happy smiles. "And I can be Gay Uncle Isaac to Roxy's kids, and her husband, Brian, can have me over to watch hockey, and...." His eyes darted around his plain, boring, large house. "And anyway, yeah, it's a good system."

Luca was hit suddenly with a terrible sense of loneliness. Not just from the aftermath of his husband's death, but from the void the man seemed to have left before.

Tread carefully, Luca. This isn't some guy you dragged home from a bar and then decided to keep seeing.

"So what plans you got for the place now?" he asked, and Isaac's eyes went from his all-in-neutrals kitchen and living room back to Luca's face.

"I don't know," he said softly, thinking about it. "I..." He glanced into the living room again, at the prissy little couch up on peg legs and the two not-so-comfortable wingback chairs. Everything was done in ecru, and underneath a couple of different yarn-project baskets, the table looked like it was made of glass and mirrors.

"I guess I could go shop for some more comfortable furniture," he said, sounding surprised at himself. "And maybe an area rug that...." Suddenly his eyes went dreamy again. "They come in some lovely colors. I wouldn't mind something like a traditional Persian rug, with deep reds and blues, and maybe some blue-gray couches and a love seat—nobody likes wingback chairs, right? And... and one of those coffee tables that pops up so you can eat dinner on top and keep magazines or crafting stuff inside?"

His smile at Luca was no longer dreamy—it was *intense*. "Oh wow. Where did that come from? It was like I *forgot* I could order stuff *I* like now."

Luca gave a happy little shrug. "But I guess no time for Allegra's blanket—"

"Oh no," Isaac said. "No, don't think that at all. Blankets take a couple of weeks. It's the sort of thing you do when you sit down to watch television or listen to music or podcasts. You pull out your knitting. So if I plan now, I can purchase the yarn after school tomorrow, depending on what you want, and get a start on it. It'll be great to have a project between this year's hats and scarves for the students and next year's."

"And no more brown sweater?" Luca asked hopefully.

Isaac frowned. "I... you have to understand how *expensive* that yarn is. And for brown, it's very pretty—there's lots of blues and reds and greens in the fibers in the sunlight. It's just that there's *so much* of it. I...." He shook his head. "I'll have to ponder it for a while," he said with some resolution. "I don't believe in throwing away perfectly good wool—it's bad karma—but I *do* believe in repurposing it. That's what that wool needs. A new purpose."

Luca couldn't have agreed more, but at this point he thought it was best to dig into his soup and nod appreciatively.

His NEWLY resolved quiet lasted about half an hour.

He offered to do the dishes since Isaac had cooked, and while he was loading the dishwasher and finding his way around Isaac's orderly kitchen, Isaac ran to organize his yarn bins. After Luca had wiped the last crumb off the counter and packaged the leftovers in the containers Isaac had provided, he walked past the staircase that started in the front room and down the hallway, where, he saw, there were two guest bedrooms, a bathroom, and a den.

The yarn bins were in the den—the smallest room of the house.

But this, Luca thought, taking in the accent wall in shades of royal blue and magenta, the brilliantly colored wall hangings, and a truly delightful stained glass piece capturing moonlight over a pond full of lily pads, was where *Isaac* lived.

"Oh wow," he said quietly, feeling like he'd just fallen through an IKEA catalogue to land in a fairy grotto. "Isaac, this room—"

"I know it's terrible," Isaac said, ducking his head and keeping his attention on the contents of one of the big plastic bins absolutely full of the fiber Isaac loved so much.

"Terrible?" Luca replied, stunned.

"Too loud, too gaudy, too precious—it's not a room for grown-ups."

"Too…?" Luca couldn't breathe, he was suddenly so angry.

Isaac shrugged, still looking abashed. "It's the one room I got to decorate—"

"I can *tell*," Luca said. "It's the best room in the house!"

Isaac glanced up, surprise all over his face. "You think?"

"My God, I was wondering where your soul was," Luca burst out. "I… the rest of this house is so bland! This room"—and it was barely big enough for a desk, an armchair, and the yarn bins—"*this* room is just glorious. This room needs to spread to the rest of the house! *Every* room needs to be an Isaac room. You need to get more than new furniture. You need to do *this* to the rest of the place. It will be *amazing*."

Isaac stared at him, big hazel eyes wide and a little starry "Wow," he said, his expression a cross between elation and absolute dismay. "That's… that's the nicest thing anybody has ever said to me."

Luca gaped, fighting the temptation to fall to his knees, kiss the guy, and make wicked sexy love on the brilliantly hued area rug, surrounded by plastic yarn bins.

And that was when he knew he was *really* in trouble.

Distractions

"Whatcha working on now, Isaac?"

Roxy Michaels had wide hips, frizzy brown hair, and her clothing—button-down shirts and stretchy slacks—was constantly askew.

Isaac adored her, and his only regret about their friendship was that they'd met while they were both married, teaching, and respectable, because he thought the two of them would have been *fabulous* at the club scene.

And because when Roxy met Brian, that might have pulled Isaac into respectability without him having to meet Todd, who literally yanked Isaac out of his post-college ecstasy rave haze with the force of an annoyed parent yanking a child out of traffic.

It would have been great to have been teaching and respectable—both of which Isaac adored—without having to be married first, because the more Isaac lived without Todd, the more he wondered what had happened to Isaac during the last ten years.

That moment in his yarn room had been a revelation.

Here was a guy Isaac barely knew, telling Isaac that the world needed to see *more* of his heart after being told for ten years that he had to show rather *less* of it, and Isaac's only response had been to….

Well, he'd cried, but he'd kept his face averted as he'd focused on the totally mundane and secretly wonderful task of picking out soft, fine baby yarn for the patterns in the books that Luca liked best.

And he'd been so considerate too.

Appalled at his own audacity at taking full advantage of Isaac's impulsive offer, Luca had been asking about the easiest blankets, the ones that would take less of Isaac's valuable time. And the more Isaac thought of making a blanket for Sophia and Geordie's great-grandbaby, the more he wanted this blanket to be *amazing*.

In the end their compromise had been… well, Isaac felt a little sneaky, because he felt like he was *sneaking* more of Luca's company, but….

"Isaac?" Roxy said, calling Isaac's attention back to her original question. They'd both finished their lunches and were cozied up on the couches in the back of the teachers' room while the rest of the staff got into politics. Isaac needed to ignore politics. He'd started teaching at a time when gay teachers could be subtly fired for a million reasons that magically had nothing to do with gayness and everything to do with, "Well, he just didn't click."

Yeah, his skinny twinky ass.

Anyway, the quickest way to find that he "just didn't click" was to suddenly be interested in which administrator was a total tool, who was sleeping with who at the district office, and how they should protest all testing because it didn't work.

He had a sixth sense for avoiding tools, he didn't actually give a shit about who was sleeping with who at the district office, and he knew for a fact that *some* testing worked, so he ignored what didn't really seem to matter.

Which was why he and Roxy got along so swimmingly. She kept him apprised of all the gossip (okay, it really *was* kind of fun to know who was sleeping with whom), and she also told him who was a total fucking tool and should be avoided at all costs.

And in return, he continued to keep her apprised on what the world was like when you weren't elbows-deep in diapers and Desitin after you left your students.

And part of that was talking about his yarn work, because she'd always been the one person interested in it—and she had two different sweaters with flowered embellishments and a complete layette for each of the three kids to show for it. He would have made something for Brian, her husband, but he worked from home and wore, by her reports, a frayed hoodie and cargo shorts even in the deepest, darkest winter.

And part of his duty as best work friend was to tell her what he was working on and why it was making his face hot—and probably pink to boot.

"Isaac?" she asked, sotto voce. There were always those hidden teachers who were "fine with his sexuality as long as he doesn't rub it in our faces," which was code for not mentioning his husband or his dating or even celebrities who were gay or shows that had gay characters. His first year he'd almost gotten fired for telling a student he liked *Glee*, and he'd since tempered any public utterances accordingly.

"It's nothing," he said, still not able to fight the flush. "Just, do you remember those nice Giordanos who lived next door?"

"That older couple who moved? Isn't the grandson remodeling their house to sell?"

Isaac nodded. "Yeah, well, he came over to chat while I was out on the porch last night and…." *I almost trauma dumped my bad marriage and nonexistent self-esteem all over him.* "And anyway we got to talking, and it turns out his sister's pregnant, and her boyfriend dumped her and… well, I offered to make him a baby blanket for her so she could remember that she's always wanted kids, and she's going to do just fine."

"Aww," Roxy said, holding her hand to her heart. "That's sweet!" She checked out the many, *many* tiny squares he'd already crocheted. "So this is going to be what? I mean, you sew the squares into a blanket but… Isaac, those squares are awfully *small.*"

They were, in fact, two-round squares in sport-weight yarn. They were tiny. And Luca hadn't been blind to that fact when he'd seen the book that showcased blankets that used the small squares as pixels on a grid to make pictures. In this case, a rainbow under the sun. He'd said, "Oh, this is cute—but look at it. It's probably super labor-intensive, right?" And without waiting for an answer, he'd set the book aside.

And then Isaac had apparently suffered a nonlethal brain lesion or had an out-of-body experience, because like that, he lost his mind.

"Yes," Isaac said to Roxy now, "but I'm not the only one making them. Or I won't be. Luca—that's Allegra's brother—is coming over Saturday, and I'm going to teach him how to crochet so he can help me make them."

He saw Roxy's eyes widen. "Luca?" she said.

"I don't want to talk about it," he said with dignity, finishing off a square and snipping it with the little attachment he kept on his key lanyard. So far everybody thought it was a charm—only Roxy knew it was scissors.

"Okay, then," Roxy said. "Let's walk around the quad and not talk about it." And with that, she packed up his lunch detritus—reused Ziploc bag, aluminum water bottle, and insulated lunch box—and grabbed it by the handle before standing up, allowing him the moment to pack up his knitting.

"Where you guys going?"

Both of them turned toward Paula Lamphere, their department head, and pasted on smiles. "Out for a wander," Roxy said breezily. "There's ten minutes left, so I thought we'd walk around the quad before we stare wistfully out the window for the next two hours." It really was a beautiful day. Roxy taught Geometry and Algebra II, so she was stuck inside like Isaac, but they understood one of the senior English teachers let her kids sit out on the sidewalk on days like this, while she read book excerpts to them and led discussions. It was the only time Isaac wished he'd majored in the humanities, actually.

"Just make sure you get to your room on time," Paula said, as though she was speaking to students.

"Of course," Isaac said, his hand on Roxy's bicep before she could shoot off at the mouth. Hating Paula was one of those things they both saved for "walks around the quad."

"Sure, Mom," Roxy muttered under her breath as the door swung shut behind them. "Be sure to round up your flying monkeys before you go back to your classroom."

Isaac snorted at their standing "Wicked Witch of the Math Department" joke, then coughed and then had to endure three of his students staring as Roxy pounded him on the back.

"Okay," she said when he was done. "That's it. We're heading for the soda machine—I swear, all water and no cola makes Isaac a very dull boy."

"I thought you were going to say coke, and I was gonna say not in this decade," he told her, and it was her turn to spit-take. By the time they had their shit together, they were halfway to the H-building and the last soda machine on a high school campus in California, because sometimes parents liked to suck the joy out of kids' lives, that's why.

"So," Roxy said as they caught their breath, "tell me about this Luca and trauma dumping. After all of that, you owe me some tea."

Isaac laughed a little. "He was nice," he said after a moment. "I… I was having a bad Todd moment. I kept hearing his voice in my head. He was telling me what to knit."

"Asshole," she muttered, and then gave one of her mom smiles when he looked at her sharply.

"He liked to keep me from spending too much on—"

"Isaac?" she asked.

"Yes?"

"Do you have lots of money in the bank?"

"Yes."

"Buy all the fucking yarn you want. Buy some more art. Buy more of those glorious stained-glass pieces. Whatever you do, don't knit whatever shit-brown masterpiece your ex-husband told you would make your poops better, okay?"

Isaac gave her a bemused smile. "You know, that's funny—that's almost what Luca said. Except for the reference to poop, but then—"

"He's not up to his elbows in diapers when he gets home from work," Roxy muttered with a sigh. "So anyway, this Luca guy, he asked you to—"

"I offered," Isaac told her. It was important, and Roxy knew that. Paula asked Isaac to knit her a sweater the year before, said the kids would love it if they knew their favorite pre-algebra teacher had done that for the department chair! Roxy had almost gotten herself fired by producing a breakdown of the cost of making the sweater, by material cost for both the cheap stuff (as Paula told him *not* to use) and the expensive stuff, and then added an hourly wage.

Paula had yelled first, added, "It was just a stupid joke," and then thrown the wadded-up invoice into the trash, but she hadn't apologized, even when the rest of the staff told her it hadn't sounded like a joke when she'd done it.

"Again, why?" Roxy asked. "Seriously? I know how jealously you guard your crafting time. Why offer it to this guy?"

"His grandmother is lovely," Isaac told her. "And his grandfather is lovely to *her*, so he also gets my approval as a nice guy. But it's...." He let out a breath. "There I was, trying to knit that sweater Todd asked me to make him—"

"The shit-brown monstrosity," she said.

Isaac bit his lip thoughtfully. "Did you ever see it?"

"No," she said. "But Isaac, it's been a year and a half. It's time to start speaking ill of the dead. If I say nothing else about your late husband, I'll tell you that his affinity for brown, tan, ecru, and crème was the least of his sins. Why you would want to pull that out now to finish it is beyond me."

Penance, because I was thinking far worse before I reached for a new project.

"I don't know," Isaac told her. "Self-flagellation. Whatever. But Luca walked up and said, 'Whatever is making your face do that, don't,' and I was so grateful I offered to make him something, and then *he* told me about his problems, which was nice—"

"Because you weren't alone with the problems," she said, and he nodded.

"And…." He sighed. "I don't know. I guess anything was better than working on the shit-brown monstrosity."

Roxy's disappointment was palpable, and for a moment it was just the two of them in the cool of the early afternoon sunshine with the sound of kids' shouts and the eternal hum of conversation, even if nobody was near enough to hear.

"That's it?" she asked. "Was he even cute?"

"Oh yeah. I mean *built*, and with this sweet little face and brown eyes and—" He stopped himself. "He was pleasant," he finished weakly, conscious that Roxy had perked up next to him.

"Pleasant?" she asked. "*Pleasant*?"

He let out a breath. "I," he said, "am still grieving."

"And I'm still a virgin with a twenty-eight-inch waist," she retorted.

He glanced at her squishy, comfortable, *happy* body. "You never had a twenty-eight-inch waist," he said critically.

Her laughter burbled into the early afternoon air, and he was reminded again of why he'd knit for her again and again. "You bitch, I did too! Childbirth does terrible things to your body, trust me. But"—she sobered—"even if I was a size zero and had hipbones that could pierce steel, that wouldn't change the fact that what you just said was a lie."

"I am too grieving." But even the word was hard to say.

They neared the soda machine and waited patiently—and quietly— while a small group of students made their purchases. One of them—one of Isaac's favorite kids, actually—glanced up as he grabbed his illicit soda and grinned.

"Hey, Brown-man. You coming to walk on the wild side?"

Isaac gave him a warm smile. "Caffeine and sugar—next it'll be the hard stuff and a one-way ticket to the big house!"

Marcelle gave a delighted cackle and walked up for a fist bump, which Isaac happily gave. Smallish—his freshman growth spurt had been more like a growth wave—and African American, with his tightly napped hair dyed blond, then purple, Marcelle had been out and proud practically since the cradle. Isaac admired everything about the kid, from his enthusiasm about English lit to his dogged determination to pass pre-algebra, which he was fixing to do this year, as a junior. He'd bonded with Isaac when Isaac had given him after-school help, a thing he did readily for any student who needed it. But Marcelle had really put his back into math. And Isaac had put his back into helping the boy learn math, pulling out every trick he had, from manipulatives to trips around the school looking for math examples, until Marcelle had not only passed pre-algebra, he'd determined to pass algebra in summer school so he could sneak one more math class in as a senior for better hope of a college admission.

This was the kind of kid teachers lived for.

"So what are you two gossiping about?" Marcelle asked, giving the girls with him a bawdy wink. "You got plans to go clubbing this weekend?"

That made Roxy laugh, and she said, "The closest thing I get to clubbing is chaperoning school dances, but nice try. I'm taking the kids to the park and hoping they take a long nap."

"I will babysit anytime," Marcelle told her. "I've got siblings coming out my ears—I've even got a first aid certificate so my mom doesn't freak out when I'm in charge! And Sheryl"—he nodded at one of the girls—"and me, we watched Mrs. Halford's kids last week, if you want a reference."

For a moment Roxy's face was taken over by wistfulness, and Isaac felt for her. He'd babysat for her plenty, but usually for family stuff or work things, and Roxy was careful not to impose too much. A date night probably sounded like the ultimate in luxury.

"You should do it," he said quietly. "You and Brian could go see a movie or, you know, have an uninterrupted meal." Marcelle threw a friendly arm around his shoulders, and Isaac returned the move so they could stand together in brotherhood. "I've got Marcelle's digits, if you want to call Brian and then call him up. I'm a reference. I guess Kim Halford's a reference." Kim Halford was a science teacher—nice lady, they agreed, but her room was on the other side of their large campus. "Come on, Roxy," he said quietly. "You deserve a weekend out."

"We come fully equipped," Marcelle said. "First aid certificates, cooking classes—Sheryl here even took some childhood ed classes this year so she could look after her sister's kids."

Which was impressive, because Isaac was fully aware that usually the only requirement to babysit for family members was a pulse.

Roxy laughed, the sound full of a sort of relieved joy. "Let me call my husband," she said. "And Mr. Browning can give me your number." She nodded. "Thanks, Marcelle. I promise, we'll pay you right."

Marcelle waved a hand. "For Mr. Browning's friend here, we'll do it for free."

"Hey!" protested Sheryl. "I'm trying to go to college here!"

"We'll pay you right," Roxy repeated. "But let me double-check. Now move so we can get our soda fix before the bell rings!"

The students departed, laughing, and Isaac gave her a fond glance as she used her phone to buy them both a Coke. "Thanks for that," he said. "Marcelle's a great kid."

"I know Sheryl," she told him. "And you're right—they're both awesome kids." You couldn't know Marcelle without knowing Sheryl, Isaac was well aware. "But the real question is…," she said, raising her eyebrows, "is he gayer than you?"

Isaac snorted. "No boy's gayer than this boy," he told her, allowing some of the vamp and swish he'd so carefully squashed over the years to escape.

Roxy laughed, and then, as she handed him his soda, said, "You wouldn't have done that two years ago."

He swallowed, knowing it was true. "It would have gotten me fired in short order before I got tenure," he said evasively.

"But you had tenure eight years ago," she told him, unrelenting. "And you wouldn't have done it at home, and you wouldn't have done it when you and I were taking the kids to the park, and you wouldn't have done it when watching television. You…." She sighed. "I don't want to be a bitch, Isaac. I *want* you to have a healthy grieving period for your late husband. He died too young, and it's not fair." High blood pressure wasn't called the silent killer for nothing. Todd had been so arrogant— the simultaneous stroke and cardio infarction had dropped him dead at fifty. "But sometimes," she continued, her voice terribly gentle, "I think the worst thing about his death and its timing is that you were just starting to realize how… how wrong he was for you."

Isaac stared at her, his tongue cleaved to his mouth with two impulses—the impulse to deny it and the impulse to burst into tears and bless his friend, bless her with his whole heart, for saying what he hadn't been able to, not even in a year and a half of supposed grieving.

For a moment they stood locked in a gaze of tortured understanding, until the bell rang.

She sighed, and they both started to move toward their building. "I'm sorry," she murmured. "That was real personal in a real bad place."

"It's fine," he murmured.

"No, it's not," she said, as always, harder on herself than any student or administrator could be. "Just know that… that if you've got a chance to be happy, or even to make a new friend, do it. The only thing that should hold you back is whether or not this guy is worth your time."

"I like him," Isaac admitted painfully. Roxy's squeeze to his shoulder grounded him, made them human and okay again.

"Good, Isaac. Even if it's just a friend—or even if it's just a date—this whole 'teach a stranger to crochet' thing sounds like moving on."

ISAAC'S SIXTH period pre-algebra class was unusually quiet today. Part of it was that they were nearing finals, and all the work was review, absolutely dedicated to helping the kids know what they needed to have learned for the last big test before finals, and part of it was that Isaac let the kids listen to their music on their AirPods or do other homework if— and only if—they'd finished their seatwork for the day. He considered a really good day the kind where every kid had five minutes at the end of the day to breathe and call their own. It didn't happen often, but when it did, he'd walk up and down the aisles, often with a knitting project in his hands, stopping to chat quietly with whoever had questions or sometimes just wanted to talk.

Marcelle *always* wanted to talk.

"Whatcha working on?" he asked as usual, his pretty face all animation.

"A baby blanket for a friend's sister," he said, liking the short answer very much.

Marcelle eyed the yarn—white with sprinkles—critically. "Nice," he said, "as long as there's other colors."

"This is only the beginning," Isaac promised him solemnly. "There's going to be a whole rainbow, and a teddy bear and a pot of gold." He held up the tiny square. "Think of this like a pixel in a picture. The pattern calls for five hundred of these."

"Wow," Marcelle said, cocking his head with interest. "That's... I never thought of that. So, you get enough squares in different colors, you can make anything."

"I've got *books* full of patterns," Isaac confirmed. "You can also do half-color squares."

"Huh," Marcelle murmured. Then, brow wrinkled like he was thinking hard, he pulled out a sheet of graph paper from his binder. "Hey, can we design our *own* blankets and then figure out how many squares they take?"

Isaac blinked. "Mmm... yes, but you can't do it by counting only. You'll have to show me how you used algebra to get it done."

"Ooh...." Marcelle's eyes got big. "I'm *on* it. Can I get credit for this?"

Marcelle was currently working on a C, which for him was a big furry deal, but Isaac was impressed—damned impressed—by the kid's initiative, and by his ability to *see* math in everyday things—including art.

"Mmm... I'll add fifty points to your lowest test grade," he said, thinking that should pull the boy's grade up nicely. As he glanced around, he saw a number of kids pulling out their own graph paper and the colored pencils they were required to bring to class and gazing at him with expectant expressions.

"Okay, then," he said, walking up to the whiteboard. "Here's the deal. The blanket I'm working on is twenty squares by twenty-five squares. You can make yours twenty by twenty, but no smaller." He wrote the assignment down and then outlined it. "No fewer than five colors, with three algebraic equations showing how you figured out how many squares of each color you'd have to make to create your blanket."

"Are you going to make the best one?" asked one girl, and Isaac grimaced.

"Honey, something like this takes me a *month*, and my friend already picked out the picture he wanted—"

"But what if we make something *really* good?" Henrietta asked, and Isaac figured he'd let the unseen Luca be the bad guy.

"I'll tell you what," he said soberly. "I'll *ask* my friend if he'd want to take a look at the designs and see if one of them would work instead of what he picked out. And if I *do* make it, remember, it's for somebody else."

"That's okay," Henrietta said happily. "My grandma can teach me how to make granny squares. Maybe I can make my own blanket instead."

And that set them off—but in a quiet way. As each kid planned and plotted and sketched, they talked about somebody they knew who crafted and how if they'd known, *they* could have been making their own pictures with squares and half-squares too.

Isaac watched magic happening and turned to Marcelle, who was grinning at him with absolutely no shame.

"Look what you did," he said softly. "Aren't you proud of yourself?"

Marcelle nodded. "Absolutely always," he said.

"You should be," Isaac told him. As the bell rang and the kids packed up their colored pencils and graph paper reluctantly, Isaac texted Luca to tell him what he'd inspired, thinking the man had been kind, funny, and good company the night before. Maybe he'd enjoy knowing—

Awesome! Can I—I mean, can I come to your classroom and judge? Like a contest and everything? When is the assignment due?

Isaac stared at the text, absolutely gobsmacked.

Two days before the final, the last Friday in May.

Great! I'll be there! Can we still work on the blanket even if we don't know what it's going to be?

Isaac thought of the two hundred tiny white squares he'd need for the majority of the blankets in the pattern book.

Sure. If we make too many squares in one color, we can sew them up to be a sweater or a stuffed animal.

Awesome! Tell the kids yes! And I'll be by your house on Saturday to learn so I can do my part!

Isaac gave a thumbs-up to that, because he didn't want to… to… give the (right?) wrong impression, and then glanced up when he realized he wasn't alone in the room.

"Marcelle?" he asked.

"Did your boy say yes?" Marcelle countered.

Isaac grimaced. "He's not my boy—"

Marcelle rolled his eyes. "Well, he should be. That look on your face when you were texting—it had 'That's my boy' written all over it."

Isaac resisted the urge to shift his eyes left and right, like some sort of deviant. "I should be quieter about expressions like that," he said, then felt compelled to add, "And he's not my boyfriend—and he's only thirty."

His reward for that was a snort. "Yeah, don't give me that. You're making a *five-hundred*-square blanket for this guy's sister. He'd better be important. But why didn't you make him a sweater?"

Isaac thought about the crap-brown thing he'd shoved in the back of his yarn bins the night before. "Sweaters are an awfully big commitment," he said. "For somebody I'm not dating yet. No, he did something nice for me, and I offered to make him something, and he *really* wanted a baby blanket for his sister, and he was willing to help make it." Isaac shrugged. "It's more like I found a new friend than a new *boy*friend."

Marcelle's pixyish features took on the calm superiority of the wisest sage. "What was the nice thing he did?"

Isaac swallowed. "How old are you?" he asked, because damn if this kid wasn't just pushing into his business.

"No—this is important," Marcelle said. "You are the only teacher here that's out. Did you know that?"

Isaac sighed. "Do I *ever*."

"Yeah, and you don't… we didn't even know you *had* a husband until he passed away last January. You get to be happy. Like Ms. Michaels with all them kids. She's happy, and her husband's a computer programmer, and she's run off her ass. We know that because she tells us that. You don't *tell* us anything."

Isaac knew that was the trend in teaching—to be a real person to your students. Todd had hated that trend, hated that Isaac had to host clubs or spend his time after school supervising activities. In spite of the fact that other teachers brought their significant others to things like football games and plays, he'd never shown the slightest interest in Isaac's job and had insisted, with a faint curl to his upper lip, that Isaac keep his name out of any class discussion.

And now….

Isaac thought about his boring house and his quiet life and how the highlight of his day was knitting on his porch with his audiobook or going yarn shopping with Luca's grandma. Hell, babysitting for Roxy was a big deal on the weekend.

"I've got a small, boring life," he said apologetically. "I—"

"Yeah, now." Marcelle's eyes had narrowed. "I bet you were hell at a rave back in the day, weren't you?"

Isaac should have said no to that—he should have. But Marcelle was looking at him with… admiration. And camaraderie. And for a moment, Isaac wanted to feel young. He didn't want to be *grieving*; he wanted to be *hopeful*.

So Isaac held his finger to his lips and pulled out his phone, calling up Katy Perry's "Part of Me," which had been his anthem in his twenties.

Then, after setting his knitting and his phone on the table in front of the whiteboard, he stood in the space between the table and the student desks and…

Danced.

Marcelle came up next to him, watched his feet, and started parallel footwork, following him through the first half of the song, when Roxy—who had apparently heard the music from the hallway—walked in and joined them, her own moves not bad at all.

And she was joined by Sheryl before the song finished winding down.

The song came to an end, and it was the four of them, a little breathless and definitely warm in the spring afternoon, laughing.

"Yeah," Marcelle said, grinning as he grabbed his backpack. "You were a hell-raiser. You too, Mrs. Michaels. Don't deny it. You guys give us hope that being a grown-up isn't all the suck, right?"

"Sure," Isaac said, still catching his breath. He was reaching for what was left in his soda as the kids walked away laughing.

"That was fun," Roxy said, taking a swig of her own soda. "Why'd we do that again?"

Isaac gave her a bemused smile and indicated the extra credit assignment on the board. "Apparently," he said, as surprised as anybody, "I am not allowed to be dead yet."

He watched her smile grow. "You never will be. Now explain what this is to me so I can do it too."

He did, and she got impressed, which he felt like she shouldn't be, because dammit, the *kids* had thought of it, but even after they called it quits and went out to their cars, he realized he'd dodged a bullet.

Marcelle had asked him what Luca had done that had made Isaac *so* grateful he'd go to such an awful lot of trouble for a near stranger.

He told me it was okay to be angry.

And that's something Isaac hadn't had permission to do in a long, long time.

Learning Curve toward June

Luca swallowed and looked unhappily at the teeny tiny hook and teeny tiny yarn in his thick work-roughened fingers and thought, *I am going to suck so bad at this.*

Next to him, Isaac grunted and sighed. "Okay," he said, like he'd thought about it for a minute. "You're brand-new, and you've never used these tools. I feel like we're starting you out with the advanced set. You don't give a kindergartner a ball-peen hammer and a chisel, you give him a plastic hammer and a peg board. You're smarter than a kindergartner, but the theory is sound."

Luca set the tiny yarn and tiny hook down and felt a rivulet of sweat slide down his back, which spoke more to his discomfort than to the temperature in Isaac's climate-controlled room.

"Yeah," he said dispiritedly, "but I can't help you build a blanket with a plastic hammer."

Isaac gave him a gentle smile. "No, but right now I'm just excited somebody wants to do this with me who's not your grandma. How about we start you off with thick yarn and thick hooks—something that won't make you feel like you'll rip it up if you breathe on it? Once you get good with that, we can work our way down. And in the meantime, maybe some moisturizer on your hands at night so your cuticles don't catch the yarn?"

Luca felt totally inadequate, which was why he said the next thing. "Well, I haven't had any complaints so far."

The flat-eyed gaze Isaac gave him was absolutely glacial. Luca couldn't remember being this intimidated since Mrs. Schraven in the second grade.

"You said you wanted to help," he said with that same teacher tone he remembered from Mrs. Schraven.

"I do," Luca told him sincerely. "I just feel like… like I'm too dumb to do this."

Isaac's expression softened. "Nonsense." Such an old-fashioned word. "Stay right here for a second. I've…." He stopped. "Never mind. Set that down and come with me."

"Where we going?" Luca asked.

"The yarn store. You look like a bulky-weight acrylic sort of learner."

Luca would find out later that it was like Mrs. Schraven saying he needed to take a "special" sort of math, but Isaac was so nice about it—about everything, really—that he actually took that the way it was intended, with compassion and his best learning style at heart, and not like "special" was the exact opposite of special.

The craft store was sort of fun.

Luca had been with his sister before, for things like putting together a photo album for his grandparents or picking out a silk-flower arrangement for her apartment. But his grandma—and Isaac—both usually bought their yarn at smaller boutique sort of local businesses, of which there were only a few in the area. His grandma had a thing for natural fibers—wool, alpaca, organic cotton—and Luca figured Isaac might too, although the baby yarn had been acrylic, just finely spun. (Apparently acrylic yarn was easier to wash and would last longer than the baby would be a baby through multiple washes. Luca was a fan.)

The craft store carried bright, sturdy, beautiful yarn, a lot of it *much* thicker than what Luca had been so terrified to work with earlier. Isaac smiled as Luca started to stroke a furry strand of something that appeared to be a densely packed caterpillar of fiber and said, "No, not that yarn, Luca. You need to learn what your stitches look like, and that sort of hides them." He gestured to a couple of shelves with thick yarn wound into both cakes and skeins. "Here, but make it something bright. People don't realize this, but color makes a big difference in how easy it is to see what you're doing, and being able to see what you're doing—or feel it— makes a big difference in how you learn. So something big and bright."

"How much?" Luca asked, and Isaac frowned briefly.

"How about three skeins or two cakes?" he said after a moment. "We can start with making a scarf. Then once you learn the stitches, you can learn how to make a granny square for one end, and then one of the blanket squares for the other end. By the time you're done with the scarf, you'll be able to help with the blanket."

"But who's the scarf for?" Luca asked.

Isaac grinned. "Anyone you want. Including *you*."

"I'll make it for Allegra," Luca said, grabbing a striped cake in pink, purple, and white. "I'll be able to see this just fine, and that way I can give her something nice for her birthday in October. It'll give me a deadline." It was his turn to shrug. "I'm a contractor—we work better with deadlines."

Isaac's laugh was starting to… do things to him. Pleasant things. Happy things. Things that made him wish he hadn't gone for the clumsy, swaggering come-on and had bided his time instead.

"How's she doing?" Isaac asked, putting Luca's yarn in the red basket he held by the handles.

Luca followed him down the brightly colored shelves and watched as he stopped, searching a shelf of yarn that seemed to call to him.

"She's doing okay," he said. "She's—well, my apartment is tiny, and I'm bummed I can't give her a pay raise anytime soon. I mean, we're going to need a better place for her before the kid comes along. I thought you and Nonna didn't buy yarn here?"

Part of the diversion was that he didn't want to talk about how Allegra spent all day every day looking like she couldn't stop crying, but part of it was true interest. He got that there were politics and snobberies in every craft known to man, but he just didn't understand his grandmother's yarn prejudices, and he was hoping Isaac could give him the key.

"We both like wool," Isaac said absently. "But I'm going to need some more of that baby yarn to make the blanket you picked out—or even any of the ones the kids are designing, and it's really sad, but I want to make them *all*, because they are *really* stunning."

Luca noted that the baby yarn was down on the other end of the shelf.

"So what's this?" he asked.

"This is a wool/acrylic combination," Isaac said. "And it's in a lot of bright kid's colors. See, I make the kids hats and scarves every year, and I can get this kind of yarn at my usual yarn place, but this is on *sale*, and I'm trying to decide how much I want to pick up."

Luca noted that it was 50 percent off, with extra discounts for volume. "Well, given how much you do yarn stuff for the kids, wouldn't you want to get *all* of it? That looks like a *really* good price."

"It's an *amazing* price," Isaac said and gazed woefully at the handbasket in his hand. "We're gonna need a bigger basket."

Luca cackled at the *Jaws* reference. "You start picking out colors—I'll go get you the bigger boat."

By the time he returned, Isaac had stuffed his handbasket and was busy shoving more of his picks into an empty shelf. The racks containing the sale yarn looked nearly picked clean, and Isaac was giggling to himself in a way that was not quite sane.

"Okay," Luca murmured soothingly, dumping the chosen yarn into the basket. "Here we go. Don't forget the baby yarn or you'll just be back here later."

Isaac complied, but he was still giggling to himself as he went, and Luca wondered what the deal was.

The giggling stopped when they got to the counter, the basket *stuffed* with yarn and Isaac carrying a whole extra plastic bin in his arms. As soon as Luca stepped up to pay, Isaac shoved the bin in his arms and darted to the register, going for his own wallet.

"Nope," Isaac said, proving surprisingly fast for someone who looked so sober and grounded. "Nope. I'm getting this one. It's *my* pleasure."

Luca didn't want to argue with him in the yarn store—while he'd always known he was gay, there was something so *extra* gay about quibbling with your crush at the counter of Michael's, and he might be willing to go there someday with this guy, but not yet.

"Sure," Luca said, and he listened, bemused, as Isaac and the woman behind the counter gushed at the amazing price, and how great the product was, and what did he plan to do with all that yarn.

"Why," Isaac said, sounding almost breathless, "*anything*. It's *anything*. It's… it's all the possibilities in the world, all in a big squishy pile, right?"

The sales associate smiled, and Luca stared at him, trim and adorable and sweet and… and… *hopeful*, all over armloads of cheap yarn.

Isaac didn't start giggling again until they got out to his little Kia Sportage, and Luca really needed to hear about it.

"What's the deal?" he asked, helping Isaac shove the *many* bags into the back. "Why are you so… so giggly?"

And then Isaac's face shut down, and Luca could have kicked himself. "I mean, it's a great price," Luca hurried to add, "and I *love* what you said to the girl about, you know, possibilities? I thought that was great. I think it's great that you can *see* those possibilities in a big squishy pile of yarn. I mean, that's awesome. But… but you sound almost like you're trying not to cry."

The… the *shut-down* part faded, but suddenly, to Luca's horror, tears actually formed in Isaac's eyes.

"I just," he whispered, staring at the piles of yarn, "I-I never did this when Todd was alive. He… he made me stick to six boxes. He *hated* when I bought yarn. I had to write—*write*, mind you—a justification, a plan, a *reason* for all the yarn. That's why… that alpaca? It's such good stuff. And I wanted it. I wanted to make something with it. So I wrote, *I'll make a sweater for my husband*, and Todd… he was like, 'Okay, but it can't have a design in it, and no colors, a simple goddamned brown pullover, Isaac, do you think you can do that?' and… and I wanted to work with the yarn *so much*, and now when I touch it, it feels… it feels like I sold my soul for a pile of shit-brown yarn. But I don't have to do that anymore. I can buy *bins* of yarn. I have all the money in the world. I can buy *all the yarn I want*. I just…." Oh no. Luca heard the wail building. "I don't have anybody to knit for!"

Luca had his arms around Isaac's shoulders and was holding him, sobbing in the parking lot at Michael's, as he used one arm to shut the hatch over a giant pile of discount yarn.

Eventually Isaac's tears subsided, and for a moment they stood in the bright May sunshine, uncomfortably warm but—at least on Luca's side of things—not wanting to part. Luca stepped back, smiling grimly to himself when Isaac wouldn't meet his eyes. Then he gently but firmly held his hands out for Isaac's keys and, when he got them, ordered Isaac into the Sportage.

Then he drove them to a local sandwich shop.

As Isaac got out of his own vehicle and followed Luca obediently, he said, "Why are we here?"

"Because it's easier to talk while you eat, and brother, I could eat."

Isaac gave him an amused glance through puffy eyes and a face swollen with weeping, and Luca offered his best, most comforting smile.

"What do you want to talk about?" Isaac asked.

"Well, for starters, what kind of sandwich do you want?"

Fifteen minutes later they were seated outside in the shade, with a scenic view of the parking lot but a lot of fresh air and early May sunshine that definitely lifted the spirits. Luca had paid, his treat, because he said it was his turn, but also because he liked to pay for his dates, even when he was broke. That probably made him a controlling bastard, but he also liked to think it made him Italian.

After a few bites, Isaac set his sandwich down and said—as if surprised—"This place is really good."

"I like it," Luca said.

"Todd never wanted to come here. Said Jersey Mike's sounded pretentious in California." Isaac sighed. "I'll have to bring Roxy here. It's close to the school, and we're always looking for a good place to run away to on Friday."

"You mean they let you out of the building?" Luca asked, feigning big eyes. "They don't lock you in the basement and pipe in the federal allotment of sunshine?"

Isaac laughed—a real laugh this time and not an insane giggle.

"No, no locking in the basement. But usually there's not enough *time*. We get thirty-five minutes to eat, so most of the department has somebody with an early prep go out and get food."

"But not you?" Luca asked perceptively.

Isaac shrugged. "Most of our department is sort of a conservative toolbox. Roxy and I have a prep period that backs up against lunch, so we go early. And we still remember what it was like to be young." He took another bite and chewed ruminatively. When he was done, he said, "I had a master teacher when I was coming up through the credential program. She was on the verge of retirement, but you wouldn't know it with the way she played with the kids. She took me aside and told me to watch out for the teachers' room. 'Sometimes,' she said, taking a drag of her Virginia Slims in her car, mind you, because she wasn't going to stop smoking at sixty if they arrested her, 'sometimes, those people are the lambs of God, and you couldn't imagine a finer bunch of sheeple in the universe, doing the bidding of the man. But sometimes,'" and he mimed taking a drag and letting it out on a blissful sigh, "'sometimes, kid, they're a cancerous lesion on the collective consciousness of education. And the thing is, you'll never know what it's gonna be. Are you going to walk into the teachers' room and find your friends and colleagues who will give you solace and support and tell you how to be the best teacher you can be? Or are you going to find a bunch of conservative bigots who laugh at the gay kids and are still pissed that you can't teach the Bible in California? You don't fuckin' know.'"

Luca stared at him in shock. "You are shitting me," he said. "It can't possibly be that—"

"Oh, but it is," Isaac assured him. "The trick is to find somebody—even if it's just one person—you can talk to. Someone who loves the job. Loves the kids. Can tell the administration to go suck rocks when you've got a toolbox in the front office. Carly Vogel taught me that, God love her, and I hope she's in a retirement villa somewhere warm, wearing nicotine patches and getting laid, because it was the best advice going into the profession that I could have gotten."

"So, you and Roxy?" Luca surmised.

Isaac shrugged. "Me and Roxy," he said. "We were both in the same credential program. Masomat High School was hiring math teachers—they had a twenty-to-one program—"

"What's that?" Luca asked, curious.

Isaac rolled his eyes. "Common sense. Most schools have to apply for grants to get it. Basically it's a policy of only having twenty students in basic freshmen classes—pre-algebra and English, although they should include everything else. But this was a grant for only twenty kids per pre-algebra classroom, and the grant is to pay the extra teachers. It's how a lot of teachers get hired on, and then the school loses funding, and of course the profession eats its own, so the few teachers left after the initial hiring burst are there to teach thirty-six kids per class. It's awesome—"

"Oh my God," Luca said, feeling like his brain had been assaulted by too much bad information at once. "Let's go back to 'the profession eats its own.'"

Isaac took a glum bite of his sandwich. "It's... it's not for the weak, Luca. Besides knowing math *really* well, you also have to know politics—which I don't and Roxy sort of does, but she doesn't like to fuck with it—and they throw kids at you who have third- or fourth-grade skills—"

"But shouldn't they be in remedial classes?" Luca asked, appalled.

Isaac set his sandwich down regretfully. "Do you remember maybe fifteen years ago—probably when you were back in high school—there was a thing called No Child Left Behind?"

"Yeah."

"Well, what it was—what it *really* was—was a way to blame teachers for every kid who had a problem learning. That philosophy and a lot of those policies have hung around. If a kid, or even an entire class, isn't at grade level, the teacher isn't allowed to go back and reteach the lesson, or make sure half the class has the skill. The *entire class* must move up, and if not, the teacher takes the heat. So the result is, when the kids get moved up to high school, your supersmart, A-level kids are in the honors classes, and that's about fifteen percent. And the other eighty-five percent, who needed help or, hell, a little bit of slowing down, weren't *allowed* to get help or a little bit of slowing down, and they are either below grade level or so disillusioned that it doesn't matter. And if you complain about it—see, politics—you're considered part of the problem, and you're fucked."

It was dawning on Luca that Isaac swore a lot, but hearing him talk about his profession, he was beginning to understand why.

"That's awful," he said, dazed. He could vaguely remember taking classes, passing classes, having teachers tell him he was a good student, and figuring that was nice, but he couldn't wait to get out and get a real job. He'd had no idea what his teachers had gone through for any of that to happen.

Isaac shrugged and reconsidered his sandwich. Took another, more enthusiastic, bite.

"It's got its hard parts," he confided. "About a week before school starts in the summer, I have a series of nightmares: My alarm doesn't go off and I sleep through the first week, my pants fall down in the middle of class, or—and this is my favorite—I'm standing on top of a desk, screaming at the top of my lungs, and they keep talking over me. And the worst part of that one is that it actually happened during student teaching."

Luca's chuckle rumbled out from his stomach, surprising them both.

"That's terrible," he said, holding his hand over his mouth so he didn't spit food. "Is that true?"

"Yeah." Isaac nodded. "Yeah. I… I mean, I was the twinkiest of twinks. What high school kid was going to listen to me? Half the juniors had thicker mustaches than I did at twenty-three. But I had a degree in math and nothing to do with it, and everybody said, 'Hey, you're gonna be a teacher, right?' So I thought, 'Why not?'" He blew out a breath. "And my parents died when I was right out of college, and I was a mess. I mean, a *mess*. I spent three months after their car accident hitting every club between here and San Francisco—I'm lucky I survived. They didn't have PrEP back then, and I'll be honest, sometimes I was too high to be safe."

"What made you decide to clean it all up?" Luca asked, suddenly curious—and aching for the lost young thing he could still see in Isaac, for all that he tried to be a boring, quiet little widower.

"I don't know," Isaac said, sighing and falling back into the hard patio chair. "I met Todd, and he was… well, he was solid. He was steady. He… well, he treated drug use with disdain, which was funny because I *met* him in a club. I wondered sometimes if he was there twink-fishing so he could have someone young and pliable, you know? Somebody to form in his own image." His mouth hardened, turning down at the corners, which was too bad—he had a mouth for smiling, or kissing, or giving… uhm. Never mind. Luca veered away from the crude sexuality. Isaac was cute—oh God, was he—but he was still a "mess," as he put it.

But a mess worth knowing.

"Obviously he didn't know how to cook a twink," Luca said, keeping his face straight.

Isaac's eyes lit up, and then that mouth—that puffy-lipped, mobile mouth—widened into a joyous smile. "Lightly pan-fried so he's still a little flaky," he said, and the angry moment, the bitter moment, eased.

Their eyes locked, and Luca knew what was in his own face—he'd never been particularly mysterious, but for a moment, he saw the softness he'd been hoping for. He saw recognition.

He saw *want*.

As if surprised by his own emotions, Isaac jerked his head, breaking contact before he closed his eyes and turned his face to the sun.

"You are so cute," he said after a breath. "And I could like you so much. But right now I'm *so very angry*. That wouldn't be fair to you."

Luca's heart skipped, and he tried not to be afraid. "Hey, buddy—don't worry about me. I'm just here for the yarn."

Isaac smiled, still scenting the breeze. "Okay," he said softly.

"Okay what?" Luca asked suspiciously.

"That's what we'll be for now. I'll teach you yarn, and you teach me…."

"Acceptance," Luca said, thinking about all the things Isaac needed to overcome for them to be a couple.

Isaac opened his eyes, and Luca got a glimpse of how intense they could be when he focused. "You… you're a lot smarter than you pretend to be," he said, cocking his head.

Luca gave him a lazy grin. "Dumb and hung. You're not the only one who's spent time being stupid and getting laid."

Isaac's laughter—both wicked *and* understanding—burbled up. "Good," he said, turning back to his sandwich with gusto. "One of the things Roxy and I have learned over the years is we cannot *stand* the kid without flaws. Straight A students are great. Straight A kissbutts are the *worst.*"

"Let me guess," Luca said, going back to his own sandwich with relief. "You guys are the C and B students' best friends."

Isaac's attractive mouth made an attractive moue. "I have actually grown *really* fond of some kids who never did end up passing my class. Some teachers take that personally, but you look at kids, and some of them have so much going on in their own lives. Foster homes, abusive parents, good parents who can't make ends meet, boyfriend or girlfriend trauma, gang pressure, cyberbullying—so much bad shit. And I get them a grand total of four hours a week, with twenty to forty other students—*if* they can show up that often, because sometimes they just fucking can't. The fact that they *do* show up, do the occasional assignment, and are civil and kind and often funny—that shows more character than most teachers give them credit for. My department head, for one, assumes they're doing it because they hate her. I mean, not that *I* haven't bailed on some meetings because *I* hate her, but these kids, they've got too much going on to think that much about her at all. If they show up and say, 'I'm sorry I'm failing—you're a nice guy but this semester is the *worst,*' that's… that's some consideration right there. A lot of kids say, 'Fuckin' class, fuckin' teacher, fuck off.'"

"Still not personal?" Luca hazarded.

"Still not personal," Isaac confirmed before taking another bite. He let out a blissful breath. "You," he said, wiping his mouth on a napkin, "are really easy to talk to. You have to do me a favor and not tell your nonna how much I swear."

Luca's laughter surprised even him. "I promise," he said, after he'd covered his mouth and made sure he hadn't done anything embarrassing with his food when he'd opened it.

But inside he was thinking that this—this was it. This was the day he determined that, as much of a mess as Isaac was, he could wait. There was just… just… *so much potential* there.

Isaac was apparently his own basket of yarn. Some of it was a little bit frayed and angry, and like most people, some of it turned brown and sad with age, but with a little work and some care, he had all the potential in the world.

BACK AT Isaac's house, the first thing they did was put away the yarn, and Luca derived a lot of satisfaction from watching Isaac, hands on hips, admiring his seventh box.

"Isn't it pretty?" he asked, with no irony whatsoever, and Luca glanced from the big clear plastic box with all of that "potential" inside to Isaac's shining eyes and agreed that it was beautiful.

Then they sat back down on the couch, and Isaac—patient and funny—taught Luca how to move his big work-roughened hands with gentle poetry so he could make things with a hook and colorful string.

When he left, he had a sturdy canvas bag with his yarn, his hook, and a little pouch with scissors and big-eyed metal needles in it, and strict instructions to keep working on it in the quiet hours so he had questions for Isaac next weekend.

"Yeah?" Luca asked. "Next weekend?"

Isaac's fair complexion washed a sweet pink as they were standing at the door. "Uhm… if you still want to—"

And Luca made his move, swooped in, and kissed him on the cheek. "Of course I want to," he said. "You want to plan for lunch next week too?"

Isaac stared at him with big eyes, touched his cheek like a teenager, and nodded wordlessly.

"Awesome."

And then Luca left, whistling, with plans to bring his work in the evenings too so he and Isaac could sit and yarn and watch the neighborhood as the sun went down.

Unexpected Purrings

Isaac was sitting at his desk, grading papers and listening to Green Day—and reflecting woefully that "Holiday" was a great song, and nobody seemed to have learned anything in the twenty or so years since its release.

Roxy had come in and was using his TA's desk to do the same thing, while both of them hummed along, enjoying the breeze and the sunshine coming in from the open door. Next week the temperature was going to be in the nineties or hundreds, but this week, it was topping out at eighty-five, and before three o'clock, life was downright pleasant.

And that's what they were doing when a half-grown orange tomcat wandered in, sat down about three feet from Isaac's left shoe, and meowed imperiously for his attention.

Isaac stared. "Well, hello," he said.

"Meow."

"Can I, uhm, help you with something?"

"Me*ow*?"

"Are you hungry?" Because lunch was coming, and Isaac had a tuna sandwich sitting in the cooler in his drawer, and he'd been thinking about reasons not to eat it.

The cat cocked his head, so Isaac reached into his drawer for the sandwich.

Which was when Roxy glanced up. "No… wait, Isaac, you don't really want to—"

Isaac pulled off a little piece of sandwich, and the cat took it delicately from his fingers.

"Feed the cat," Roxy finished, grimacing.

He stared at her. "Why?"

"Because, you idiot, that's how the cat distribution system works! The cat sees you, you feed it, and you are obligated to the thing for life."

Isaac paused, the next piece of tuna sandwich on his fingertips, and the cat stood up on its hind legs and relieved him of the burden.

Isaac stared down at the thing, who was licking his whiskers with a fastidious pink tongue, although he appeared a little bit dusty and travel-worn.

"Really?" he asked the cat. "Do you have some sort of nefarious agenda to become my cat?"

The cat reached up, claws sheathed, and started to pull at his fingers for more sandwich, which Isaac quickly gave.

"I guess so," he said, surprised, before looking back at Roxy. "Uhm…."

Roxy was already packing up her stuff. "I'll be back," she said resignedly. "With some pet supplies, a box, and some takeout so you eat. Don't worry, Isaac. I've got three kids, two cats, and a Labrador retriever. I know how this works."

And she was gone before he could feed his new cat another piece of sandwich.

By THE time Roxy got back, loaded down with a crate and flea treatment and a week's worth of food, Isaac had a feeling for this cat. Handsome, vain, unflappable, Euclid (as Isaac was calling him now) seemed to have an innate "chill factor" that had apparently garnered him more than one tuna fish sandwich.

But that didn't mean he wasn't willing to leap into Isaac's lap to petition for more.

Isaac got a good look at him while he was there, saw some battering around his ears, a few scars under the fur of his face, and felt a certain boniness under his dusty fur, all of which indicated tuna sandwiches might be few and far between.

He was also—quite obviously—intact, and Isaac knew enough about *that* aspect of cats to know that condition needed to be nipped in the bud—or nipped under the butt, as it were. To that end, he was balancing the cat on his lap and his cell phone in his ear as he called the vet near his house to see if they could book an appointment for a new rescue for—as the receptionist called it—a bath and snip.

They had an opening that very day after school. He could pick the animal up at seven.

He thought regretfully about his knitting time with Luca. It had only been two days out of the week, but Luca had promised to be by that evening to get help on a tricky part of the scarf.

But then he held out his finger, and Euclid rubbed his whiskers against it and purred, and then did it again.

"Sure," he said into the phone. "I can be there at three thirty."

The receptionist signed off, and Isaac gazed helplessly at Roxy. "Are you sure this is how the cat distribution system works?" he asked.

"I dare you to contradict me," she told him. "Now give me the cat, go wash your hands, and eat this teriyaki bowl before the bell rings. You owe me a lunch hour, so you know."

The cat had an entire fan club before fifth period was seated, and Isaac was relieved that, once the lid of the crate had been taken off and a cat bed—laced with some catnip—had been installed, Euclid was content to sit there and be stoned for his people.

So maybe more kids stared at the cat than heard his instructions—fact was, this close to summer vacation, having an excuse to keep them quiet during seatwork was the *real* miracle, and he was calling it a win.

For sixth period, Marcelle strode into the classroom, gave the cat a double take, and then laughed low in his throat like he'd just gotten laid on the drama room couch and nobody had caught him. (At least Isaac knew that was how *he* had spent his lunches in high school, and he had it on good authority from the beleaguered drama teacher that a blacklight would make the couch look like a Jackson Pollack painting, and she didn't even want to know.)

"What's so funny?" Isaac asked warily.

"Well, for one thing, I see the cat distribution system is still working," Marcelle told him. "And for another, that department head lady who thinks she's hot shit—"

"Ms. Lamphere?" Isaac clarified.

"Yeah. Anyway, she was getting all loud in the quad during lunch about some disease-ridden animal running around and how she was going to ask the custodian to make sure he ended up in the shelter."

Isaac stared in horror at his cat, appearing self-satisfied and still very stoned after eating a tuna sandwich, having a little bit of water from Isaac's bottle, and enjoying the drugged cat bed very much.

"Euclid?" he asked in a small voice, and Marcelle patted his shoulder.

"Don't worry, Mr. B—you got him a box and everything. She can't take him away from you."

Except she *could.* This was blatant defiance of Paula Lamphere and her adherence to all things school-related.

Isaac rubbed Euclid's whiskers again and thought about dumping him outside or calling the humane society or any of the things that Todd would have insisted he do rather than bring the creature into their home.

Which was where Isaac had been *really* excited about Euclid ending up!

"Maybe," he said, with a worried glance at Marcelle, "we should move his crate into the corner by my desk so, you know, if somebody comes in, they can't see him."

Marcelle nodded sagely. "That's a good idea. And how about if I put the lid on it, since he seems so…." Marcelle stared at the cat and then grinned at Isaac. "Stoned, Mr. B. Did you give your cat a gummi?"

Isaac snorted. "No, I did not," he retorted and then lowered his voice. "But the bed is laced with catnip."

Marcelle laughed throatily and then moved to hide the cat while Isaac got everybody else started on their seatwork.

Twenty minutes later, everybody was quiet and working—although part of that was that Isaac had promised to let one or two people go visit the cat when they were done with their seatwork. He was, as he had been last week, bemused. It was one of those moments—as the week before had been—that proved to him that students could be very, very good people, and that all of the hard work and frustration was worth it, because helping very good people was what being human was all about.

Then Marcelle's crush (yes, Marcelle had been crushing on Domingo, everybody knew it but Marcelle and Domingo, but Isaac didn't gossip) gave an urgent stage whisper.

"You guys! It's Ms. Lamphere!"

"Oh shit!" Marcelle burst out, and if he hadn't been suddenly terrified for poor Euclid, still snoozing in his box, Isaac would have mourned the days when he'd hoped his students would actually fear him enough to not swear. "Mr. B! Go talk to her. I'll sit at your desk and pretend to… to…."

"Be my TA," Isaac said and handed him a stack of papers with an ever-present felt-tipped pen. "Put a smiley face on these if there's any work on them."

"Hee, hee, hee…."

Which meant Marcelle had just cracked the code of how Isaac managed to grade 150 sheets of seatwork every day, but whatever. It said in the teacher bylaws that seatwork was *practice*.

So when Paula burst through the door, Isaac was walking amiably up and down rows of silent students pretending to do seatwork.

"Isaac," she demanded imperiously, and he strolled up to her, as innocent as a lamb.

"Yes, Paula," he replied, knowing it bothered her that he called her by her first name in front of the students. Yes, she'd done the same thing to him, but that's what made her the Wicked Witch of the Math Department.

"Keep your eyes out for a… a *cat* that's been wandering around here. If you see him, let me know. I've got the humane society on speed dial, and they can take him to the nearest shelter."

Isaac nodded sagely. "How… humane," he said, wondering if his tone of voice gave away his disgust.

"Don't give me that shit, Isaac," she said. "It's unsanitary to have an animal roaming around campus, and you know it."

Isaac snorted. "Anybody who's walked into a high school classroom at the beginning of summer knows that a cat is the least of their problems," he said. Poor kids. They didn't ask for sudden onset BO, but that was what happened with adolescence, and that was God's honest truth. "Paula, has it occurred to you that we all have better things to do than harass poor felines because they had the misfortune to wander around a high school? I mean, think about their view alone. All those feet. That's got to be a treat."

Paula stared at him in horror, but Marcelle and a few other students made suspicious noises, and there were a few sniffs, snorts, and coughs scattered around the room.

"Isaac, it could have *fleas*!"

"So could you," he replied shortly. "But I give you the benefit of the doubt."

"Your sense of humor is not appreciated," she said with a delicate sniff. "It would be nice if you took these things seriously." She glanced at his busy hands in disdain. "If nothing else, you could at least put down your knitting."

"I'll take it under advisement," he said blandly. "Did you have anything else you needed, Paula?"

She glared at him. "I'll be talking to the principal about this," she warned.

"Oh no, no, not the principal," he said flatly. "Paula, there are kids in my morning class afraid to come to school because they cut off bus service. Three-quarters of my students won't eat if the proposed cuts to SNAP funding go through. My God, don't we have better things to worry about than a *cat*?"

And then he saw it—the thing that made him only dislike Paula and not loathe her entirely.

The stricken expression that told him she was fixating on the cat because fixating on anything else was an exercise in futility.

"But the cat I can control!" she burst out, her voice wavering. "I don't want to see his… his *body* in the parking lot because he got hit!" and he took pity on her.

"I know," he said. "That's why I'm taking him to the vet and taking him home. Now that you know that, can you maybe get off my case?"

The grateful, limpid look she gave him made him almost forgive her for all the sniffing, superior things she said in the staff room. "Really?"

Isaac glanced over at Marcelle, who sighed and stood up.

Euclid regarded them through half-closed eyes and purred.

"Roxy got me the crate during lunch. He wandered in and…."

"Kitty…," she said wistfully.

"Yeah," he said. "Kitty. I promise, he's getting de-flead, fixed, and, if he'll have me, homed. I understand this is how the cat distribution system works."

And then Paula, who was in her mid-forties and groomed like a cartoon character, with stiffly sprayed hair and granny spectacles, gave him a smile that made her seem… young.

"It's already given me four," she said with a little hiccup. "I can't have another one or they'll evict me."

"Do you want to go pet him?" Isaac asked. "He's stoned stupid, but—"

But she was already booty bumping Marcelle out of the way to rub Euclid's whiskers. Goddammit. Isaac might really have to knit her a sweater. She was, what? A size 2? It would take him two weeks.

SO IT was an unexpected development in the day, and the vet's office gave him a blessed, blessed discount for a rescue cat. When the super-extra-super-*young* technician at the reception desk sounded out the name (Yuuuuukllllit?), he corrected her gently, telling her, "He was the father of modern geometry."

"Oh," said the girl. "I should remember that—I like math." She was Black but had dyed her hair white-blond and styled it to swirl in straight flyaway bangs, and Isaac had worn a Bieber for a while (Todd had been so embarrassed) and knew the combination of vanity and determination it took to get even mildly curly hair to do things it wasn't designed to do, and was impressed.

He felt like Euclid was in good hands, whether or not she could pronounce his name.

"I teach it," Isaac said apologetically. He and Roxy had enjoyed long, bitter discussions about why that *shouldn't* make them the most boring humans on planet earth but somehow did.

"Math teachers are the greatest," she said with a smile. "We'll make sure Mr. Yuclit here is treated right."

Isaac gave the cat one last look through the slats in the plastic crate, and Euclid blinked still-sleepy eyes at him. "Alrighty, Mr. Yuclit," he murmured. "You and me, we got a date at eight—don't be late."

He glanced at the girl again. "He's had a *lot* of catnip," he admitted.

Her laugh tinkled. "Also, he's an orange boi," she said, and he heard the *i* in *boi*. "You understand, they're sort of dumber than the average cat. They share three communal brain cells—you never know when your boy's going to be using one or when they're all out on loan."

Isaac laughed, delighted, and decided he had to remember to tell his class that. "He wandered into my classroom when I was grading papers," he said softly, "and proceeded to eat my lunch. I think he's got just enough brain cells."

Euclid purred back, and Isaac left him reluctantly.

It wasn't until he got home and prepared a casserole to bake for an hour that he realized that the visit—and the return to pick up the cat— would put his entire evening with Luca out of whack.

Once the casserole was in the oven, he went outside to see if Luca was working on his grandparents' place yet. What he saw was the man sitting in his truck—some sort of big, battered extra-cab wide-bed affair—with the windows down and his head tilted back, the wind ruffling his hair as he napped.

For a moment, Isaac was completely arrested.

God, he was handsome. High cheekbones, strong chin, a plush mouth still meant for smiling, and the Italian complexion that tanned so nicely, along with the toffee-colored hair. "Dumb and hung" he'd called himself, but he was more than that. He was funny, he was kind, he was… well, game to try, even if he wasn't great at yarn work yet. Maybe *ever*. But Isaac was starting not to care. Frankly, he'd make thousands of little squares in hundreds of colors and sew them all together in whatever configuration Luca asked him to, just for his quiet companionship when they were working on their projects in the early evening.

You could probably kiss him, and he wouldn't object, taunted a little voice in his head, but Isaac thought of the way they'd met and of the hated brown yarn and how he still couldn't get himself to wind it into balls and give it to an upcycling place, or repurpose it for charity or… or *anything*. Nope, it sat there, this tangled mess of anger at Todd, at himself, at his inability to change things before Todd had dropped dead of a brain aneurism because he'd been too goddamned self-sufficient to take his high blood pressure medication.

Yeah. He should probably let go of some of that before he made room for a Luca in his heart.

But that didn't mean he didn't want to still have him in his life, on his porch—hell, in his kitchen, eating his food.

Isaac had complained about the time it took to cook all those super gourmet dinners, and Todd had insisted on buying those gourmet single-serving dinner things from a service six days a week. That way they could have a nutritionally balanced, constantly revolving array of prepared food that Todd didn't have to worry about.

Isaac *liked* worrying about food, but cooking for one was depressing, and the one time he'd tried it, Todd had refused to even *eat* with him, since they were eating different things.

And this casserole—which consisted mainly of chicken, mayonnaise, and pimentos—was one of his favorites. Luca worked so hard all week, and he'd been so worried about his sister. Isaac had looked forward to sending some of it home so neither of them had to cook.

He watched as Luca startled in the front of his truck, yawned, and sat up, glancing around a little wildly before he oriented himself. He swung his eyes to where Isaac stood on his porch and gave a half-embarrassed smile before waving.

"Come on in," Isaac called.

Luca yawned again as he got out of the truck and tried to talk. He finally managed as he came even with Isaac's little gate through his front yard. "I was going to—" *Yawn.* "—try to get some work done."

Isaac gave him a sympathetic nod. "Your nonna wouldn't be happy about you getting hurt if you were so tired you slept in your truck. Besides, I'm going to have to leave early tonight, so you might as well get your crocheting in now."

Luca grimaced, quite apologetic. "My sister stole it," he muttered, letting himself into the gate.

"Your sister *what*?" Isaac asked, surprised.

"I was working on it last night, and my sister came in and said, 'Wait a minute, I've seen Nonna do this,' and the next thing I know, she was making her own scarf. I was going to take it back, but she was working on it during lunch, and it made her happy." He let out a sigh. "I may have to steal some more of your yarn."

Isaac shook his head. "I'm telling you," he said, "this is the weirdest day. But okay. Fine. Bring your sister over tomorrow and we can *all* do yarn. It'll be fun."

Luca's grin told him that, against all odds, he really *did* think that was fun. "You think? I mean, I still wanted to help with the blanket—"

Isaac shook his head. "Listen, you may not know this, but your blanket has helped five more kids pass my class. They're willing to do math and algebra like you can't *believe* to figure out how many squares we need to make for their designs. And wait until you see what their designs are. I will make your sister *all* of the blankets if these kids can do this actually *relevant* extra-credit project and show me they've mastered equations."

Luca's grin faded, and it was his turn to seem bemused. "That's amazing. You are, like, the *best* teacher."

Isaac felt himself flushing from the compliment. He tried to remember if Todd had ever told him he was good at his profession.

Isaac, you should learn how to mingle more with your administrators—it's the only way to work your way up.

Isaac, why aren't you getting your MA in administration instead of physics? It's not like any of these kids will appreciate those extra letters after your name.

God, Isaac, is this all you wanted to be—a lifer in a shitty high school?

"What?" Luca asked. "What'd I say?"

Isaac shook his head and let out a sigh. "You paid me a great compliment," he said, "about something I'm super proud of. I…. Roxy's the only one who ever tells me I'm good at my job." Roxy was *amazing* at teaching. Isaac always thought that getting the kids to connect with math was, like, her superpower. She once got an entire class to understand vectors by talking about a stroller rolling downhill and into the street, because that was her worst nightmare.

Luca swallowed. "What you're not saying," he observed cannily, "is that Todd probably thought it was no big deal."

Isaac let out a sigh. "We're not going to talk about Todd right now," he said, and then he pulled that happy bemusement he'd been feeling back around him like a comfy Mr. Rogers cardigan. "We're going to talk about why I have to leave right after dinner, because *somebody* has to hear this story besides Roxy."

"Let me wash up," Luca said, toeing off his work boots in front of Isaac's porch. Isaac thought of putting stuff there—one of those things with scrub brushes so Luca could get dust off the soles, and one of those wedges that helped people remove boots with leverage. He could tuck it right next to the porch swing so Luca would always feel…

Welcome.

Isaac regarded him yearningly as he stepped aside to let Luca in.

Please, let Luca feel welcome here in his big bland stupid house until Isaac got his shit together enough to ask for more.

Isaac hadn't kissed anybody in so, so long. He'd really love to explore that plush, smiling mouth. Maybe kissing had gotten better since he and Todd had gotten married. Todd hadn't been great at it—he seemed to treat it as an alpha male contest, and Isaac had never been great at those. He'd never gotten the point. He was five seven and slender. Why would he want to mash teeth together to prove he was strong? If he'd been that strong, he probably wouldn't have let Todd bully him into bed for most of his adult life.

He seemed to remember—back before Todd, before his parents had passed, when he'd been an undergrad crushing on his fellow students and necking at parties—kissing had been fun, hadn't it?

Suddenly he wanted to kiss Luca in the *worst* way, to see if it could be fun again. He felt that magnet pull of the man as he strode through

Isaac's house in his stocking feet. Kissing him seemed like it could be *really* fun.

But Isaac remembered that tangled ball of Todd—uhm, of yarn—again and resolved to simply make Luca feel welcome until he could sort that shit out. It just wouldn't do to wrap those tendrils of shit-brown yarn around this nice man.

Isaac had his plan firmly in place by the time Luca came into the kitchen to sit at the island.

"So," Isaac said, his voice brimming with excitement, "let me tell you what happened today...."

As he launched into the telling of Mr. Euclid, the father of geometry, in relation to stoned orange kitties, his brain went on record to tabulate all of Luca's expressions as he listened.

Not once was he bored or disgusted (except by Paula, but even then he showed a certain delighted incredulity that the woman was not *actually* the Wicked Witch of the Math Department). Instead, he was interested, bemused, and, in the end, so very happy.

"So you're getting a cat?" he asked.

"Yes," Isaac said, and by that time, the casserole was done, and Isaac pulled it out and set it on the stove to cool. "In fact, I am *waiting* for my cat to finish his, uhm, operation"—he lowered his voice and whispered the word so Luca would know they were talking about poor Euclid's balls—"so I can go fetch him home." He paused. "They were going to give him his first round of shots and flea treatments and a bath too." He glanced at the clock and saw he had about forty-five minutes before he was due at the vet's. "In fact, we have just enough time to eat before I have to go pick him up."

As he turned to get the salad mix from the fridge, Luca said, "Hey, can I come with you? I'm super excited. I *love* cats."

"Really?" Isaac grabbed the salad bowl from the shelf above the counter. "You want to see him?"

"Well *yeah!*" Luca regarded him with puzzlement. "Who wouldn't?"

Isaac knew his expression closed as he busied himself with the little bags that made up the salad mix.

"Of course," Luca murmured. "The whole reason you don't have a cat in the first place."

"I was going to go get one after summer vacation started," Isaac told him.

"But the cat distribution system had other ideas," Luca said, perking up again.

Isaac shook his head. "What is this cat distribution system everybody keeps talking about? Why didn't I know about it until now?"

Luca shrugged. "Because you don't know about the cat distribution system until it distributes a cat to you. It's like kitty karma—very Zen."

Isaac snorted. "Yes, it's so Zen this cat just wandered into my classroom to get fed, fixed, and baked. Where was the *boyfriend* distribution system when I was in high school, that's what I want to know."

"Same place it was when I was in high school," Luca said reasonably. "In the cheerleader's pants, pretending it was straight."

Isaac snorted and put the salad on the table. "You were not," he said.

"Well, for a couple years, yes. And then it hit me that it probably shouldn't be that hard, and I shouldn't have been dreaming about the school quarterback while I was doing it." He sighed and moved the salad so there was room for the casserole when Isaac took it from the stove. "The years after that were muddled. I think even if the distribution system had been working, it would have skipped me entirely. I was not fit for distribution for a couple of years."

Isaac *hmm*ed, because he doubted Luca had *ever* not been fit as boyfriend material. Even those cheerleaders had probably had nice things to say.

AFTER DINNER, he dished up the extras and put them in the refrigerator in a big container, showing it to Luca as he did so.

"This is for you and your sister," he said seriously. "I will not eat it—it will go *bad* if you don't take it, do you understand?"

Luca chuckled. "I understand I'm bringing Allegra by tomorrow so you can teach us both to yarn is what I understand, so don't panic. Now let's go get the cat."

On the way out the door, Isaac realized that he'd spoken to a grown man the way he spoke to his students. Oh God. Oh *God*. He did that sometimes—he knew it. Todd used to get cold. Cold and disdainful and superior.

When we met you were too stoned to remember the rubber, Isaac—don't talk to me like a student.

Except Isaac had never *meant* to talk to him that way—it just slipped out!

No amount of apologizing to Todd had made that better until Todd had frozen Isaac out for at least two days, but that didn't stop Isaac from apologizing now.

"I'm sorry for the lecture on the leftovers," he said as he locked the door. Mid-May had fallen with full force, and even at nearly eight in the evening, the heat coming off the pavement was suffocating.

"That?" Luca's perpetual goodwill was untarnished. "Naw, I figure most teachers do that at one time or another. I mean, don't you people have to take *classes* in how to give instructions? I dated a guy in the credential program once, a few years ago. He had this bit when he was pretending to give instructions on how to wipe your own ass—I can't do it like he did, but it made me laugh until I cried. And then one night *he* cried for real, because apparently the whole thing was taking over his brain. You got a tough gig—control issues, they gotta be a blowback, right?"

Isaac gazed at him wistfully, forgetting for the moment that they were going to go get one of the most wonderful things to happen in Isaac's life in a really long time.

Except for Luca coming to talk to him the week before. That had been wonderful too.

"Do you know how badly I needed to hear that when I was starting out?" he asked, his eyes almost shiny. "I thought I was some sort of mutant, and Todd…." He snapped his teeth together and gestured to Luca to get into the Sportage.

For a moment they were silent as he piloted through the quiet, still-sun-dappled streets to the vet's office. Then Luca spoke.

"Look, Isaac?"

"Yeah?"

"I get that you're trying not to bitch about your late husband too much. But I don't think it's doing you any good *not* bitching about him. I mean, there *had* to be some good about the guy, but you're never going to see it for all the resentment you're holding on to."

Isaac sighed. "Yeah."

"So maybe, when you're mad at him, you just keep saying whatever he did that pissed you off. And then, even if it's not to me, you finish off with a thing he did you liked. Then you won't feel so guilty, but you won't feel so… so *obligated* to hold on to all the bad stuff. What do you think?"

And Isaac's eyes grew hot. "I think you're a genius," he croaked. "And that's super good advice. But you've got to… I don't know, remind me, I guess. If someday all I do is talk about Todd, you've got to tell me to stop. I'm… I'm afraid I'll get stuck on loop. Like I was when he was alive. It was all about Todd. I got up in the morning, and I couldn't set a certain alarm because of Todd. I couldn't sing in the shower because of Todd. I could only eat fruit and yogurt because Todd couldn't stand it if I ate toast and peanut butter instead. I-I want to think about somebody *else*, because God, he's been gone for a year and a half, and wouldn't it be great if I could remember who I was without him?"

Luca's voice was infinitely gentle. "Is he the reason you never got a cat?"

"Yeah," Isaac sighed.

"Then how about you tell me more about this cat?"

Isaac brightened. "He's orange," he said happily. "Did I tell you the girl at the vet counter told me that orange cats have three collective brain cells, and they only get partial custody? So you never know if you're going to get the smart orange cat or the idiot orange cat who just sits and bakes in all the catnip."

"Sounds like me, post–high school," Luca said. "I think me and this cat are already destined to be friends."

"I was too cool to smoke pot," Isaac said primly. "Not when gummies tasted better, and I could get the ones with the extra THC."

Luca's hearty laughter was what he remembered about the trip to the veterinarian. And then he got the box with his new best friend, Euclid, who seemed a little dopier but just as sweet and poised as he had been when he'd been eating Isaac's sandwich, and as much as he liked Luca, Euclid sort of sucked up all the attention.

"What do you think?" Isaac said as they belted themselves back in the Kia, the cat purring—*purring*—in the box behind them.

"I think you've needed a Mr. Euclid all your life," Luca said. "This could be a once-in-a-lifetime orange cat."

Isaac smiled, feeling almost as happy and almost as dopey as the cat. "I wonder if he likes to play?"

Learning to Play in Summer

Luca sat cross-legged on Isaac's floor, enjoying the new brightly colored area rug very much as he taught Mr. Euclid to fetch a catnip mouse with a bell on its tail. The cat absolutely crushed the game, right up until the catnip *really* kicked in, whereupon he simply lay there, eyes half closed, drool dribbling from his thin cat lips, absorbing all the pretty cat colors in the room.

"You put the cat in a coma," Allegra said. "Achievement *unlocked*."

Luca chuckled and turned to her, a little dismayed but mostly pleased to see that she'd taken the simple scarf Isaac had given *him* to create and had whipped out the vertical part and was now working on the horizontal part. Because the yarn made its own stripes—and because Isaac had promised to teach his sister how to make squares for the end and middle—it was going to be a great scarf. Different. It wouldn't look like a beginner scarf at all, but like something bold and fun and very feminine.

And his sister was so delighted with it that even the fact that *she* was the one who would probably be helping with her own blanket wasn't enough to make Luca regret asking Isaac.

Hell, getting Allegra moved into Luca's apartment had made a difference in her life. She'd been funnier and freer and more *Allegra* than she had been in the last year, and Luca thought of Isaac's lingering anger at Todd the Terrible, and he couldn't help it.

Luca wanted to vent about the guy. Todd, who made fun of Isaac's yarn hobby and his students and his job. Todd, who wouldn't let him help decorate the house. Todd, who wouldn't let him cook because he might not do it perfectly.

Todd, who made him feel like it was his job to be the quiet little house-husband, because forever ago, Isaac had been young and lost and had needed direction.

Luca was starting to learn what Isaac had probably known for the last year and a half. There was *nothing* more frustrating than anger at the dead. It was completely unproductive. There was nothing you could *do* with it. *This* was the reason Isaac tried to bottle it up, to not talk about it, to not mention that, say, Todd's taste in home decor was boring and Isaac had true taste and a love of color that made this living room *so* much more exciting with a rug and some drapes that used earth tones—cinnamon, autumn purple, cantaloupe—to jazz up the furniture that Isaac reluctantly admitted still had some years of use on it.

Raging at Todd would have resulted in… poor choices.

For example, Luca would have put the furniture on the side of the road and gone out and put new furniture on his already-stretched-thin credit so he could get rid of that ass-boring tan stuff.

But with the rug and drapes, they could wait on replacing the expensive stuff, and the room still looked way better. Luca rather slyly suggested an afghan for an accent, and Isaac had almost instantly been transported to "design his own knitting" land, which made Luca wonder if Todd had told him that afghans were tacky and he didn't want any of Isaac's work in the room.

And see? Getting mad at *that* was counterproductive because it wouldn't have let Isaac plan something beautiful that might be more healing than raging at the dead guy who was *still pissing Luca off.*

Wow.

This was tangled. This was complex. No wonder Isaac interrupted himself and didn't finish sentences that began, "Todd used to…."

Isaac was probably as ready for Todd to be well and truly out of his life as Luca was, but dammit, he was like a demon that needed to be exorcized.

First they had to say his name; *then* they had to find the right combination of words and deeds that would make his presence fade from Isaac's house!

But as Luca sat on the rug Todd would have hated and threw the catnip mouse for the cat Todd would have hated and helped Luca's sister make a scarf Luca knew *for a fact* Todd would have hated, he was starting to see that the subtle approach might be best.

They'd started with the giant box of yarn that Todd would have hated, and Luca was there for that.

Look at what had happened in the two weeks since Luca had given Isaac permission to *not* knit with that ass-ugly shit-brown yarn.

"What?" Allegra asked. "What's that crinkly expression on your face?"

Luca shrugged. "You're doing a good job with that," he said. "I mean, I was *not* doing a good job with it, and I felt like shit, but you're doing a good job about it, and now I'm not obligated to feel like shit, so everybody's happy."

Allegra laughed. "Well, Nonna tried to teach me when I was a kid, and I think I drove her batshit. This feels like… I dunno. Redemption in yarn." She aimed a brilliant smile at Isaac. "Thanks, Isaac. I can't tell you how much this has settled my nerves. Have you figured out what picture you're going to make with all the tiny squares?"

Isaac stood up abruptly, suddenly excited. "Wait!" he said. "I've got to show you guys something! Here—let me get my briefcase. I barely remembered it in the excitement about Mr. Euclid, but I was *so excited* to show them to you!" He ran out of the room, leaving Allegra and Luca to stare at each other in bemusement.

"I sort of adore him," she whispered into the sudden silence. "Find a way to keep him."

"Working on it," he mouthed back, and at that moment Isaac returned from the yarn room/office with his briefcase, sat down, and started rifling through it.

What he produced from the center zipper pocket was worth all the fuss.

"Wow," Luca said. "Are these all of them?"

"No!" Isaac said. "These are just the first batch—the ones that came in early. I gave them until the week before the final to turn them in, but I thought I'd bring these home to show you. What do you think?"

He handed the batch to Allegra, who looked at them one at a time before passing them on to Luca.

"Wow," she said, after looking at only a couple. "These… these are *amazing*. Isaac, can we really do these?"

Isaac laughed. "Well, some of these are big enough to cover a large bed, so I may have to, you know, draw a line…."

"Right?" she laughed. "Luca—what do you think?"

Luca stared at a depiction of the Little Mermaid using squares as pixels and shook his head in impressed disbelief. "I think these are *really* awesome!" he said. "Allegra, how're we going to pick one?"

Allegra bit her lip while checking out an ethereally lovely depiction of a bouquet of flowers, all done in squares, with, Luca assumed, embellishments for the stems and bow.

"Maybe," she said slowly, staring at that one longingly, "we should ask Isaac which ones are actually *do*able. Which ones are, you know, crib sized." She glanced at Isaac. "They all get extra credit, right?"

"Oh yes," Isaac said, smiling. "If you turn them over, you can see their algebra work. They were really thorough. It's why they're due a week *before* finals—I want time to get all their extra credit entered into the gradebook before we do the judging."

"Turn them over? Absolutely not," Allegra said. "That's *your* part of the business. But maybe we, you know… make criteria?"

Isaac nodded. "That's what I thought too." He reached into his briefcase and pulled out a pen and a legal pad. "So, we've got *practical* to make," he said.

"This one's really simple," Luca said—not critically, because it was pretty, but it wasn't as involved as some of the others.

"So, we've got *interesting* to make," Isaac said, adding it to the pad.

"And some of these…." Allegra held out one which would have required a whole lot of different yarns that Luca wasn't positive even *Isaac* could find.

"*Possible* to make," Isaac said. "So that's three criteria—practical, interesting, and possible. Let me look at these, and then you can judge from the stack that's only got all three, how's that?"

"Yes!" Allegra said. "That sounds much easier." She paused and glanced at Luca. "But Luca's got to have a say too, because it was sort of his idea."

Isaac nodded. "Oh yes. Absolutely." He flashed Luca a quick grin. "Just because he's opted out of the making, that doesn't mean he's not *amazing* yarn support, right?"

Allegra's laugh burbled out of her, and for a moment, Luca just gazed at his sister in profound relief.

She'd been *so* disheartened in this last week. Steve had stopped by Luca's apartment to "drop the last of her shit off," and Luca had needed to get in the guy's face to make him go away.

He'd had to hold his sister while she wept against his chest, saying, "Jesus, Luca, how could I have given that douchebag my *time*," and he'd been so sad for her. And he'd thought of Isaac, working on his knitting and his crocheting and doing things for his students and trying so hard to let go of a ten-year relationship that had obviously hurt him as much as it had helped.

Bringing Allegra here felt like bringing her to a place where she could learn, like Isaac was learning, how to heal.

Except Allegra had seven months to get where it had taken Isaac a year and a half to get—although Allegra had a lot less time invested, if that made things any easier. And she had something to show for that time.

Luca could already see her getting excited about the baby.

"He's been outstanding *everything* support," she said happily, before shooting him a playful glare. "Now if only we could do something about the bathroom situation."

Luca grunted. "Sorry, honey. It's a *really* small apartment."

Isaac frowned. "Wait… you only have one bathroom?"

"Yup," Luca said. "I… you see, I've been spending all my money trying to get my business to run."

"He sleeps in the trailer a lot," she said, reaching down to ruffle Luca's hair as he sat on the floor. "And to his credit, he uses the bathroom and shower there more than he does at home." She grimaced. "I just have to pee a lot, and, well…." She made a sweeping gesture with the same hand she'd used to tousle Luca's hair. "One bathroom."

"You know," Isaac said slowly, glancing around his big house, "I've got more room than I can handle here. You're welcome to stay here until you can find a place of your own."

Luca and Allegra both stared at him.

"Uhm, that's really nice, Isaac," Luca said slowly, "but that's also crazy talk."

Isaac shrugged. "Believe it or not, Todd and I had a giant argument in my head right before I said that, and then I remembered he was dead and had no say." He laughed quietly to himself for a moment before sobering. "No. I stand by it. If I were to run a classified and advertise for a roommate, I could run a background check, stage interviews and meetings, and still know less about that person than I know about you. Allegra, I know your grandparents—they're lovely. I know your brother— he's a stand-up guy. And I know that if you and I have a problem, they will both give you a place to stay while you figure out another solution." He smiled at her kindly. "Although I'm not sure if you and I are going to have any problems."

"She's a slob!" Luca blurted, at the same time Allegra said, "I'm *messy*!"

To his credit, Issac thought about it. "I know it seems like it," he murmured, glancing around, "but I am not, in fact, particularly meticulous." His eyes fell on the window that overlooked the porch and the front room. "That window is clean because Todd hired people to wash them, inside and out, once a month. I like the look, so I kept them on. Same with the rest of the house—maid service once a week. And the rest of it is, you know, simply *me*. My bedroom has unfolded laundry on the bed, and"—his lips twitched—"I've been folding my stuff and putting it *on* the dresser instead of in it."

Luca felt a small measure of warmth at this. "I take it Todd would not approve?"

Isaac shuddered. "No, he would not have," he said, and Luca felt again that terrible combination of anger at the dead and helplessness because it would forever go unresolved. But Isaac was excited now and on a roll, so Luca let it go.

"It's a fine solution," he said. "I know where your office is, Luca— it's on the way to the school. Luca comes by in the evening to work on your grandparents' place, so he could drop you off. I cook four or five nights a week, and usually I give leftovers to Roxy—you'll love her, by the way." He paused. "And she's got three kids, all of them still in diapers. She's got life hacks like you can't *believe*. But anyway...." He gave Allegra an almost pleading smile. "Look at the place, you guys. It's *huge*. The backyard is big, and it's fenced, with a porch and shade. This place is *made* for a family, and all it's got right now is *me*." He set his yarn work on his lap and raised his hands in supplication. "You can decide on rent, but I swear, I'd do it rent-free. We could do yarn work in the evenings while listening to audiobooks or watching TV...."

"All the murder shows," Allegra said promptly. "Please tell me you don't watch documentaries."

"Only if they're about murder!" Isaac said, his face almost transported with happiness. "I think we could make it work. There's a suite downstairs—a large bedroom with a bathroom and a smaller bedroom on the other side—and something similar upstairs. Right now, the upstairs one has Todd's office in it, but...." And now there was a dawning joy. "But it would force me to clear that out! I think it's down to two file boxes and his computer, which could be repurposed anyway." He smiled prettily at Allegra. "Feel free to snoop around. With the exception of the yarn room and the master suite, the rest of it can be redone."

Allegra bit her lip, glancing around. "How about I start with a bedroom and a bathroom?" she said hopefully. "And then, if it seems to be working between us, we'll make plans for, uhm…."

"Seven months from now?" Isaac supplied so she wouldn't have to.

Luca realized that for one reason or another, they were both looking at him for permission.

He glanced at Euclid, who was still baking in a sunbeam, super pleased with himself.

"You sure you're ready for this, Isaac?" he asked. "You, uhm, just got a cat."

Isaac shrugged. "I remember right after college—I mean, I was a mess, but I shared a two-bedroom flat with four other guys. Can you imagine? One of us always ended up on the couch."

"Which one?" Allegra asked.

"The one who didn't have a hookup that night," Isaac said. "And only two of us were gay. Trust me. Awk. Ward."

Allegra's laughter burbled through the house, and Luca had a sudden shaft of good feeling, as bright and clear as Euclid's sunny spot.

"You won't be lonely," Luca said, still doubtful. He'd had one of those flats too—he seemed to recall he wasn't speaking to any of those guys anymore. But then, he'd been young and prideful and wounded by his parents' rejection. Like Isaac kept proclaiming about himself, Luca too had been a mess, and even after he'd spent two years at his grandparents' place, he'd still lived in his office trailer for a few months before getting his own apartment.

"I'll think about it," Allegra said, but she giggled to herself for the rest of the afternoon and evening.

ON THE way home, after Isaac cooked for them and they watched two episodes of one of Allegra's favorite "murder shows," which Isaac was rewatching, Allegra sat next to Luca as he drove them back to the apartment, her yarn bag with her WIP, as Isaac called it, (short for Work In Progress) at her feet, along with some extra yarn for the thing she was planning to start next.

She kept making happy sounds that Luca could barely hear under the classic rock station, and he liked those sounds better than the knowledge that the "classic rock" he was listening to had been cutting-edge when he was in middle school. Like Isaac, his "I'm a mess" days were further and further behind him.

"What?" he asked finally, turning the music down.

"I really wanna," she said, smiling into the warm spring night.

"You really wanna?" he asked. He didn't even have to ask what she wanted to do.

"He's nice, Luca. And he's right. He knows our grandparents, he's part of our community. And he's got *stupid* amounts of room there. And he seems...."

She paused to ponder, and he tried not to grip the steering wheel too tight. He *really* wanted her opinion, good or bad, of this guy he'd been crushing on.

Isaac still seemed like that giant box of yarn.

Tangled, yes, but so, so full of... possibilities.

"Seems what?" he asked, in agony, when it appeared pregnancy brain was about to eat what she'd been thinking of saying.

"Seems... open to a new life," she said thoughtfully. "I know his husband passed, and you say the relationship wasn't, you know. Happy. But this is more than that. It just feels like his house is becoming more colorful, and he got a cat, which is amazing, and... I don't know. Like he wants more than color in his life. He wants *people* in his life. And jeez, Luca, doesn't that sound like exactly the opposite of the people we grew up with?"

Luca grunted. "You'd think—" He stopped in the middle of the sentence and then had a solid epiphany. "Huh."

"What?"

Well, Luca had insisted Isaac finish *his* sentences. "Mom and Dad," he said, and even when he said it, he remembered the mom and dad from their childhood. "They were good parents, right? I'm not crazy stupid about that, right? I mean, aside from the church thing, which drove us a little nuts, they were... they were *good.* There were trips to Disneyland and family jokes and new clothes. Mom taught me how to cook, Dad taught you engines—we had a good childhood, *right*? I'm not deluded about that?"

"No," she said, her voice aching. "No. They were good parents. I thought so. And then...."

And then Luca had come out to them the summer after he'd graduated, thinking, *Hey, I'm eighteen, and they've been good parents. They'll still love me, right?*

"They kicked me out," he said, and to his shock he heard the same bewilderment in his voice *now*, twelve years later, that had been in his voice *then*, when Allegra had met him in the backyard with his bank book and his money and a suitcase full of clothes.

"I don't understand," she said, sounding exactly like he did. "I'll *never* understand why they thought that was okay. Why it was okay to kick you out, just like that. Why it was okay to kick *me* out when I was eighteen, because they found out I was still talking to you. How…?" Her hand rested protectively on her abdomen, and she said, "This is why Isaac can't finish a sentence that begins with his late husband's name, isn't it?"

"*Yes,*" he exploded, grateful for his little sister in many, many ways. "I was just thinking that."

"Okay," she murmured. "Okay, then."

"Okay what?" he asked, not sure what they'd resolved.

"Well, we know that me and you and Isaac have a lot more in common even than we first thought, and moving in together might be a good thing for him and me, right?"

Luca grunted. "It's weird when you read my mind like that."

She gave a delicate little snort. "And we learned that before I have this baby, Luca, you and me, we've got to go talk to Mom and Dad, at least once, and tell them why we're mad."

Luca was an amazing driver, which was good because anybody else would have wrecked the truck. "I'm sorry? You took a left turn while I was still going straight. The hell?"

"Because as much as that conversation might suck, Luca, at least we can still *have* it. Poor Isaac—it's taken him a year and a half to start to figure out all the stuff he wants to say to Turkey Todd, and the guy is *dead.* The least we can do is go say our piece to Mom and Dad while they're still alive. So we can finish our goddamned sentences, you think?"

Luca grunted again, hating what she'd said. Hating it. Hating. It. "Hatechu," he muttered, even his inflection right back to when that word had meaning in middle school.

"Yeah, Luca. You hate me. What'd I do?"

"Right," he grumbled. "Goddammit. God*dammit*, Allegra Maria Carolina Giardino, why do you have to be right?"

She chuckled without joy. "Don't get too upset about it," she said. "First we've got to move me into Isaac's, then we have to see if it will work, and then we've got to beat the Todd out of poor Isaac so he can see what a catch *you* are."

"Why does all that come first?" he asked, not that he minded that plan, really.

"Because," she said with a sigh, leaning back in her seat and rubbing her still-flat tummy some more. "Because we don't want to walk up to them pregnant and scattered and crammed in the same apartment with no happy ever after in sight, do we? Your business is gonna make it—hooray! And I'm going to have this baby—also hooray! But we want to walk up to them in a place of power and say, 'We can organize our lives, bitches, and aren't you sorry you didn't want to be a part of them!'"

Luca chuckled. "How very dramatic," he said. "I swear, you got me so charged up I could go do that right now."

"No." She yawned. "Tomorrow, I go tell Nonna and Pop Pop. That's going to be hard enough. Seriously, I like this plan. Let's do this plan."

"Mmm... it's too easy to back out of this plan," he said shrewdly. "There will always be a reason to back out of it. Let's say... let's say October. Your birthday. You'll be seven months pregnant and twenty-six, and no matter where we are in our lives, you and me, we can go visit the 'rents and say our piece. That way, when this baby comes into this world, *you'll* know two things."

"What's that?" she asked.

"The first is that you're strong enough to clear the air with Mom and Dad, so you're strong enough to raise this baby," he said, and he saw her nod.

"The second?"

"That you're strong enough to raise this baby and be happy with who *they* are, not who you thought they would be. You can be a good parent through and through—you can see this kid to *their* kids and beyond. You don't need all the old memories to do this right. You can goddamned go make your own."

"Righteous," she said, nodding some more. "Okay. Fair. You don't need a boyfriend to do this. I don't need a man. We can go announce our adulthood and walk away."

It sounded *great*. Grandiose, but *great*.

And then Allegra brought him right down to earth.

"But I still hope you and Isaac get together, because he's a sweet guy, and today was a lot of fun."

He smiled to himself. "It was, right?"

"Seriously. I can't wait to show Nonna my scarf. She'll be over the moon that somebody could finally teach me. I can't wait to start helping with the crib blanket. I'm going to have so much fun."

Yeah, Luca thought, liking the idea more and more. *Yeah*.

And the Winner Is….

"Really?" Marcelle said, disbelieving and ecstatic. "You guys really like it?"

Allegra and Luca had dressed up to come to the campus and announce the winner on the Friday before finals week, and Isaac was so, so proud of his class *and* his friends.

His class had been excited and polite and all smiles as the people who had mapped out a pixel drawing for the blankets all stood up and showed off their pictures to the rest of the class. Each entry had gotten extra credit *and* a vinyl sticker of a heart-shaped ball of rainbow yarn with knitting needles stuck in it. The kids *loved* a good sticker—they went on laptops, binders, water bottles, and seriously, they were one of the purest rewards Isaac could give.

After the sharing phase was over, Isaac explained to the class that, while all the designs were awesome, for the contest, they'd developed criteria for judging.

"This doesn't mean the pictures that didn't match the criteria were bad in any way," he told the students. "It just means that since Allegra and I have to make the blanket, it needed to be something we wouldn't hate by the time we were done, and something that a baby could use." He chuckled. "You guys, some of you had pictures that would need *thousands* of squares, and frankly, I'm not that dedicated to this project."

The class laughed like it was supposed to, and Isaac was hopeful there would be no hard feelings.

Isaac named the kids whose pictures had met the criteria, and they stood up proudly, while Allegra and Luca walked by each kid and told them something they'd really loved about their drawing, while giving out another tiny prize—a tiny square (Allegra's first efforts) on a key ring.

The kids had gotten excited about *that* too, and it could have been because it was the last week of school before finals, but Isaac liked to think that it was also because he had nice kids.

And then they'd named their winner.

Marcelle was practically floating.

"You really like it?" he asked for probably the twelfth time.

"It's great," Luca said. "I love the rainbow fish and the little boat—it's super cute without being too intricate."

"It's so fun," Allegra said to the boy. "I love your sense of design—and it feels like you know little kids, right? Like you know they don't like things too complicated, but they love color?"

Marcelle gave a modest little smile. "I got *four* brothers and sisters—two sets of twins. I go home to watch them all the time. They're so much fun. I made a copy of this to put on the fridge so they could see it."

Isaac wanted to clutch at his chest. *He'd* known Marcelle's homelife had its challenges, but hearing him talk about his siblings with so much pride made his eyes burn. *This* was why he loved teaching. Not the steady paycheck Todd had said was adequate, and not the summers off. It was just nice, as a human being, to see the best of human beings as they launched into the world.

Isaac had to settle everybody down then to give them last-minute reminders about the final next week, and to congratulate everybody who'd entered the contest for extra credit all over again.

As the last bell rang and the kids ran out excitedly, Isaac stopped Marcelle before he disappeared.

"Hey," he said. "I know the ultimate prize was supposed to be having your blanket made—and we'll do that! But I wanted to give you something for *you* since we're keeping the blanket."

Marcelle took the gift certificate and looked suspiciously at him. "What's this?"

"It's a gift certificate for the local art supply place, with another one for a basic craft store. Luca and Allegra contributed too. We figured this way you could get the super-nice art supplies and all the plastic beads you could ask for."

Marcelle grinned at them, practically glowing. "Solid, Mr. B. This is *solid*. Thank you so much—you guys, wait until I tell my mom!"

He went tearing out of the classroom, and Allegra sank down into Isaac's comfortable chair while Isaac and Luca rested on desktops facing her.

"Wow," she said. "That was *intense*. I can't believe you do that five periods a day. *Wow*."

Isaac laughed. "Yeah, well, I was *exhausted* my first two years. By the time I had tenure, I knew I'd earned it, because I'd stopped sleeping through my weekends."

"I *bet*." Allegra shook her head. "But they were so great! I can see why… you know. Teaching's such a passion."

Isaac grimaced. "Well, you *did* see them on their best day. I pulled the kids who'd participated in the extra credit out of their other classes for this—it was pretty celebratory."

"What's a worst day like?" Luca asked perceptively.

Isaac shook his head. "Nope. Nope, nope, nope, nope… not gonna talk about a worst day."

At that moment Roxy bounded in.

"Oh my God!" she crowed, and Isaac nodded.

"Right?"

"Like, *way* amazing!"

"*Right*?"

"Like, they got—"

"*So excited*!" They both said in tandem, and Isaac wondered if he was glowing like she was.

"That was a rush, Isaac," Roxy finished breathlessly. "Not gonna lie. We gotta do that next year. And you *gotta* take pictures of the blanket you finish. It'll be *amazing*. In a million years, I never thought they'd get so amped up over your sticks-and-string thing. I'm *boggled*." She turned to Allegra. "And you must be the lucky recipient of the blanket. Congratulations!"

Allegra gave her a shy smile. "Thank you. You must be Roxy— Isaac talks about you a lot. And the kids, uhm, Falcon, Pigeon, and Sparrow?"

Roxy grimaced. "Yeah. My husband—I mean, I get having a passion, but not once has Isaac suggested naming the kids something like Worsted or Acrylic. Sadly, I'm not married to Isaac, so…."

"Falcon, Pigeon, and Sparrow," Allegra said, nodding like it made total sense.

Isaac and Roxy called the kids by their middle names, which were a *little* better. Justice, Patricia, and Anne. When Isaac had learned that the third one—also his goddaughter—would be named "Sparrow Anne," he'd glared at Brian and said, "Just so you know, when she runs away, she'll be at my house, and we'll be filling out change-of-name forms. But you do you."

Todd hadn't been there, of course, because Isaac had known Brian would laugh at that but Todd would have been mortified.

"Brian wanted to go into the forestry service so badly," Roxy said wistfully. "I wonder, sometimes, if we'd been on an isolated hill in the middle of The Devil's Woodland Anus, if he would have let me name the boy Brian Junior."

"If you have a fourth and he names it Vulture, I'm abducting that child before you sign the paperwork," Isaac said, meaning it. He felt like it was the least he could do.

"I'd slip the kid out the back to keep him from having that name," Roxy said, nodding. Then she glanced up at Allegra. "And lucky you, you can name your little up-and-comer something sane."

Outside, the sound of kids pelting by and chattering had died out, and Roxy looked wistfully out Isaac's window and sighed.

"You guys," she said, "It is almost the weekend, and thanks to Isaac, I've got a babysitter tomorrow night so I can have a date with my husband. But right now, I'm *dying* for a drink with my friends. You guys game?"

"Not your teacher friends?" Luca asked.

Roxy shrugged. "Isaac and I are sort of a matched set. That a problem?" She tilted her head at Luca, and for a moment Isaac had a flashback to when Todd had told Isaac not to call Roxy at home more than twice a week because it wasn't socially appropriate. They'd had to *coordinate* their calls, and they'd gotten *really* good at texting, because *Todd* didn't want to feel bad about Isaac's social life.

"Not a problem at all," Luca said, smiling. "I didn't want to get in the way. I know when I take my crew out for a drink, we get very… I can't think of the word.…"

"Groupie," Allegra said.

"That's not the word." Luca stared at her.

"Clannish," she said instead.

Luca grimaced and glanced at Isaac and Roxy. "Okay, that's sort of the word. But this isn't like intruding on a group," he amended. "This is like having a drink with friends."

"There you go." Roxy smiled at him and then glanced at Isaac and raised her eyebrows.

Isaac gave her a flat look, although secretly he was very pleased that she seemed to enjoy Luca and Allegra's banter. "Of course I'm coming," he said. "I thought we agreed that I'm not dead yet."

She shrugged. "You were a little dead for a while. We've gone out very few times in the last year."

Isaac shook his head. "She was preggers," he told them. "Knocked up. Quickening. *With child.* I may have been dead, but on the days I was ready to go out, *somebody* was gestating."

"Uh-oh," Allegra said. "We'd better go soon, or gestating will be *my* excuse. I don't want alcohol, of course, but I could eat you all under the table right now."

Roxy grinned at Isaac. "It's like you brought her here just for me." She helped Allegra out of her chair and linked arms with her. "Come on, sweetie. I'll tell you bibles full of truth about the one thing that will make the two of them run screaming in horror."

"Hoohas," Allegra said soberly, and Luca and Isaac both shuddered while the two women laughed their way out of the building.

DINNER AND drinks—all nonalcoholic, because for all her talk, Roxy was still nursing the youngest one, and Luca didn't want to knock back a beer while his sister couldn't, and Isaac didn't want to feel like the only heel getting buzzed—was far more fun than Isaac had anticipated.

Luca and Allegra didn't merely laugh politely at Roxy's infectious humor, they contributed to it. They *enjoyed* it, and Isaac listened to the three of them tell stories avidly, remembering that time in his life when this was the best part of whatever event had brought him to a restaurant. It didn't matter if it had been a concert, a rave, or a passed final—sitting at the table, listening to other people's stories, had always felt very communal.

They were down to their last sip of virgin margaritas (and who didn't love a sour lime Slushee?), and Roxy was winding down the unlikely but true story of when her first student-teaching class had rebelled against her, staging a revolt that included talking and ignoring her, standing on desks and yelling while she was alone in the room without her master teacher to back her up. Luca and Allegra laughed at the appropriate parts and winced sympathetically, and then Luca said, "But you came back? I can't believe you came back after the little bastards did that to you."

Roxy sighed. "The thing about teaching," she said, leaning back and wiping out her drink, "is that it's about belief. I spent all summer looking at myself in the mirror, saying, 'I do not deserve to be shit on. I know my subject. I'm older than these little assholes. If anybody's going to cry today, it's not going to be me.' And then I walked into my next student-teaching class that fall saying that to myself. At first I was sort of an unbearable bitch, but eventually you find that balance, you know? Between belief in yourself and the need to assert authority." She glanced at Isaac. "It helps when you admit your weaknesses. I don't exude natural authority. Isaac doesn't either. Which means the kids have to listen to us because there's something in it for them."

Isaac nodded thoughtfully. "You have to make damned sure your lesson plan is ready to go. I mean, sometimes you have room to experiment—the extra credit assignment today. But sometimes if you get one instruction the least bit fuzzy—"

Roxy snapped her fingers.

"Like that," he said. "The class will go like that. And if you've got any strong personalities…."

They both shuddered.

"That was bad," Roxy said. "I… damn. Isaac, you walked back into the classroom after that. Bravest thing I ever saw."

Luca cocked his head. "What was?" he said. "Isaac never told us that story."

Roxy glanced at him, and he shrugged, making the time-honored "go on" gesture with his hand.

"Two bad things happened at once," she said, turning to Luca and Allegra. "The first was the front office got the schedule wrong for when progress reports went out. Nobody had entered their grades, and the computer just sent out progress reports that had half the kids failing, and we hadn't even talked to the kids about what they were missing or how to fix it. It was bad. The whole school was *pissed*. You could smell it in the air. It was bad."

"That's serious," Allegra said, straightening. "That's *dangerous*."

Roxy and Isaac both nodded. "The day was hot, and there was this dry wind blowing down in October—even the weather had everybody's back up," Isaac said, remembering.

"What was the other thing?" Luca asked.

"The other thing was that fuckin' hate group," Roxy muttered. "You know, the one that keeps trying to make it illegal to be gay or trans?"

Luca and Allegra both raised their eyebrows. "Yeah, we know that one."

"Well, there was a Proud Boy rally at the local park, supporting their favorite hate group," Roxy said. "And there was a kid—sweet little thing, right? Trans. If these kids hadn't grown up together, practically from the cradle, not a soul would have guessed she wasn't a she from birth."

Isaac tried to keep his breathing even. He thought he could deal with this story, but his heart still ached.

"And there was the whole school, just this one big ugly grumble, and there was the ten percent of the school whose parents thought the Proud Boys were the *shit*, and there was Angel, running through the quad in a rainbow miniskirt, calling Isaac's name because she was scared."

Luca and Allegra both stared at them in horror.

"What happened?" Luca asked.

Roxy glanced at Isaac, and her eyes were dark with memory. "It was terrifying," she said. "Isaac saw Angel from his room—saw the crowd after her, like in a movie, but scarier, and he ran to his door to let her in and then slammed the door shut behind him and locked it."

"You were right there with me," Isaac said, finding his voice. "You must have sprinted—you were, like, seven months pregnant. Scared the shit out of me. There we were, our backs to the door, and the crowd...." He shuddered.

"Someone took a swing at me," Roxy said, "and Isaac stepped forward and caught it in the face. At that point the principal stepped into it, started shoving kids out of the way, telling them to break it up and go back to their classes. Other teachers stepped in, started doing the same thing, and eventually the mob broke up." She glanced at Isaac. "Isaac was a *mess*. He had a concussion, his eye was already swelling, his nose was bleeding, his lip was split open."

"Poor Angel," Isaac said. "She had to change schools." He gave Roxy a sad smile. "John—the principal," he added to Luca and Allegra, "he... he was really good. But he started drinking shortly after that. We didn't blame him, but he finally quit so he could dry out and parent his own kids. I think he sells insurance now."

"And you guys kept teaching?" Allegra asked, wide-eyed.

"Who else is going to help the Angels?" Roxy asked, a faint smile at the double meaning. "And honestly, that was one instance out of a handful—but seventy percent of the time, you have days like today. Quiet miracles. Those are the reasons to stay."

Luca frowned. "I'm not great at math, but… five percent of the time it's terrifying, seventy percent of the time it's wonderful—what's the other twenty percent of the time?"

"Admin," Roxy and Isaac said together and then laughed.

"God, meetings are the suck," Isaac said, with feeling. "I swear to God, after that thing happened, there were at least ten meetings in which I was trotted out as the poor soul who was injured in the line of duty, and Roxy and I were the first people cut off whenever anybody looked for a solution to the root of the problem. Gay-Straight Alliance? Too radical. Town meeting where we talked about hate speech? Too divisive. How about just a letter to parents where we put the blame on the kids who were shouting slurs the entire time and a zero-tolerance policy? Nope. And you gotta give props to the English and history departments—they were fighting along with us the whole way." He shook his head.

"What'd the administration do?" Luca asked softly.

"Nothing," Roxy murmured. "In the end, nothing. That was five years ago. As you may guess, it's getting worse again." She grimaced. "Brian begged me to quit. I managed to leverage the moment into some extra paid maternity leave, which was good for both of us, but if I hadn't done that, he might have won that argument."

"What about Todd?" Luca asked.

Isaac looked away. "Todd actually wrote my letter of resignation. He picked me up from the hospital, and it was all written, on official stationery, and notarized. All I wanted was a fucking hug, and he put a pen in my hand." Isaac snorted. "I almost stabbed him with it." He paused and remembered what Luca had said about remembering the good things too, and suddenly, he saw Todd's handsome, patrician-featured face, with the strain around overbright, red-rimmed eyes. "We didn't talk for a week. It took me that long to recover from the concussion, and by then I'd figured out that he'd been worried about me. Yeah, taking time to write the stupid letter while I was waiting in the ER was a douchebag move, but… you know. I think his heart was in the right place."

"It's a good thing you waited a week to tell me that," Roxy muttered. "My blood was so hot by then, the only thing that kept me from coming over to stab Todd with a pen myself was that I was on bed rest." She gave half a laugh. "I begged Brian to do it—I seem to recall referencing *Strangers on a Train*. Nobody would suspect him—it would be the perfect alibi. He went out and got us both cookies and ice cream instead."

"Ben & Jerry's," Isaac remembered with a fond smile. "And E.L. Fudge. He put them in my lap himself when I was sitting on the couch, and then he went to fetch a spoon. Todd just stared at him, but Brian gave me a napkin and winked and told me to come visit you as soon as I felt better and then left." He gave Roxy a grateful look. "It's a good thing he's a keeper, because otherwise, you need to tell him to stop getting you pregnant."

Roxy cackled. "Nope. We want a basketball team with a bench player. It's a goal."

There was general laughter, but the story had brought the tone down a little, and it was getting late.

When they got out to their vehicles, Roxy drove away first, and Allegra got in the passenger's side of Luca's truck. Luca walked over to where Isaac was setting his leftovers on the console and waited for him to stand up to speak.

"What's up?" Isaac asked. "We're still on for tomorrow, right?"

"Oh yeah. Uhm, Allegra was wondering if we could bring Nonna and Pop Pop over too. That way I could show them how the house is going, and you and Nonna and Allegra could do the yarn thing, and they could get out of the old folks' home for a day. I can cook, if you like. I've got a pesto dish that's a pain in the ass, but if I'm cooking for five of us, it'll be worth it."

"Cook?" Isaac asked, suddenly absolutely pleased.

"Well, *yeah*. You cook for us all the time. My apartment's tiny, but, you know—"

"That would be awesome," Isaac said, staring up at him. The day had been warm, but a breeze had picked up, and it fluttered Luca's toffee-brown hair, riffling it just a tad. His eyes—that dark, dark brown that could appear black in some light—hadn't strayed from Isaac's face, and Isaac was suddenly assailed by his warmth, pulled into the sphere of this nice man who was bringing laughter and family into his life, with barely a kiss on the cheek as encouragement.

God, he was beautiful.

And then he smiled, and his beauty grew exponentially. "I look forward to it," he murmured, and then, without warning, he dipped his head and captured Isaac's lips. Isaac gasped, leaning forward, and before he could have the predictable tiny war with himself, Luca pulled back.

"Isaac?"

"Yeah?"

"You said something nice about Todd tonight."

Isaac shrugged. "He couldn't have been *all* bad." But inside, he felt the enormity of that.

"You spent ten years with him. It's okay if you talk about him. Remember that, okay?"

Isaac nodded, his lips tingling. "Okay," he whispered.

Another kiss—lingering, aching, and sweet.

This time, when Luca pulled back, he said, "You and me, we can be a thing. An amazing thing. It can happen. Todd's always going to be there, but, you know… in time he'll be less important than he is now."

Isaac gazed into his eyes. "He's already faded," Isaac murmured. "All I can see is you."

One more kiss, longer, Luca's tongue invading his mouth, Isaac clinging to his collared shirt, and then Luca pulled away. "So sweet," he murmured, rubbing Isaac's lower lip with his thumb. "See you tomorrow."

Isaac watched him hop into his truck, and he saw Allegra's joyful thumbs-up as they drove away.

He took an extra minute, though, staring at the pink sky of late spring, smelling cut grass and the river, which was close by.

It didn't smell *brand*-new, pinks and crocuses new, and the mustard flowers and almond blossoms had long since come and gone.

But it smelled ripe new. Summer hay new. Sleepy afternoons and dappled shadows new. Fall was a long way off, and winter but a fluttered harbinger of rain.

Isaac turned his face to that promise of summer and smiled.

THE NEXT morning, he woke up with Euclid breathing cat breath in his face, begging for his breakfast. Isaac made him work for it, petting him until he forgot about breakfast, flopped over, and drooled so Isaac could go back to sleep for another half hour.

But only a half hour.

He needed to spend an hour cleaning off the kitchen table, down to the tablecloth, which was… dusty, at best. He found another one—something bright and green and yellow—and a table runner that he'd crocheted with orange cotton yarn that Todd had kept hidden in the back of the linen closet out of mortification. When the table was set, he grabbed the vacuum and made an extra pass—the maid service came on Wednesday, and he had a cat now, so company on Saturday meant a little extra effort.

And speaking of cat….

He changed Euclid's litter out, wiped down the bathroom and put fresh soaps in the dish, and got out his good towels, making sure the pretty little flower insignia was turned out.

Todd used to insist on the good linens, but they never had guests. Isaac had gotten used to using the regular, comfy, faded towels in the last year and a half, but now, with guests coming over, he was remembering some of the joys of a little formality.

Little touches—*his* touches—helped make his home welcoming.

It felt like a whole new house.

With an hour left to spare, he made a quick trip to the market—crackers, cookies, tea, and fruit—as well as, just for himself, a bouquet of flowers.

By the time Allegra knocked on the door, he felt like *he'd* bloomed, for the first time after a long, long winter.

Allegra came in, carrying groceries and ushering in her grandmother, while Isaac peered around them, wondering where Luca and his grandfather were.

"Luca's taking him on a tour," Allegra said. "He's redone the bathrooms, the kitchen, and the hardwood in all the bedrooms. Painting comes next, and they can put it on sale by the fall. Grandpa's really excited."

"Not you, Mrs. Giordano?"

"Call me Sophia," she said happily. "Since my Allegra and her baby are going to move in here, you can call me Sophia, and I can call you Isaac." She smiled, her lined face showing off the same dimples she must have had as a girl.

"Of course, Sophia," he said, offering his arm. She allowed him to escort her to one of the stuffed chairs, which had a small coffee table next to it at the perfect height. She could work on her project and sip tea and chat in perfect comfort. She could also (and Isaac had seen her do this before) fall asleep mid-sentence, tilt her head back, and snooze without needing to be moved.

"Well, *I'm* moving in first," Allegra said from the kitchen. "Isaac and I are going to see if it will work before we commit. I'm something of a slob, you know."

Sophia laughed softly. "I know," she said, leaning her head conspiratorially toward Isaac. "I used to watch her and Luca when they were children. Luca, he could be counted on to clean up his toys. This one? She would get so unhappy. 'Nonna!' she'd say. 'I want to wake up and have my dolls in place to play the same way!'" She laughed, and Isaac nodded, but inside he was thinking that was a very wise way to play.

"Oh my God, Isaac!" Allegra called, coming down toward the dining room so she could peer out at Isaac and Sophia. "The flowers, the clean table—it's so wonderful! And this table runner. Did you show Nonna?"

"Is it the orange one?" Sophia said. "With the flowers worked in filet crochet?"

"Yeah," Isaac said, unable to hide his proud smile. "It looks *really* good. You'll see it when we eat. In the meantime, stay right there and I'll get you some tea and cookies."

"You spoil me," she said happily, getting out her yarn.

Isaac had already put the kettle on and was pleased to see it was almost boiling so he could set up the tea service while Allegra put away groceries. Together they achieved a sort of dance around the kitchen where they each accomplished a task without getting in each other's way.

"The place setting really is special," she said as she pulled out a covered glass bowl full of vegetables soaking in some sort of dressing. "Now I'm going to put this in a sunspot and leave it, okay? It's part of the pesto, but it doesn't need cooking, it just needs warming."

Isaac gave her a bemused glance. "You can cook pesto without cooking?"

"Very funny. No—you cut up the cherry tomatoes and the cilantro and the garlic and then add oil and vinegar. You leave it in the sun for a few hours to season, and then you cook the pasta and grill the chicken. When it's all cooked, you cut up the chicken and toss it with the pesto and the pasta, and voila! This really good fresh dish that's not too hot for summer."

"That's amazing. Luca knows how to make this because?"

"Because Nonna told him about it once," Allegra said, laughing. "Luca's funny. He doesn't cook on the regular, but he'll watch YouTubers and TikTokers, and sometimes he'll see something that makes sense to him and he wants to see if it will work. The only drawback to this is you have to praise him to the skies—like, *forever*—when he does it, or he may never cook again."

"Good to know," Isaac said. He pulled the kettle off as it started to whistle and poured the boiling water into three rose-themed porcelain cups. They'd been a gift from Todd, Isaac recalled, stunned still for a moment.

"They're lovely," Isaac said, pleased as he pulled the wrapping off the set of six. The matching teapot had been in the first box he'd opened, surprised to see the two big Christmas gifts under Todd's small and tasteful tree. "Thank you!"

"The neighbor is always commenting on how plain the white is," Todd said with a sniff. "This way she can just drink the damned tea."

Isaac ran his finger over the rim of the cup, noticing that there was a tiny rosebud at the bottom of each one, with little green leaves, to match the motifs on the outside. He half expected the pretty cup to be darker somehow, sullied with Todd's sulking, but it was, in fact, still delightful.

Isaac had made a point of using the cups the next time Sophia had come to visit, and Todd had given him a kiss on the temple, telling him his service looked perfect, a rare public display of affection and a very rare compliment.

It wasn't until that moment that Isaac realized that the sulking had been a front. This was, indeed, a gift of thoughtfulness and beauty, and Isaac had almost missed it.

"Isaac?" Allegra's voice penetrated his thoughts. "What's up? Where are you?"

Isaac shook himself. "Nothing," he said softly. "I just remembered when Todd gave me this tea set."

"Good memory?" she asked carefully.

"Believe it or not, yes," he said, and then he picked up the tray and took it into the front room so she wouldn't see his shiny eyes.

But he made a resolution to tell Luca about it when he could—he thought Luca would want to know.

LUCA AND his grandfather ("Call me Geordie now, since you're giving Allegra a place to stay!") came in half an hour later, and Luca shooed Isaac back into the living room while he brought in some tea and cookies for his Pop Pop.

What followed was… well, the same visit Isaac had enjoyed dozens of times with Sophia, but with the added happiness of Allegra and Luca mixed in.

In fact, the entire day was a success, from the yarning to the snacks to Luca's amazing dinner, which included a salad course, the pasta, and a small dish of ice cream at the end—and wine.

"Nonna and Pop Pop are crazy about wine with dinner," Luca told him almost apologetically as Isaac helped him prepare. "You're not obligated to drink it, and trust me, I'm driving Pop Pop's Caddy, so I'll be taking little tiny sips, but I'd better have wine or I'll hear about it later."

Isaac had nodded seriously, because hey, he didn't know the rules!

But as they moved around each other, as smooth in the dance as Isaac and Allegra had been earlier, Isaac found himself telling Luca about the tea set, and how it was a good memory, and how he'd almost forgotten.

"Really?"

Isaac was, in fact, washing the tea service as Luca prepared dinner, and he moved over Isaac's shoulder to get a better look at the delicately beautiful cups.

"I'm not going to touch them," he said softly. "I just wanted to see. You're right—they're lovely." He leaned over Isaac's shoulder, and Isaac set the cup down in the warm soapy water so he could lean back against Luca's heat without fumbling the cup and losing it. Naturally— so naturally—Luca kissed his temple.

"Is that… that okay?" Isaac asked, welcoming Luca's arms around his shoulders as this quiet moment—intimate in a way he hadn't known his heart was chambered for—enveloped them.

"I'm glad," Luca murmured, rubbing their cheeks together. "It's good, Isaac. Like you said, you spent ten years with him. I'm so glad they weren't all bad." He nuzzled Isaac's temple again and then stepped back. "I've got to finish dinner or the chicken'll burn, but thanks, Isaac."

"For what?" Isaac turned to watch him, fascinated by how smoothly his solid muscular body moved, how comfortably in Isaac's borderline fussy home.

"For telling me about that. I... I mean, I'll be afraid to pick those cups up from now on, because God forbid I break one, but thanks. I mean, it's *easy* for me to hate the evil ex. But finding things—good things—to like about him? That's important. It means you know how to love. Someday you'll know how to love someone else. That's all. So thank you. It was a good memory. That makes me happy."

Luca went back to work, and Isaac finished drying the tea set and putting it away, but inside, he was feeling that kiss on the temple, the gentle rubbing of cheeks, and reliving Luca's words.

How was it he had met such a man, who was so simply interested in Isaac's well-being that he could be happy for a good memory of another relationship?

Isaac wasn't sure, but that evening, as he sipped wine and listened to Nonna and Pop Pop tell more stories about their grandchildren, he felt a certain resolution.

More of this. More of Luca and Allegra's family in his life. More evening meals and Saturday afternoons yarning. More *life* in his life.

Maybe—just maybe—more of Luca's soft touches, his warm arms, the breadth of his chest.

More of that too.

Gentle Crucibles

Luca moved Allegra in the Friday after that first afternoon with Nonna and Pop Pop. The day had gone so nicely that Luca was already trying to schedule another one, asking apologetically if Isaac could do that once a month.

He'd been warmed by how excited Isaac had gotten—and also a little worried. So easy. Their lives seemed to fit together so easily, the construction worker and the nice widowed teacher. Where was the glitch?

But as Luca and Jimmy Bob, his best worker and best friend, moved Allegra's furniture into the bottom bedroom—which had been empty of all but a guest bed and an end table—Jimmy Bob's comments about the house stirred up all the possibilities.

"So, he just invited your sister to move in?" Jimmy Bob said dubiously, looking around. The day was in the low hundreds, and Jimmy Bob's shaved head gleamed with sweat. Luca would remind the guy to put his hat on when they went outside, but right now he was probably enjoying the air conditioning.

"And he's not here now?"

"He's a teacher!" Luca protested. "And today is graduation. He couldn't get out of it, but I got the key—it's fine."

"Are you sure he's not, uhm, after your sister's virtue?" Jimmy Bob wrinkled his nose, and Luca resisted the urge to smack his bald pate. Yeah, the guy was a good worker—and a genuinely good guy who gave his time and building skills to charity and had started no fewer than three grassroots lawn-care guys into their own businesses by letting them borrow his oldest mower—but he wasn't particularly educated, and he wasn't particularly socially conscious.

"Jimmy, he's as gay as I am," Luca said, shaking his head. "Probably gayer, if that's a thing. His husband died, they have this giant house, he's all alone, and he and my sister get along. Since I don't hate either of them, I think this is a win."

Jimmy Bob glanced at him. "Are you sure you and him aren't...?" He waggled his eyebrows. "I understand widows and widowers can be pretty hot stuff."

Luca's eyes were going to dry out. "I'd remember if we were having sex, Jimmy Bob. He's cute. You don't want to forget that."

Jimmy Bob cackled. "Yeah, yeah. But you can—" He waggled his brows again, the gesture particularly noticeable on his shaved head because his entire scalp wrinkled. "—even without the *poketa-poketa*, you know what I mean?"

Luca *forced* himself to blink. "Sadly, yes, I *do* know what that means," he said and decided if Jimmy Bob wasn't going to drive him bugnuts, he should come clean. "And we've had some nice moments— no *poketa-poketa* necessary."

"So?"

"So what?" But Luca knew. For a guy who could pick up girls at a bar with a lazy-eyed glance and a "Hey, darlin', it's looking slow tonight, do you wanna?" Jimmy Bob could be surprisingly perceptive.

"So why aren't you and Mr. Widower a thing yet?"

"Do you want some ice water?" Luca asked. They'd pretty much moved their last item—a vanity and a bench, as well as a couple of dressers Allegra had finished herself because her useless ex-boyfriend couldn't be assed to help her—and Allegra and Luca would bring in her bedding and clothes when he dropped her off that evening.

His apartment was already breathing a little easier, and he'd moved his computer desk and weight set back into his guest room with a sigh of relief.

"Am I allowed in the kitchen? This place is pretty choice."

"Yeah, sure," Luca said. "Just—and I mean this—don't touch the good teacups, because his late husband gave them as a gift, and if I ever break one, I have to kill myself. It's in the rules."

Jimmy Bob looked properly terrified, which was good. It meant he took Luca seriously and let Luca grab the serviceable sturdy glass tumblers from the cupboard that carried *all* of Isaac's everyday glasses and plateware so nothing delicate was at risk.

"Well this is pretty fancy for me," Jimmy Bob said, taking a swig of simple ice water. "And I'm grateful."

"Oh...." At that moment, Luca saw the note on the fridge in Isaac's legible but not meticulous handwriting. "Oh!" He opened the fridge and pulled out a plate with three sandwiches on it, each one cut in half, the whole thing covered with a layer of plastic to keep it fresh. "Oh my God."

He set the plate on the island and then reached into the fridge again and came out with a small plasticware bowl filled with fruit salad. Then he closed the fridge and grabbed the small bag of potato chips on top of the bread drawer.

"Is all this for us?" Jimmy Bob asked, eyes bulging.

"Well, one of these sandwiches—the one with the extra tomatoes, I bet—we need to take to Allegra," Luca said, taking the plastic wrap and using it on the one sandwich. He grabbed a fork from the drawer that he figured he and Jimmy Bob could pass back and forth and put it in the fruit salad, and for a few moments, they settled down to a working man's feast of *amazing* Dagwoods, cut peaches, grapes, yogurt, and chips. When they came up for air, Luca put the lid back on the fruit salad and started to load the dishwasher and wipe the counters while Jimmy Bob formulated a thought.

"That was amazing."

"I know it," Luca said with a sigh.

"This guy left you a *feast* in the fridge, an extra sandwich for your sister, and leftovers."

"He asked nicely that we return the plasticware," Luca said, his lips twitching. It was sweet.

"And you've only had *moments*? What—and I ask this nicely, with all the respect in the world—the fuck, sincerely, are you waiting for?"

Luca gave him a smile even *he* knew was a little dreamy. "This guy's a keeper," he said simply. "You don't one-and-done a guy like this. His last relationship—it wasn't so great. And it ended when the guy *died*, so, you know…."

"Ouch," Jimmy Bob said. "It didn't really end."

"No, it didn't." Luca sighed. "He's got to get all those 'My late husband used to do this…' moments out of his bloodstream before he can look at me and think 'Luca,' not just 'Not Todd.'"

"Todd? As in 'Why is the floor wet, Todd?'"

Luca snorted at the line from *National Lampoon's Christmas Vacation*. That movie was forever old, and still any poor schmuck named Todd had to deal with that line.

"This guy would *not* have appreciated that, believe you me," Luca said.

"How bad was he?" Jimmy Bob, for all the roughness around the edges, hadn't been born in a barn. He took over where Luca left off, making sure they left the kitchen cleaner than they'd found it and that his tumbler wasn't going into the dishwasher with big greasy fingerprints on it.

Luca suddenly needed someone to talk to who *wouldn't* talk to Isaac. He'd lost Allegra, he knew—she was now firmly Team Isaac, no matter what, because the guy had pretty much offered her free rent in a nice place.

"Here," he said. "Follow me."

He took Jimmy Bob past Allegra's room and opened the door to the yarn room. His friend glanced around and whistled lowly. "Pretty," he said, taking in the colors, the art, the stained glass, and the rug.

Luca nodded. "You saw the living room, right?"

"Yeah. It's nice. A little bland, but your guy did some stuff to spice it up."

"Yeah—see, all that oatmeal, cream, and tan?"

"Yeah?"

"That was Todd. Isaac—and I mean, in the last five weeks—he actually *remembered* that Todd doesn't live here anymore. And wait...."

He went to the downstairs bathroom, knowing what he'd find when he opened the door.

Euclid burst out like the Kool-Aid Man, crashing against the door as Luca opened it, giving an imperious "Meow!" and hauling ass down the hallway, probably in search of the bed in the living room and all his toys.

"Oh wow!" Jimmy Bob loved creatures—dogs, cats—he had five of each, and they all had an uneasy truce under Jimmy Bob's roof. Luca surmised they were the reason Jimmy Bob was still picking up women in bars, because very few sane women would jump into his furry mess like that, but it *did* make him a sucker for a friend with a cat. "Kitty!"

Like a five-year-old, Luca's forty-year-old drywall specialist trotted through the house, looking for a new friend.

By the time Luca got to the living room, Jimmy Bob was on his knees, playing zoomies with Euclid, and Euclid had absolutely bought in.

"And a right!" Jimmy Bob said, going right, "And a left! And a right! And a left! And a mouse! And a ball! And a *go!*"

With that he threw the little ball with the bell inside across the floor and Euclid went running right past it, up the stairs, and they could hear his claws ripping a new path in the upstairs hallway as Jimmy Bob laughed himself silly.

"Wow!" he hooted. "What an awesome cat!" He paused. "Also new?" It wasn't a hard guess. The cat was young, and the house was—relatively—unscathed.

"Yes," Luca said, listening to make sure he didn't hear dressers toppling or mirrors breaking or anything untoward happening. Isaac had asked him to let the cat out after they were done moving stuff in, but Luca hadn't anticipated Jimmy Bob's absolute weakness for all things furry.

Jimmy Bob rocked back on his heels, like Luca being careful to keep his work boots on the hardwood and not mark up the nice new area rug.

"So your guy is… sort of trying new things," he said carefully.

"Yes," Luca agreed.

"And you think he's the one."

Luca sighed. He'd always known Jimmy Bob wasn't stupid. He knew with every animal rescue—or loyalty to gay bosses—that he made himself potentially less attractive to available mates, but he made that choice anyway. "Yes."

"So you gotta wait," Jimmy Bob said in understanding.

"Yes," Luca sighed, his lunch sitting heavily in his stomach.

"But still…." Jimmy Bob grinned as the cat raced down the stairs again, heading directly for the ball, which had stilled in the corner on the hardwood. With a happy "Meep!" Euclid leapt on the ball and started batting it around the floor, obviously intent on being his own best friend.

"It's worth it," Luca said, watching Euclid fondly. Give the cat five more minutes and he'd find his favorite sunbeam to nap in, and Luca and Jimmy Bob would be able to leave without worrying about Euclid even trying to escape.

"You said he was cute?" Jimmy Bob asked hopefully.

"So cute." Luca pulled out his phone and found the pictures he'd taken on Saturday, featuring Isaac, Allegra, and his grandparents all sitting in the living room talking. They hadn't noticed Luca, coming in from the kitchen, and the moment had been so charming. The perfect tea set and all his favorite people in this sunshiny moment of grace.

One of the pictures had been of Isaac, his brown hair curling a little at his crown and in the front, his giant hazel eyes open and earnest as he spoke to Luca's nonna about something Luca didn't understand. He was wearing slacks and a button-down, conservative clothes obviously picked out to impress Nonna and Pop Pop, and Luca's heart had just swelled.

This man—baggage and all—was so pretty. So smart. So kind and funny.

A keeper.

"Nice," said Jimmy Bob, taking the phone from him and rifling through the pictures. "Oh wow—Luca. This is nice. I mean, *I* don't understand it, but...." He glanced around at the front room, which was so much more Isaac's than it had been a month ago. "Your guy. Once he finds himself, he's going to be so worth looking for."

"I know," Luca said softly.

"Gonna be a *loooong* summer," Jimmy Bob warned. "Good thing I got a pool."

Luca grinned at him. "Really? You'd be willing to let us come over?"

"Bring your sister," Jimmy Bob said. "And not for creepy reasons either—she's fifteen years younger than me, there should be a law. But because she's pregnant, and I understand that sucks in the summer. So yeah. Come over. Bring your guy. Let him pet all the cats and play with all the dogs and find himself some more. He'll be worth it."

Luca laughed a little. "It was only a sandwich, Jimmy Bob."

"Yeah, sure. But it was a *really good* sandwich."

But Luca knew it was more than that. Jimmy Bob had chosen animals over people in his personal life. But that didn't mean he didn't like people too, Luca's family included.

LUCA PARKED in front of the house to drop Allegra—and her clothes— off, and while he was not surprised to see that Isaac had already started dinner for the three of them, he was pleased.

He hauled in random shit and set up her little TV and entertainment system, and then she shooed him out of the room so she could put away her clothes and put her girl stuff on the shelves, and he found himself in the kitchen while Isaac, wearing a plain red apron over his button-down and slacks from graduation, pan-fried chicken.

"That smells *amazing*," Luca praised. "Want me to do anything?"

"Salad in a bag?"

"Salad in a bag," Luca confirmed, and he went to the fridge to get it. "You're quiet—too much sun?" Isaac had obviously put sunscreen on his nose and cheeks, but his ears were a little crispy.

Isaac glanced up from the chicken and shook his head, giving a melancholy smile. "No," he said. "It's… you know. Anticlimax. Letdown. You work so hard to get them to graduation, to the last week of school, and then boom! All done. And you're a little lost afterwards. This happens every year."

Luca blinked. He'd never really thought of what it must be like to have his heart beat in the pulse of the school bell. "What… what do you usually do?" He hated to ask it like this, but… "What did you do with Todd?"

Isaac shrugged. "Well, I used to go out with Roxy, and Todd and Brian would have to come fetch us because we were sloshed. Then she started getting pregnant, and that was out, so… I don't know. I came home and sort of powered through it."

Aw!

"What do you *want* to do?" Luca asked, pulling the salad out. "I mean, are you in a 'Go out and dance!' mood, or a 'Snuggle and watch movies!' mood."

"Todd used to *hate* it when I watched my end-of-the-year movies," Isaac said, and then he smiled a little. "Probably because they made me sob like a baby."

"Catharsis?" Luca asked. Made sense to him!

"Yes!" Isaac said. "You get it!"

"What are your movies?"

"Mmm… they're all old. *Say Anything, Dead Poet's Society, Stand and Deliver—*"

"I have heard of none of those," Luca said seriously, wondering how bad this could be.

Isaac brightened. "Really?"

Luca chuckled. "I'm going to hate this, aren't I?"

"So much," Isaac said, nodding. "Is it…. Is it okay if we do it?"

"Course," Luca murmured. "Just know I've got my own sad day and my own movies. You good with that?"

Isaac's smile was still sad—but it was also luminous. "It's a deal," he said.

FOR THE first movie—an old teen comedy that Luca had never seen but really enjoyed—Isaac and Allegra each took their places, Allegra on the couch and Isaac on the chair he'd settled Sophia in, while they did their yarn thing.

After the first movie, Allegra yawned and excused herself, after telling them both they were on to help her pick out curtains and a new area rug in the morning.

After she left, Luca, who had sprawled on the opposite corner of the couch, spoke up.

"Isaac?"

"Hmm?" Isaac paused while piloting the remote control.

"You and Allegra, you're making progress on your blanket, right?"

Isaac smiled. "Yeah—both of us are working pretty fast. Why?"

"Because I was wondering if you, uhm, maybe wouldn't want to sit next to me on the couch?"

Isaac paused and frowned, but he stood up. "Why would I have to stop yarning? I could simply move—"

"Okay, let me rephrase that. I was wondering if maybe you wouldn't want to sit *on* me on the couch."

Luca shoved himself back into the corner and lifted his leg—and his bare foot—so that Isaac could fit himself in the vee of his legs. "I'll behave, I promise."

Isaac's smile went shy, and he set down his project and moved to fit himself against Luca's body. Luca sighed, the other man's weight just so, so sweet against him.

Carefully he wrapped his arms around Isaac's shoulders, giving him a chance to wriggle and make himself comfortable before using Luca's chest like a pillow and turning toward the TV. Euclid got into the act by draping himself over Luca's shoulder and purring in his ear, but still, they managed to achieve a pretty comfortable equilibrium in a short time.

"Luca?" Isaac murmured, before pulling up the next movie.

"Yeah?"

"You only have to behave a little."

Luca *hmm*ed and took advantage of that invitation. While they watched the movie—and God, it was horribly sad—Luca thrust his hand under Isaac's shirt and rubbed his concave stomach, up over his ribs, along his hips. He didn't tweak any nipples or tease any waistbands, and when Isaac twined their fingers together and rested them both atop his abdomen, Luca stopped.

"Tickling?" he murmured.

"Turning me on," Isaac confessed. "I'm working on catharsis here—I've got twenty minutes before this one makes me a sobbing wreck, and I have to be in a mood."

Luca chuckled, and then he got as immersed as Isaac in the movie.

And then he held Isaac while he cried, and he shed a few tears himself.

When the movie was over, Isaac hit pause on the algorithm, and lay quiet in Luca's arms. Euclid continued to drool, and Luca was uncomfortably aware that there was a drool spot about the size of a quarter on the shoulder of his T-shirt.

"Feeling better?" he asked. "Or falling asleep?"

"Both," Isaac murmured. "I… this is the most wonderful moment. I can't remember the last time I was this content."

Luca couldn't help it—he let a wicked laugh escape. "You want to be more content?"

Isaac froze, and Luca could have kicked himself. And then, to his shock, he heard Isaac say in a small voice, "Eventually, yes."

"Yes?" Nobody was more surprised than Luca himself.

Isaac turned in his arms. "Look at you, Luca. You're beautiful, you're kind, you're funny, and you're a hard worker with his own business. Which is important because it means you've got goals of your own and things that you love. You're… you're *awesome*. Did you think I'd draw a line? I've already decided I want to live—do you think I'd go find somebody else when I found a guy who will hold me while I cry through a sad movie?"

Luca stared at him in bemusement… and excitement. "I was sort of hoping not," he replied. "I just… I have to let you steer this ship, Isaac. I-I don't have any damage here. You're the one who knows how far, how fast you can go."

"That's an amazing metaphor," Isaac said with a playful scowl. "Too bad I'm a math major."

That made Luca laugh. "Yeah. I can tell you let that limit you."

Isaac's smile was boyish, delighted. "You're doing fine," he said softly. "I… I need to make sure, in my heart, I'm being fair to you. That you're getting one hundred percent of me in a relationship, and not seventy-five percent Isaac and twenty-five percent Todd's Husband."

"You'll get there," Luca murmured, and unlike that afternoon, when he'd been talking to Jimmy Bob, he could see sunshine at the end of this tan and ecru dawn. Which reminded him…. "By the way, my buddy Jimmy Bob extended an invitation today. He wants you and Allegra to use his pool at least once a week this summer—and to pet his cats and play with his dogs. He's got five of each, so hopefully he'll be a cautionary tale on why Euclid should remain an only child."

"Oh wow," Isaac said, but he sounded excited. "That's amazing! And yes, I'd be happy to go to the pool with Allegra." He sobered a little. "And to pet all the creatures. That's really generous of him. What prompted that?"

Luca grinned and dropped a kiss on the corner of his mouth, which was the nearest place he could reach from this position. "You made us sandwiches, Isaac. I mean, don't leave a working man sandwiches unless you want a marriage proposal. In this case Jimmy Bob is straight and I'm a little possessive, so you got an offer of a pool instead."

Isaac laughed in his arms and then—not surprisingly because a couch was only so big—had to stand up as he slid off the couch. He stretched, and Luca stood and rubbed his hands up and down Isaac's stomach as Isaac stretched too, hands over his head. Then, unable to resist, Luca lowered his mouth to Isaac's and tasted.

Isaac answered, moving his arms to wrap around Luca's neck as they explored, took in each other's breath, responses, moans.

After a few moments, Luca pulled back and grinned. "I could get *so* used to kissing you."

Isaac kissed him again, and for the moment they just stood, kissing, allowing their attraction to grow until it got urgent enough for Luca to pull away.

"You promise?" he asked, panting a little. "You promise this ship is heading to Fantasy Island?"

Isaac moaned a little. "I can't imagine anywhere else we'd dock," he muttered. Luca rested their foreheads together and then tore himself away.

"In that case," he said with regret, "I'm going to take myself home so I can be back in the morning with doughnuts. You get some sleep, okay?"

Isaac nodded. "I'm the dumbest person in the world for not dragging you upstairs *right now*."

"I'm even dumber for not doing the same thing." Luca leaned forward, took his mouth again, and then started toward the door so he could put on the boots he'd been leaving on the porch. Isaac had gotten him a boot block and scrubbing brush and everything. "Soon, okay?

You tell me when, Isaac, but boy, I gotta tell you, I'm wanting this with everything in my body."

Isaac sighed. "Same," he said. "Drive safe."

Luca glanced up and grinned. "Like an *angel*," he promised. "You can't get rid of me that easy!"

And then he was gone, knowing he'd dream about more kisses for the rest of the night.

Epiphanies in July

Isaac had never felt more like twenty than he did at Jimmy Bob's pool.

He and Allegra went together during the weekdays, when the office was slow and Luca didn't have enough for Allegra to do, or when she was too sick or too tired to move in the morning.

Isaac had been the one to call Luca that first week, when Luca had dropped her off four days running so she could collapse on the couch and sleep. Isaac would feed her, she'd thank him groggily, eat everything he put in front of her—usually on a TV tray—and then she'd wander off to bed. Saturday morning, he'd called Luca and told him that the two of them should go out, get some lunch, and bring some home to Allegra, because if anybody needed to sleep in, she did. And after that he considered himself the family mole. If she was too tired at night, he'd call Luca and tell him that he was going to have to answer his own phones for a day.

When Luca wasn't able to make it to work on his grandparents' house, Isaac started going in for her.

And when it was too slow—or when Jimmy Bob's niece could be pulled from her summer vacation between college classes—Isaac would take her to the pool, with the animals, the shredded furniture, the never-ending supply of canned sparkling water and apples, and, oh my God *yes*, the pool.

Isaac started to make food for Jimmy Bob too, which either he or Allegra would leave in the man's fridge if they visited, using the key he had given Luca.

Something about lying out in that pool, in that comfortable, battered bachelor pad, with a couple of giant mixed-breed dogs who loved to swim, and two tiny Chihuahua rescues who preferred to hang out on the floaties with Isaac and Allegra, made Isaac remember his own idyllic days back in college. Somebody's parents or apartment complex or rich uncle *always* had a pool. Or there were trips to the lake or the river— frolicking in water had been something they'd taken for granted back then, and something adults seemed to lose.

But this summer, between Jimmy Bob and Luca bringing burgers to grill or Isaac and Allegra hitting the place in the morning before it got too hot, Isaac's normally vampire-pale skin was a soft brown, and his hair was streaked and a little long, so his ringlets looked tinted.

And the sheer hedonism of treating summer like *summer*, instead of like that time he felt guilty for not working because Todd had work, made him feel all glowy and healthy, inside and out.

So there he was, Friday evening toward the end of July, four weeks left before school started again, eyes half closed on the floaty while the wet dogs all snoozed in a pile in the shade, when a hand, cool and firm, cupped the back of his neck and reminded him he needed to put sunblock on.

"Getting crispy," Luca murmured in his ear, and Isaac turned a dreamy smile to him.

"I am feeling like a golden-brown chicken on a rotisserie," he said with some satisfaction, and Luca's throaty chuckle warmed his stomach—or, well, his *groin*—with such a natural arousal he didn't even question it.

True to his promises, Luca had been kissing him pretty much whenever he came over. In front of his sister, there were chaste kisses on the cheek, but once she went to bed? Long, drugging kisses on the couch, lingering, aching kisses by his door, or—once—a hot, blatantly carnal kiss in Luca's truck after a date—an *actual* date—which had included dinner, a movie, dessert, and hands in low places, until they had both practically *leapt* across the bench seat of the truck to pant in their corners.

"Isaac?" Luca had finally breathed, unbuckling his belt and adjusting himself—blatantly and without apology—inside his jeans.

"Yeah?" Isaac's Dockers were really roomy, and he was grateful, because otherwise he'd be in Luca's same predicament.

"Don't take this the wrong way, because I swore I wouldn't push you, but have you thought maybe we should take this inside at some point?"

Isaac had closed his eyes, and for a moment he was lost in all the places his skin was tingling—his lips, his cock, his taint, the inside of his thighs. Even his hands from their perusal of Luca's nicely furred chest.

Suddenly it was all he could do not to lunge across the seat and ruck Luca's shirt off in an effort to taste his surprisingly pink nipples.

"Yes," he breathed, not even aware he'd said the word. "Yes. God yes. We should take this inside."

"No!" Luca moaned. "Not tonight—of all nights!"

Isaac started to pull himself out of his sexual haze. "Not tonight?" he almost whimpered.

"Yeah. No. God, after what? Two months? May, June, half of July—yeah. After two or three centuries, Isaac, I want it to be *good*. I gotta get up early tomorrow so we can get this guy's swimming pool done while he's still on vacation."

Isaac had heard about this job. It took a good six weeks to install a pool, and while this installation had gone well—and more than helped to make up for the mother-in-law cottage job that had gotten yanked away in May—the weather had been hellifically hot. If Isaac and Allegra went swimming, they were usually inside by noon, and Luca had been getting his workers up at four so they could take full advantage of the 5:00 a.m. daylight, and they could be home by two. Anything after that was unhealthy, and *everybody* was looking forward to the bonus they would get if they could get the pool installed, the concrete seasoned, and the thing full and treated before the homeowner returned from a trip to Europe.

But getting up at four in the morning had cut Luca and Isaac's evenings short, and Isaac was starting to realize that he wasn't going to be able to just fall into Luca's bed like a bad habit or something.

He had to make a conscious decision, plan long and plan well, and *choose* to be with this man, *choose* to make love to him.

Choose to have a relationship with somebody, instead of having *them* boss him around and into it.

Because that's what Todd had done, wasn't it? Granted, Isaac had been a hot mess at the time. He very well could have partied himself out of the credential program and into an early grave if somebody hadn't taken control of his life—*he* hadn't been doing it.

And in that way, Todd hadn't been a bad choice, really. He'd been organized, career oriented, driven. He'd been able to say, "No, we're not going out clubbing, because we both have work in the morning," and Isaac had seen this was the sensible thing to do. And eventually clubbing on Friday night had seemed too exhausting, and Saturday night had been for Todd's work friends, and Sunday was for grading papers and....

And Isaac had, one good decision at a time, grown up.

But he'd also grown *inward*. There were things he really loved— movies, for instance. Lazing in a swimming pool. Day trips to places like the beach or the mountains or the zoo. Marmalade tomcats with a weakness for kitty weed and the zoomie potential of a thousand suns. Cooking. Singing at the top of his lungs while he was doing something mindless, like washing the dishes or watering the garden. Choosing colorful wall hangings or rugs that would make his house happy. Having his stack of clean underwear in the drawer but his stack of clean cargo shorts on top of it. Going into his yarn room with pattern books and dreaming about the things he could make instead of plodding industriously through to a finished object.

Stupid things. Little things. Important things.

Things that made Isaac *Isaac*.

Those things had been forgotten. Those things had been forced inside him, and Luca's encouragement to find them again, to celebrate them—that had *freed* him.

Luca had been right. If he just finished his sentences—"Todd really hated it when I played the music out loud and sang along"—the thing that he heard back was usually… wonderful.

"Well, you're a little out of tune, but maybe if we turn the music up and both sing louder, nobody will care."

Which was what they'd been doing when Allegra had come out of her room from her nap and—instead of yelling at them—joined them.

And later that evening, after dinner, after Allegra had gone back to sleep, when Isaac and Luca were cuddling on the couch, watching something on television with explosions and hard pectorals, Isaac finished the rest of the memory.

"I think the reason he hated music," he'd said, feeling the memory out, "was that his mom made him attend church a lot when he was a kid. He never said as much, but I think she was literally trying to pray the gay away. When he came out and she told him he couldn't go back, I think the music was what he missed. He had a nice singing voice—maybe it hurt him to not be able to use it like he had when he was a kid."

"Yeah, but Isaac, isn't singing for celebration? Any celebration?" Luca's soft laugh hadn't been disparaging, which allowed Isaac to forgive him for what he said next. "I mean, you, me, my sister—we were celebrating today, right? Being happy, being together?"

Isaac remembered that moment in his classroom with Roxy and their students, and how they'd danced like idiots to a fifteen-year-old song, and how… how *affirming* that had been. For him and Roxy, sure, but for the kids too, because joy was something they had to work not to lose.

"Maybe that was it," Isaac had murmured. "Todd felt like he had to be perfect to be happy. And he had to make *me* perfect so I could *make* him happy."

"Yeah. Maybe that's it. But that's no fair to you at all, you know?" Luca's arms tightened around his chest then. "I have the best time with you. I feel like we make *each other* happy, even when we're not perfect."

Then, it had made Isaac's eyes burn, but now, on a Friday afternoon that wasn't so hot it was trying to kill them all, the feeling of Luca's cool hand on the back of his neck, of Luca in the pool with him period, the idea that you didn't have to be *perfect* to be happy, suddenly made Isaac *hungry*.

And not for burgers, although that would probably be good too.

Luca's lazy smile told Isaac that he was completely transparent, but Isaac didn't care. He'd been transparent when he'd been younger too, and that had led to frantic hookups in club bathrooms, dizzy nights that ended with waking up in a bed with too many bodies, or bad moments when he couldn't remember if there had been condoms involved or not.

He wasn't that kid anymore—reckless, grief-driven, self-destructive.

He *loved* his cozy little life and his house. He *really* loved Allegra as a roommate. When she wasn't exhausted or sick, she was much like her brother—kind, funny, genuinely good company. And when she *was* exhausted or sick, she was still kind, funny, and good company; she simply needed caring for. Isaac was surprised to find that he was good at that too. He'd assumed that since Todd had done all the *controlling* in their relationship, that he'd done all the *caring* too, or that after ten years of spending all his emotion on yarn, of all things, that he wouldn't know how to care for another person in a basic human way.

But Allegra's emotions were as all over the place as Roxy's had been (Isaac remembered those days), and on Roxy's advice, he used ice cream, funny movies, and cuddles on the couch to help get Allegra through the worst of it. To his surprise, he didn't resent a *single goddamned minute*. Not one. This person appreciated him—his cooking, his yarning, his love of movies, even time he spent reading seemed to make her happy, and she had books on her phone that she settled into when she saw he was in a quiet mood.

He'd never had a roommate like Allegra before, and she came with the added perk of being Luca's sister. *Luca* brought food and ice cream and shared in the comfort duties, and Isaac got to see him, his heart lighting up whenever he heard Luca's boots thud on the porch, or his swearing as he took them off.

Isaac *loved* his life right now. And he adored his knitting and his cat.

He didn't want those things to go away.

Staring into Luca's dark-eyed, playful gaze, it hit him that sex with Luca wouldn't kill those things. In relentless afternoon sunshine, Isaac thought that maybe lying down in a bed, smooth, cool body to smooth, cool body, would make those things he loved even lovelier.

And wouldn't it be worth it to try?

"What're you thinking?" Luca asked softly, his body bumping the floaty Isaac reclined on.

"I'm getting hot," Isaac murmured, and Luca gave a sexy, throaty chuckle.

"You need to get in the pool hot, or…."

"Or you need to spend the night hot," Isaac said, not dropping his eyes. Then he frowned. "But the other kind too—here, move and I'll—whoa!"

Without ceremony, Luca tilted the air mattress and Isaac went tumbling into the pool, the cool of the water surprising and refreshing on his overheated body. He came up sputtering and laughing and *splashing*, and Luca whooped and splashed him back. The fight was fierce and epic and ended when Luca seized his hips under water and dragged him closer, and Isaac wrapped his arms around Luca's neck and raised his face for a kiss, hot and sweet and drugging.

Isaac sighed and melted into him, and Luca wrapped his arms around Isaac's shoulders and whispered, "You think?"

Isaac's eyes burned. Fun. This man was so much *fun*. And living proof that you didn't have to be a mess, or irresponsible, or exhausting to be fun.

How much fun could they have together—in bed, in each other's lives?

God. Isaac had been so cold, so *alone*, for so long. Didn't he get to play, laughing, in the sun for a while?

"I think," he said, resting his cheek against Luca's bare collarbone. "It's Friday. You can sleep in tomorrow—we'll have all the time in the world."

"Mmm…," Luca murmured. "And tomorrow, we're having Nonna and Pop Pop over again. I can help you get ready for once. I can't wait."

Isaac wanted to cry. "Sounds perfect," he said, not sure what the tears were for. Happiness? Excitement? Terrible, gut-wrenching fear that it would all be taken away? Or even worse—prove to be a lie!

It didn't matter. Luca was holding him so close right now. And tomorrow he'd be hosting family in his home, which was feeling more and more *homey* every day.

The Sunday before, he and Luca had hit up thrift stores and had found Tiffany bedstand lamps for a *steal*. During the days Allegra had worked, he'd spent some of his time restoring the lamps, cleaning the glass, researching how to repair the joins, even asking Luca for help when it came to soldering tape, and now the lamps were *in his bedroom.*

And the day before, he'd ordered a bedspread to match them. Bright, with a glorious blue and some purple and green and peach and magenta and yellow. Todd would have hated the room now, he knew, but as he started to shop for artwork on the walls—which at the moment sported a modern art piece in black, white, and red—he realized Todd's dislike for something was not a factor in his choices—any more than Todd's *like* for something would have been, actually.

Isaac wasn't trying to please Todd anymore—nor was he hoping to please Luca (although Luca seemed delighted by color much like Isaac was). Isaac was wanting to please *Isaac*, and oh! This man in his arms was such a pleasure!

"If it sounds perfect," Luca murmured, "what's this for?"

Gently, he wiped away the tears that had gathered under Isaac's lashes as he'd gotten lost in the moment, in Luca's body, in the sun and the cool and….

"Joy," he said, finally daring to put a name to it. "This has been a *really* good summer vacation."

Luca nodded, and he seemed to get it. Gently, he kissed Isaac's temple. "Wait—there's more coming. Don't make a dirty pun out of it. You'll only hate yourself. Now go sit inside in the A/C with Allegra. Me and Jimmy Bob are going to cool off, and then I'll meet you at home."

"WHY ISN'T Jimmy Bob married?" Isaac asked later that evening as he put together a sandwich bar for dinner. Todd would have insisted on fish or something—but Luca and Allegra seemed to feel that working in the kitchen was completely unnecessary after 2:00 p.m. in the summer. He'd gotten good at frying up chicken in the morning, or putting together sandwich bars or baked potato bars or—when he was feeling fancy—pasta bars, for which the sauces or toppings had all been prepped in the cool of the morning and Isaac had as little to do in the evening as possible.

Isaac still spent much of Sunday in the kitchen so he could pre-make all his ingredients, as well as feed Roxy and her husband a couple of days a week. He understood that right now, her entire life was about mac and cheese and chicken nuggets, and he would show up on her doorstep on Monday morning with little meal bags, and she would honest to God *weep* on him.

And then she'd let the kids run outside and splash in the kiddie pool in the not-quite-apocalyptic morning sunshine, and the two of them would dish.

But that, he realized, was his choice. Even cooking for Allegra and Luca was his choice—and they let him know all the time.

There were no assumptions about who was *supposed* to cook. Isaac cooked because he liked it, and the people in his life appreciated it—and him.

Luca glanced up from slicing tomatoes and grinned. "Too many furry things," he said, popping half a tomato slice in his mouth. "Apparently not every woman wants five cats. Don't tell the Republicans—it'll make 'em hate us more."

Isaac set out sliced sourdough and wheat rolls and snickered.

"I'm a gay teacher—if only I was pregnant, they'd just shoot me in the street and take credit for trash pickup," he said acidly before sobering. "But that's too bad. My department head—"

"The one who let you keep Euclid?" Luca prompted, and it occurred to Isaac that his own acid humor was balanced by Luca's absolute sunny belief in the best of people. *Isaac* would have called her "Queen of the Toolbox" himself, but not Luca.

"Yeah, her. Anyway, she was almost in tears because she couldn't bring another cat home. Apparently she'll be evicted. I'm absolutely in awe of people who can keep adopting strays and feeding them and cleaning up after them. I mean, look at him." He gestured toward Euclid, who was stretched out on his back *on the table* because it had the best sunspot. "He's absolutely incorrigible."

"And yet," Luca pointed out, "I don't see you trying to move him."

"Well," Isaac sniffed, "we were eating in the living room anyway."

And that was another thing. Sometimes they ate at the island in the kitchen—usually during lunch. Sometimes they ate at the kitchen table, particularly when Isaac had cooked something more involved. And sometimes they ate on TV trays Luca had brought in one day after spotting them at a garage sale. They were sturdy, smoothly shaped, nicely sanded wood, and Isaac, who at first had worried a little about the carpet, or the informality or his furniture, had come around on one of those *really* hot days when the west side of the house—the kitchen and living room side of the house—had become an absolute inferno in spite of wooden blinds and a foil window cover. Luca had promised that when the swimming pool was done and his crew could breathe again, he'd put up an extra layer of insulation over that side of the house and then stucco it again.

Isaac had never even thought of such a thing, but he *had* come to appreciate eating in the cooler part of the house on the TV trays. They didn't even watch TV all the time—they just turned off all the lights and let the ceiling fan and the air conditioning keep them as cool as possible.

There was something to be said for informal dining. *Tomorrow* he and Luca and Allegra would clean off the table and set it nicely and welcome Sophia and Geordie into their home—

Isaac's brain scritched like a record needle skipping a groove.

His home. Right?

But it's so big!

But seriously. Allegra was temporary—

But he didn't want her to leave!

And Luca was tentative—

But he had so many hopes for the two of them!

And Todd had bought this stupid house that Isaac had hated because it was big and ostentatious and lonely—

But it didn't feel that way now.

"Oh," he said, coming to a halt in the middle of the kitchen, his hand still outstretched to his silly, presumptuous, magnificent, still-not-grown cat, who had the temerity to *smile* at him in that sunspot.

"Oh, what?" Luca said, glancing up.

"Nothing," Isaac murmured, turning around toward the fridge to see what condiments he needed. "Just… you know. Having epiphanies and shit. Life is weird. Oh, hey! We've got pepperoni!"

"Is that good on sandwiches?"

Isaac didn't even have to look at him to know Luca's fine Roman nose was wrinkled and his full lips were pulled up in skepticism.

"It's delicious," he said with a little smile. "You'll be surprised."

Which is only fair, because I think this place is your home, and it shocks the hell out of me right now, so, you know, even.

His lips twitched at his own petulance, and then he calmed down a little.

Give it time. He'll stay the night tonight. It'll be a start. Maybe when school begins and things get crazy, he'll decide he's had too much of me.

But as he set the pepperoni down on the counter and got out plates for the other deli meats and the pepperoncini, tomatoes, and pickles, he saw Luca snatch a pepperoni and toss it into his mouth with the sort of expression that said he was fine with trying new things.

Todd had never wanted to try new things. It was like he'd been so excited to have the *things* he thought were good for his life locked down in cement, trying something new—pepperoni on a sandwich or swimming at a friend's house or a new lesson plan… or a cat—was just too frightening. Too scary.

For the first time, Isaac felt sorry for Todd. All that control he'd tried to exert over Isaac, all that insistence on formality, on having the right furniture, on not being too ostentatious or too interesting…. Todd hadn't been trying to be *cruel*.

Todd had been trying to be *safe*. He'd been trying to make Isaac *safe*.

But Isaac didn't need a lover to make him safe—not even from himself. Not anymore.

Luca gave him a thumbs-up and grinned as he swallowed the pepperoni and reached for another. Isaac didn't warn him he'd spoil his dinner, because he was a grown-assed man, but he did smile and take one for himself because they tasted good, and it was his damned dinner.

Isaac didn't need a man to make him safe—but boy, did he want a man to share these moments with. Exploratory moments, simple moments—even safe moments.

There was such a difference.

There'd be time to decide if Luca wanted it to be *their* home or not. And even if the answer was not, that might just mean he wanted to keep his own apartment, not that he didn't want Isaac.

And in the meantime, Isaac was going to treat his moments with Luca like Luca had treated that pepperoni.

Simple, savory, desirable, interesting.

And added to the other things in Isaac's life, he could only make things better.

Sweetly in the Shadows

Luca's sister used to be an absolute terror, all the energy, all the excitement, none of the common sense. Pregnancy seemed to have not only knocked her on her ass, it had made her more content about knowing her limitations.

At around nine o'clock, after she'd cleaned up dinner (since Isaac and Luca had shopped and prepped) she stood and stretched, then moved to the couch to kiss first Luca on the cheek and then Isaac.

He watched as Isaac smiled at her, accepting the kiss like he'd always had a sister, like spontaneous tokens of affection were something he'd known all his life when Luca was pretty sure that wasn't true.

"When you coming tomorrow?" she asked on a yawn. "Maybe you could bring me coffee or a doughnut or something."

"I'll get you coffee if you want," he said, because she'd been limiting herself to one iced coffee a day and her doctor said that was fine. "But I'm going to be staying over."

"Mmm…." At first she nodded like this happened all the time, and then she blinked like she was trying to wake up. "Uhm… really?"

Isaac concentrated on his knitting, his already sun-kissed cheeks growing a little pinker.

"Uhm, really," he said without looking up.

Allegra met Luca's eyes, and he waggled his eyebrows, making her laugh.

"Good," she said. "It's about time. Isaac, I love living with you, but if you hurt my brother, I'll hide your body in the backyard and nobody will suspect me."

Isaac actually glanced up from his knitting, and to Luca's surprise, he seemed to take her very seriously. "Your brother's the greatest," he said softly. "I wouldn't want to hurt him in a thousand years."

"Good," she said. "No, seriously—good. Because I'll never finish this blanket without you, and that would be a real shame."

"God, you're sarcastic," Isaac told her. "Where have you been all my life?"

"Asleep in your downstairs bedroom," she retorted, and then she bent and kissed Luca on the cheek again. "Be good to each other," she said softly, and that was that.

She disappeared down the hall, and Luca cleared his throat with authority. Isaac glanced up from the crocheted square in his hand and gave a gentle smile.

"Let me finish this off, okay?"

Luca nodded. "Course." He *was* feeling impatient, but he also knew what it was like to be in the middle of a project. If you didn't come to a decent stopping place, that shit could bother you all night.

A few moments later, Isaac set the little square in the bag of them that was starting to overflow and came to sit next to Luca, leaning his head on Luca's chest.

"Mmm...." Luca wrapped his arm securely around his shoulders. "That's a lot of little tiny squares you and my sister have there. When do you start sewing them all together?"

Isaac chuckled. "Well, we've got twenty more to go, so, God willing and with your grandmother's help, tomorrow."

"Nice!" Luca paused, thinking about the pattern. "You've been keeping them in different bags, right? So, like, a palette?"

"Yeah," Isaac said. "I scanned the drawing and enlarged it—especially for your nonna. But I figured I'd finish the squares tomorrow, and your sister and Sophia can start sewing them into strips. They need to keep the strips numbered so we can sew the strips together when they're done."

"Wow." Luca was impressed. "You think that will work?"

Isaac grunted. "I think we're going to have to rip out and replace at least ten squares, but I may be a little bit pessimistic, because high school student is my default. Your sister and Nonna are smarter than high school students."

Luca muffled a chuckle behind his hand in deference to his sister, who was hopefully getting some shuteye. "Well, I'll give a little prayer to the knitting and crocheting gods that you guys can make this work." He paused, hit by something Isaac had said. "Hey—do you ever hear from your kids over summer break? That Marcelle kid who designed the winning blanket—think he'd want in on that action?"

Isaac pulled back from him and stared at him in surprise.

"What?" Luca felt his face flush. "What'd I say? Did I break some rule of teacher decorum or—"

Isaac captured his mouth then, fully, passionately, the kiss going until Luca fell back against the cushions of the couch, completely bemused.

"What was that?" he asked in wonder.

"For caring about my students," Isaac murmured. "For remembering Marcelle's name. For thinking to ask him. Yes—if you think your nonna wouldn't mind. I keep my student number phone at work, but Roxy has Marcelle and his friend Sheryl come over to babysit once a week now. She could call him up. I think he'd *love* that. Thank you."

Luca smiled weakly and searched his face, hating to bring the name up right now, but needing confirmation.

"Todd didn't ask, did he? About your job. About your kids."

"No," Isaac said, but he kept eye contact. He wouldn't have that one day in early May when Luca had caught him staring at a pile of hated yarn. "He…. I've been thinking about him. I think… I think his whole world was stunted. Made small, you know? He… like you." Isaac looked away now, but maybe that's because Luca had told him about his parents in a quiet moment, a moment of vulnerability. "You said your parents cut you off. And that was awful. And his parents did too—but more than that. They told him *God* couldn't love him. And, you know, some people don't like authority anyway." He gave a modest smile. "I was never a fan. But Todd *needed* that. He *needed* to know that good things happened if you followed the rules. So his whole life was like… like penance for breaking, you know, this *one* rule."

Luca nodded slightly, still not getting it, but he didn't want to interrupt.

"So," Isaac continued, "he… he worked so hard on making his world *exactly right*. But you can't do that with a big world. You have to keep it small. So he couldn't control my high school, or my students. He couldn't *make* me stop working there. So he just didn't ask."

And Luca got it then. Why the kiss. Why the big deal. "I… I will *always* make room in my world for you, Isaac," he promised fervently. "If you feel squeezed out, you only have to say so."

Isaac nodded worriedly. "And I'll try so hard to make room in my world for you," he said, smoothing his fingers nervously along Luca's cheeks. "I'm anxious, you know? I feel like I've spent all this time fussing about me being *me*. I want to be able to care for you too."

Luca chuckled, remembering Isaac's effusive, polite thank-yous to Jimmy Bob, and how he'd sat in the shade the week before, drinking lemonade and listening to Luca and Jimmy Bob bitch about the pool they were installing and how they wished they'd given the job to somebody who made that their specialty.

"Why did he pick you?" Isaac asked, gulping lemonade gratefully.

"The last guy he paid to install his pool left half a hole in the ground and dumped cement in it," Jimmy Bob said disgustedly. "Some people are just crooks. This guy's friends had hired us for a different job—what was it, Luc?"

"We replaced his roof," Luca said. "The one with all the gables, remember?"

"Oh God—yeah, how could I forget! Another job that people usually pick a specialist for. Anyway, we must have done a good job, because this rich guy only wants us. Luca here spent a month *doing homework, reading up on shit, calling guys known for installing pools, asking their friends, before he'd even touch the job."*

Luca shuddered. "He's paying us a fortune, *Jimmy. I mean, a* fortune. *But God, we can't screw this up."*

"Yeah," Jimmy Bob said, nodding at Isaac. "So we really appreciate how you're not bitching at him about his weird hours for this one. He's doing his best, you know?"

"Always," Isaac had said, gazing at Luca in a way that made him feel like he could accomplish everything. "He's always doing his best."

Isaac was looking at him that way now. "I… I'm putting some trust in you," he said. "That you'll tell me. If I'm not opening my world, my heart up enough for you. You're a good guy, Luca. You deserve someone who can absolutely give as much to you as you give already. I know I've still got some work to do in my heart, but God, do I want to start living again in a bigger world. I want to live there with you."

Oh, Luca wanted him. Any way he could get him, Luca wanted him.

"Check us out," he murmured, cupping Isaac's cheek in his palm. "All our talk about our misspent youth, and we're having the relationship talk before the sex. I feel like this is prime adulting here—I'm not sure if our world *gets* any bigger than this."

Isaac may have laughed then, but if he did, it was swallowed by Luca's kiss.

Deep, hard, and curiously unfettered, everything about Isaac's touch, his taste, spoke of want and yearning and a blood-pulsing joy that this time they didn't have to stop.

It was like getting in a raft and knowing that cruising the rapids was the point. Exhilarating and exciting and maybe a little bit scary, but oh, the adventure would be worth it.

Luca felt that curious sense of immersion in the moment, in the body and the touch of this one particular person, that he'd rarely felt with a lover. Almost always there was a sense of time, of place. Was there a roommate listening? Could anybody see? Was he touching this person right? Could he ignore that his nipple had been flicked twenty thousand times?

But with Isaac, in this living room he'd come to feel so comfortable in, in the arms of a man he'd come to regard as a necessary part of his day, he lost himself, as dreamy and as happy as Isaac's damned cat.

It was Isaac who had to pull back, panting, and say, "Luca, we should… you know. Bedroom."

Luca nodded, gulping air, and gazed at him helplessly. "How did this get better?" he asked, remembering their first kiss under the late spring sky. Here it was, ripe summer, and the kisses were only sweeter.

"Got no idea." Isaac rolled off him and held his hand out. "But we need…." He gestured to himself, and Luca saw the hair all mussed, the khaki shorts unbuttoned, his T-shirt rucked up, showing his tight little middle.

Luca made a sound he'd previously only heard in *Young Frankenstein*, and a half-amused, half-*starving* smile interrupted some of the kissing fog on Isaac's face.

"Come on, Monster," he said dryly. "If I'm gonna hit the high notes tonight, we've got to be upstairs in my bedroom."

Luca laughed and made that sound again, playfully following Isaac as he checked the door and turned out the lights, making sure he squeezed Isaac's backside or caressed his upper arm or snuck in a playful kiss whenever Isaac let him catch up.

When Luca got to the base of the stairs, he turned to surprise Isaac with a kiss and was pleased to find Isaac right there, ready to surprise *him*.

Their lips touched, and the kiss exploded, taking all of the playfulness, the game of catch and release, and turning it incendiary.

Isaac *devoured* him, and Luca melted, sitting down hard on the third step and pulling Isaac onto his body as he leaned back and returned the kiss. He placed one hand on Isaac's backside and pressed him into the juncture of Luca's thighs, and Isaac moaned softly, bucking against Luca's swollen groin.

"If you don't go upstairs," Isaac panted, "so help me, your sister's going to catch us here while I'm sucking your cock."

The image of Isaac's mouth on him was enough to make Luca moan, but the threat of Allegra waking up and catching them was more than enough to make him scramble upright and race to the top of the stairs, Isaac at his heels.

Together, the tumbled into Isaac's darkened bedroom and shed clothes until Luca pushed Isaac back against the door, satisfied when he heard it snick shut before he fell on his knees in front of this surprising, funny, *sexy* man.

"Oh wow," Isaac breathed as Luca gazed up into his eyes and ran his hands up and down Isaac's thighs and concave tummy. "We're doing this."

"Please God, yes," Luca murmured, before tracing his lips along the length of Isaac's cock.

Isaac let out a sigh and tangled his fingers in Luca's hair, urging him on.

Luca didn't need urging. He wanted it in his mouth more than his lungs wanted air. He pulled the length in, allowing it to glide along his tongue, relaxing his throat to take it, and Isaac whooshed out a breath as he thumped his head back against the door.

Luca tightened his mouth and wrapped one hand around the shaft, working them together while Isaac massaged his scalp, not demanding, just, Luca thought, appreciating.

He felt *very* appreciated as he gave that blow job, listening to Isaac's breathy moans, feeling his fingers in Luca's hair, or cupping his cheek, or—oh God!—tracing his own length as it disappeared through Luca's lips.

Luca could have done that forever, but Isaac's noises were getting more urgent, and Luca knew he was close. He pulled off reluctantly and gazed up, giving his own sigh when Isaac cupped his face in his palms and met Luca's eyes.

"How do you want to do this?" Luca asked breathily. His own cock ached with need, but tonight was Isaac's.

"Bed," Isaac murmured. "You inside me. It's been a long, long time." And with that he bent down, capturing Luca's mouth with his own as Luca struggled to push up and take Isaac into his arms.

For a moment they kissed, bare body to bare body, and Luca felt a sort of moonlit hush around them. His name for watching Isaac knit came back to him. *Magic hour.*

These moments here, in each other's arms, they were magic.

The kiss went on, and their feet moved of their own volition until they were sprawled on the sheets, the comforter kicked aside, their bodies and hands stroking in synchronicity.

"Lube," Luca gasped, and Isaac reached for his drawer.

"Fresh bottle," he muttered, and Luca took a moment to grin.

"Just for me?" he asked.

"Yes," Isaac said rawly. "I had to throw everything out. Apparently I forgot sex was even a thing for the last four years." Luca startled at that number, but then Isaac said, "Hurry, dammit!" And he had better things to do.

Luca slid down his body, pausing for a moment at his cock again, to lick the bell and taste the fluid at the slit. Isaac keened, needing, and Luca pushed gently at his thighs, spreading him against the sheets, before he parted Isaac's cheeks and ran slick fingers along his cleft.

"Oh my God," Isaac breathed, and Luca thrust one finger gently in. Tight—so tight—and Luca had to breathe through his own arousal, take his time, slicking and stretching, and slicking and stretching, until Isaac bucked against the bed and moaned.

"Please," he begged. "Please, Luca. I need this. I need *you*. Please?"

And Luca was there, breaching him, thrusting inside slowly, slowly, while Isaac welcomed him, pushing against him, pulling him in.

Finally he was seated, and Isaac tilted his head back, eyes closed. "Yeah," he breathed. "Oh yeah. God. Move. Do the thing. Please, Luca, do the thing."

Luca's stomach vibrated with his laughter. "The thing?" he taunted, rocking his hips, starting that primal rhythm that his body welcomed, singing with arousal, ramping with renewed need.

"The… oh God! That thing!"

Luca snapped his hips a little harder, suspecting that Isaac had probably loved a little harder, a little faster, in his wild days.

"That thing?" he whispered. "What's the name of that—"

"*Fuck me!*" Isaac gasped, and if he hadn't been breathless and wanting, Luca thought he might have screamed it, and as gratifying as that might have been, they were still sharing a house with Luca's sister.

Luca thrust faster, harder, and Isaac's gasps quickened, his quiet cries more urgent, his hands on Luca's shoulders greedy.

"Yes," Isaac managed, "yes… oh God…. Luca, I love… I love… I need… I need… oh please—please—*yes*!"

Luca felt Isaac's climax, everything in his body bearing down on Luca's cock, Luca's cock radiating pleasure until sunlight streamed from his bones, from his skin, from his very being.

He closed his eyes, explosions dancing behind his lids as his climax rushed his spine, and he came, rutting inside his lover with all the possession and need and devotion in his soul.

The comedown was rough, each muscle group unclenching, his body relaxing breath by breath, until he collapsed against Isaac, who was making fluttery petting motions with his hands. Flutter, flutter, and Luca's back was soothed. Flutter, flutter, and his neck. Flutter, flutter, and his chest was touched, and then his lower back, where he still arched, trying to stay in the haven of Isaac's body.

"The thing?" he asked when he could breathe again. "Do the thing?"

Isaac closed his eyes, collapsing against the pillows. "It felt so lovely," he murmured. "I couldn't say fuck when it felt so good."

"Mmm…." Luca nuzzled his ears. "You use that word more fluently than anybody I've ever met—unless we are actually fucking. That's hilarious. I love that."

Isaac's laughter shook them where they were still joined. "I'm glad you're amused. Was it just me, or did the earth move?"

"Oh yeah," Luca murmured, kissing along Isaac's jaw. His cock, sensing that the fun was not over, began to do some stretches in anticipation.

"Really?" And Luca pulled back to see Isaac's eyes on his face. "It wasn't just me, right?" Those giant hazel eyes were wide and dewy, and Luca realized he had to take this seriously.

"No, love," he said softly. "That wasn't just you. When you mean it, sex changes everything. When you mean it for the best, sex changes everything for the better."

Isaac's eyes crinkled at the corners, and he lifted up to capture Luca's mouth. The kiss was sweet, so sweet, with Isaac's soul in it. "You say good stuff in bed," he murmured. "But only because I know you'll be here in the morning."

"Oh God yeah," Luca said softly. "Will I."

Then Isaac kissed him again, and Luca's hips started to thrust on their own, and the word, the thing, the glorious thing....

They were doing it again.

AUGUST

"Isaac? Oh, Iiiiiiiizzzaaac… you in there?"

Isaac looked up from the border he was putting on the baby blanket that had been joined by group effort and blinked at Roxy. Allegra and Luca were at work, and Roxy's kids were playing at their feet while Euclid regarded them all from the kitchen counter with sleepy eyes. Yes, Isaac's whole household had given up on keeping Euclid off the table or the counters whenever it suited him, but particularly now, when there were two toddlers out for his blood and a screaming infant who would cheer them on. Isaac was definitely on the cat's side.

But that's not why Isaac was distracted. "I'm here—oh, Justice honey, maybe don't hit your sister with—"

But the wooden block came down on Patricia's head, and the wailing commenced. Isaac set down the blanket and went to comfort the little girl, who sniffled on her Uncle Isaac's shirt in a way that told him nap time was nigh, while Roxy calmly reprimanded her son.

Without looking back, Isaac carried the girl to the new baby's room that he and Allegra had set up the week before, pleased to see that the toddler bed they'd both agreed would go on one side was already made up. Having a toddler bed and a crib in there had been Allegra's idea, once she realized how often Roxy visited.

"We're going to need it eventually anyway," Allegra said with a laugh as they'd painted the trim in bright colors and planned. "Since me and Luca are buying the furniture, I figure this way the room can welcome *all* the babies, you think?"

Isaac had been tickled. The room—done up with bright red-and-blue trim and pale yellow walls—had hardwood floors but lots of thick colorful throw rugs held down by furniture and Velcro. A mom's rocking chair stood in one corner, next to the crib and a dresser, and the toddler bed lined one wall, beside bright plastic chests full of stuffed animals and teething rings. Allegra was keeping a bassinet in her room on Roxy's recommendation. "Those first weeks, before everybody's sleep schedule is down, it's just a blessing to put the baby in the basket and collapse."

In the middle of the room, Roxy had set up a porta crib, so *everybody* could go down for a nap, because the temperature outside would reach the 110s and Isaac's place was as close as these kids were going to get to outside for a while, even to swim.

Roxy had arrived that morning with an ice chest full of juice and cubed fruit, and Isaac—with Luca's help—had taped foil insulation along the outside of the west side of the house, leaving the kitchen, dining room, and living room about ten degrees cooler when the whole world got crispy.

Luca was to the point where his entire crew had filled the swimming pool with water, and they were running the filters and waiting, chewing their nails, to make sure the thousand and one things that could go wrong with a job like this had gone right instead.

The whole reason Allegra had braved the elements to go into the office was to disburse the money when the check cleared, and Isaac was both excited and anxious for the two of them. They'd poured so much into this!

He left Patricia sound asleep in the bed and passed Roxy on her way down the hall with her son, his head lolling on her shoulder.

When he got out to the living room, he saw that Annie, the youngest, had fallen asleep on her stomach, soft little baby snores coming through her mouth as she lay under the ceiling fan on her thick flannel quilt, wearing nothing but a diaper.

With a sigh, he sank back into his armchair and picked up his phone, checking to see if there was a text from Luca telling him how things had gone.

$$$ We're bringing home takeout tonight!

He smiled but shook his head. *I've got cubed fruit and cheese—you sure you want takeout?*

Good point. Take the rain check, baby—we owe you a whole lot of bacon.

Fair.

He sighed as he set the phone down and picked up the blanket again. It was not the only thing he and Allegra had made for the baby at this point, but everybody, Marcelle included, had been so excited about helping to sew all the squares together that they'd both initiated other baby projects while their helpers were helping.

Now there was nothing left but the edging, and Isaac had to laugh because the blanket didn't match the nursery *at all*, but he still couldn't help but look at it with a whole lot of pride.

"You gonna let the baby have that, or you gonna put it on a wall and make it art?" Roxy asked.

Isaac chuckled and rested the thing in his lap again. "Oh, I want this blanket to be hauled around, taken to picnics, used to wipe boogers and change diapers—this thing is going to be *lurved.*"

Roxy laughed softly too and took a sip of her own fruit drink. "That's my kind of baby gift," she said. "What's got you so distracted, honey? This should be your moment of triumph here."

Isaac glanced at his phone. "Well, for one thing, I was waiting to hear from Luca and Allegra about whether or not their big project was finalized. Apparently there's money in the bank, and Luca's business is solvent for the rest of this year, which is pretty awesome."

"Oh my God! Isaac, that's amazing. They should be so proud!"

Isaac nodded, resuming the border around the blanket, soothed by their conversation. "Oh they are—and I'm happy for them."

"You sound as happy as a heart attack," she said dryly. "What's the deal?"

"School starts next week," he said, like this was news.

"I know. This is sort of our last hurrah before we go bake in our classrooms like ratatouille." Some fucking genius had put the thermostat controls in the hands of the company that installed the HVAC systems. The company was located in Texas, and the sensors for the thermostats were *nowhere near* the mass of thirty-five kids in the center of the room generating body heat by the megajoule. The year before, teachers and students had staged a walkout when they realized they were teaching in ninety-degree heat because some pencil pusher three states away could not fathom why it wasn't seventy-six degrees in their rooms.

"I think they fixed that?" he said, ending on an "I hope" sort of note, and she grunted.

"We'll see. I wonder if they remembered to update my computer with the server this year." Two years ago, they hadn't, and her grades hadn't been saved. She'd been pregnant, exhausted, and had recorded her grades sixty-dozen times only to have Paula *and* the principal condescend to her about, "Well, if you weren't so tired, dear, maybe you could figure out how to work the computer."

Isaac had needed to hold her back, or she would have committed physical assault.

"I called yesterday and double-checked," Isaac told her, grimacing at her surprise. "Look, I don't know who you think is keeping me sane at that pit o' despond, O Earth Mommy Dearest, but if I don't have Roxy, I'm going fucking banana dumplings, and I'd just rather fucking not."

"Aw...." Roxy smiled at him beatifically. "Same with you, my queen banana dumpling. In fact"—and she grew surprisingly serious—"given how many changes you've had in your life in the last three months, I'm kind of honored. You know, when you said you were letting Allegra move in, I got kind of jealous. I was like, 'That bitch is smart, funny, and sweet as hell. She'd better not try to steal my bestie.'"

Isaac chuckled because Allegra and Roxy got along amazingly well, but if Roxy wanted to tell the story like that, well, it was funnier. No, Allegra had fit into his life just fine, and Isaac had felt an awesome sort of excitement as the two of them had prepped the baby's room the week before. He'd seen Roxy through three pregnancies, and he adored her brood, but this baby... this baby was coming to live with him, and he was so excited he couldn't stand it.

But....

"I'm going to be a parent," he said and then shook his head to reword that. "I mean, no, not the baby daddy, and I know I'm Uncle Isaac to your kids—I can change a diaper—"

"And you do a fantastic job," Roxy told him, saluting a little with her fruit juice and ice.

"Thank you," he said soberly. "I worked hard to learn that skill. But anyway, this kid is going to live in my house. And I want to help. I mean.... Roxy, I *really* want to help. But school is starting. You know... school?"

Roxy blew out a breath and fell against her chair as though suddenly exhausted. "Yeah, Isaac," she said softly. "I know school."

"That first six weeks," he muttered, and she groaned.

"Don't remind me."

The first six weeks in a school with a percentage of transient students was pretty hellish. It took a while to get the classes balanced in the first place, but when there was an influx of kids in the first two weeks whose parents hadn't signed them up for school because they didn't know they were supposed to, or figured they could just show up with a kid and it would all be okay, or who didn't give a shit, or whatever—well, that made things *extra* fun. The rosters Roxy and Isaac were given on the first day were usually *miles* away from the rosters they ended up with after that first tumultuous six weeks, and in the meantime? They still had to teach lessons, give quizzes, and make sure the kids learned something, please God *anything*, in six weeks of a school year.

It was, in a word, *exhausting*.

And that didn't include the whole "coming back to work" thing, which was *also* an adjustment. Teaching used a massive amount of energy, and teachers usually refilled their reserves during summer break. But coming back was a whole physical/psychological *thing*, and it was hard on the students and hard on the teachers. Roxy was fond of saying that whether you were having a baby or starting the school year, the exhaustion peaked at six weeks. Don't make any big decisions, don't give any big tests, and don't operate any heavy machinery in that sixth week, and after that, everything would get eventually better.

So when Isaac said, "That first six weeks," he was talking about the ordeal they had to live through to get on with their year, and for Roxy it was worse.

Because she was leaving her kids, and she hated it.

She'd hate *not* teaching, but she also hated leaving her babies. Isaac knew this in his bones—just like he knew that she would feel guilt her husband wouldn't about leaving them, and it was un-fucking-fair.

And the first six weeks only made that worse.

"So, Isaac," Roxy said, sounding sympathetic, "did you prepare them? Luca and Allegra, I mean? Did you tell them what it's like?"

Isaac grunted. "No," he said, feeling dumb. "It's just…." Randomly he said, "Did you see my bedroom?"

"Yeah—it's gorgeous. A new throw rug, a new comforter, those lamps—and the picture! It's so beautiful!" Isaac had managed to find a local artist who'd done a painting of the bridge in downtown Sacramento during the sunset. Between the gold of the bridge, the orange and blue of the sky, and the darkness of the river below it, the landscape was a study in contrast. It was bold and colorful without being tacky, and Isaac adored it.

Luca hadn't stopped praising it since they'd put it up, sliding Todd's painting, unlamented, into the same corner of the garage where Isaac was planning to put the living room furniture next year, when he had enough money to replace it.

Closing his eyes, he could remember Luca's fingertips along his bare shoulder as he'd said the words, before they'd fallen into bed again, making exuberant love in a room that felt like *theirs*, their sanctuary, their place.

"Thanks," he said, giving a small smile. "Roxy, this has been the best summer I've had since… since…." Oh God. "Since my parents were alive."

"Oh wow," she said, suitably impressed. It was so easy to love Roxy—she did get it when things were important.

"Yeah," Isaac said, finally able to actually *talk* about the thing haunting him like the ghost of a Victorian child. "I-I don't want it to end. I don't want school to start and me to get all… lost. You know how we get. Lost and tired and cranky and… and miserable."

"We get over it," Roxy supplied helpfully, and then, in the name of honesty, she added, "Most of us."

Isaac grimaced. Teachers got divorced a lot. Some of it was just that *grown-ups* got divorced a lot, but some of it was—and Isaac had seen this firsthand, in himself—that the habit of being a petty tyrant in your own domain didn't always leave a person when they left the classroom. Isaac heard it in his voice when he lectured Luca about which plasticware container to put stuff in, or why they should buy the bundles of cilantro and not the live herbs, until Isaac got his shit together and made an herb box.

Once in a while could be forgiven—even Todd had looked upon it with a certain grim tolerance when they'd first started dating. But Isaac had seen Paula Lamphere lecture the guy coming to fix the lights in her room with the same ball-shriveling don't-fuck-with-me tone she used on her students, and he'd known immediately why she was still single.

Roxy had once admitted, in a moment of absolute delirious sleep deprivation, to telling her husband how to push out his bowel movement while he was in the bathroom and she was walking an infant up and down the hallway.

The thought of inflicting that sort of cruelty on Luca—*his* Luca, who gazed at him with absolute reverence in the moonlight through his window—filled him with a deep sadness. And not a little fear.

"Todd and I…." He paused but then realized how much less he'd been saying that in the last month. "Todd and I didn't start out bad," he said after a moment. "When I was young and… and sad, he was strong and solid and dependable. I learned so much from him about how caring for someone isn't just words or putting out, you know?"

"It's being there," Roxy said, and she gave a small smile. "In the middle of the night, covered in baby puke, the guy who steps in to change the diaper and give you a towel and tell you to take a shower—that's your guy."

Isaac nodded. "Same, but without the diaper—or the baby."

"You met Todd during your party days, right?"

"God, I was so high." Isaac shook his head. "I don't even remember *meeting* him. I just remember waking up at his old apartment thinking, 'My God, I've seen more exciting hotel rooms.'" He sighed. "And then Todd brought me breakfast and ibuprofen for my hangover and told me my clothes would be out of the dryer in a few if I wanted to shower." He shook his head. "I mean, it was like my parents' house, except I'd obviously gotten laid the night before. Why *wouldn't* I want to stay?"

She chuckled like she was supposed to. "But Isaac," she said when she was done, "you're a grown-up now. And the good kind of grown-up. You've got your own cat." She petted Euclid, who had jumped up on her lap while they'd been talking. "And I gotta tell you, the cat distribution system knew what it was doing with this one. *You* may have been clean and sober for years, but your cat is the best kind of stoner."

"He's so baked," Isaac said fondly, knowing that right now the cat was stoned on sunshine, because they only broke out the catnip every so often. It didn't stop the furry orange thing from drooling on Roxy's lap, though, did it?

Roxy fondled his battered ears and then resumed speaking. "But what I'm saying is that you're… you're not that kid anymore. You sustained a long-term relationship, and it may not have been great for the last few years, but you worked hard to make it work. You know what teaching does to you. You can prep *them* for it—" She paused. "If you make one joke about stretching the rim, I'm throwing your cat at you."

It took a minute before Isaac got it, and by then he was sipping bright pink pomegranate lemonade.

He almost sprayed it all over his blanket, and he held his hand in front of his mouth in outrage.

"You bitch," he rasped when he was done coughing. "If I had gotten pomegranate lemonade all over this goddamned blanket, I would have strangled you with it and told Brian I got the kids for my suffering. Fucking *Jesus*!"

Roxy was collapsed against the back of the couch, the bombproof cat actually collapsed on his side on her lap, and she had the bright pink juice all over her white shirt.

"Worth it!" she gasped. "So worth it!"

It took them a while to regain their composure, but eventually Roxy was leaning sideways on the couch, her T-shirt blotchy but dry, resting her head on the arm of it, and Isaac had picked his blanket back up and was working quietly. He suspected Roxy was about to fall into her own nap, and he prepared himself to go get the kids at the first whimper, but given that poor little Sparrow Anne was still asleep on the floor after their terrible crack-up, he rather suspected everybody else was down for a long time.

"Isaac," Roxy murmured, "my terrible dirty joke aside, warn them, okay? Tell them what it's like so they know. It's like Brian—he makes sure he gets all caught up during the summer so he can pick up the slack when I go back to work. And then we sneak a week of vacation before Christmas."

Which beat the hell out of traveling in this heat in August; neither of them had to say it.

"Do you really want a basketball team?" he asked, wondering if she'd hear him before she dropped off.

"Yeah," she mumbled. "But I might have to go to part-time with four. I'll try to warn you."

He waited for a bit, humming to himself, and then he pulled out his phone and set it on a quiet music-streaming list. Not classical, just not "bouncy, with shouting" as the movie quote went.

About the time he was shaking out his hands, he heard a rustle down the hallway and Patricia came stumbling out, her hair sticking straight up and her eyes glazed over with sleep, clutching one of the books Roxy had packed in her diaper bag. He set aside the blanket gratefully and held out his arms.

"C'mere, precious," he murmured, and she stumbled right into him. He set her on his lap and pulled her back against him, taking the book gently.

"Book?" he asked.

"Music," she mumbled. "Sing."

He leaned against the back of the chair, that hot, sticky, solid weight in his arms, and began to hum to the Shins' "The Past and Pending."

That's where he was when Luca woke him up with a kiss on the cheek.

"Hey, baby," he murmured. "Allegra and I ignored what you said and brought takeout anyway. Kids can't live on fruit and cheese alone."

Isaac glanced around with sleepy eyes to see that Allegra had scooped up the sprawled baby from the floor and was rocking her against her shoulder. Month five had given her tummy a rise, like an emerging volleyball, and she was down to three days a week, with Jimmy Bob's niece taking the other two days. Between the heat and the baby, Allegra was beat, but Isaac watched the way her face lit up as she absently patted little Sparrow Anne's back, and he remembered Luca's assertion that day back in May when he'd thrown out the idea for the baby blanket, the thing that had started it all.

His sister was going to make an amazing mother. It was true she'd already made the decision to do that, but watching her now, Isaac thought it was the thing that would make her happiest.

He suddenly felt incredibly lucky to be part of their lives when she did so.

And then Luca distracted him with a gentle hand smoothing his hair back from his face. "C'mon, baby," Luca said throatily. "You guys can't sleep all day or the kids will never sleep tonight."

"We gotta go slow," Isaac slurred. "It's bad when they wake up cranky."

"I hear ya," Luca murmured. "Here, let me take her—looks like she woke up and fell back asleep again."

"Yeah." Isaac yawned and struggled to sit up after that warmth and weight was moved from his lap. "Here, let me go get Justice."

Luca shook his head grimly—yeah, they'd both discussed how Falcon Justice was just not going to be a happy ending for the poor kid. He'd probably change his name to Franklin Justin before he hit puberty.

"Should we wake Roxy?" Allegra asked, blowing softly in Sparrow Anne's face.

"No," Isaac said decisively, remembering the way one good laugh had wiped his friend out. "She's exhausted, and we're going back to work next week. It's still hot—it's gonna be so brutal."

With that, he managed to toddle down the hallway to turn the light on in the baby room. He'd brought his phone with him, and now he turned the volume up a tad—enough to wake up instead of lull back to sleep. He left it on the window ledge and went back into the front of the house, pleased to see Luca had set Patricia up on the booster seat Roxy left at his house and was excitedly pushing her chicken nugget around in the special sauce.

Allegra was cooing at Sparrow Anne, who was regarding her with open eyes.

"Practicing?" Isaac chided gently.

"Well, yeah," Allegra said. She smiled at Isaac a little sadly. "I… I don't have any friends who are doing this right now, you know? Have I thanked you yet, for giving me a home and a friend?"

Isaac chuckled softly, pleased that Allegra could play just like Roxy could. "I don't count?" he asked, pretending to be wounded.

"You're my brother's boyfriend," she said, rolling her eyes. "You don't get to double dip."

"Sure he does," Luca said from across the table. "He can be *your* friend, *my* boyfriend, and Roxy's friend too!"

At that moment they heard the stiff little footsteps and groggy whining of a child who wasn't quite awake yet.

"Mommy?" Justice asked, his voice just as small as his four-year-old body.

"How about Uncle Isaac?" Isaac asked, holding out his arms. Justice didn't care who it was, apparently, because he ran straight to Isaac, and Isaac hefted him up. "You're big," he said, nodding at the boy.

"Daddy says it's 'cause I eat my weight in nuggets," Justice said, leaning his head on Isaac's shoulder. "Can I eat some nuggets to see?"

"Smooth, young man. So smooth. But we just opened a hot box of nuggets, so I think you'll get away with it."

The boy giggled into his neck, and Isaac gave him a squeeze. He was almost done with the blanket, he thought happily, and enough sweaters to last Allegra's baby through the next three winters. It was time to start making Roxy's kids sweaters so he could start knitting for his high school kids in November.

Having this many people in his life to create for felt like an embarrassment of riches, and as the kids settled down to nuggets and cubed watermelon, Isaac felt himself beaming, for no reason at all, into Luca's eyes.

"You look happy," Luca said, drawing near.

"It's been a really good summer," Isaac said on a sigh. "It's going to…." Some of his happiness faded. "Have I warned you yet? About how bad the first six weeks suck?"

Luca frowned and shook his head. "You said it would be busy—"

"It's exhausting," Isaac said with a small smile. "I… I know I complain about Todd a lot, but going back to school—it's *hard* on a relationship. It's falling asleep before dinner and bitching about the coffee coming too slow in the morning, forgetting your lunch, living on Advil and caffeine, trying to control the kids in the street for playing too loud, the goddamned sunshine is getting on my nerves, and my bathroom is a science-experiment disaster. *Everybody* cries during the first six weeks, even the straight men. *None* of us are okay during the first six weeks. And Roxy and I play movies during week six while we do our grades, and we both take strategic mental health days so we don't lose our minds, but… but you've got to know how bad it's going to get. I-I just hope you can hold on through it," he said with a small smile. "I really, *really* like where we are now."

Luca returned the small smile, the expression on his face telling Isaac he'd heard, *really* heard, what Isaac was trying to say.

"Do I get a reward if I make it through the next six weeks?" he asked, teasing a little but also oddly serious.

Isaac blinked. "I… I don't know. What sort of reward do you want?"

Luca shook his head. "I'll think about it. It'll be, like, one of those awful days you claim you're going to have, if I get really pissed off, I'll think to myself, 'Oh my God, my boyfriend owes me *so much*,' and then I'll plan what it's going to be that you owe me."

Isaac had to smile, because from anybody *but* Luca, it sounded like a threat. But from Luca, it sounded like a promise that he'd still be there after six weeks.

And that made him stop smiling.

"Just promise me," he said softly, "that… that if I get too frazzled, or too awful, you'll say, 'Isaac, honey, take a breath.' Don't… don't yell." He knew he sounded wounded, but he couldn't help it. "Don't get all cold. Don't stop calling or stop coming by and not tell me why. It's okay if you say, 'Listen, buddy, you're getting a little intense, and I'm going to give you your space,' but don't—."

"Hey…." And in spite of the heat and the fact that they were both covered with the stickiness of sleepy children marinating in fruit juice, Luca pulled him into his arms then and spoke softly into his hair. "Baby. Baby, trust me, okay?"

Isaac heard the whimper and hated himself for it. It was just… just….

"Todd disappeared, didn't he?" Luca asked.

"He used to schedule his business trips in late August, early September," Isaac said. "He'd never call. I didn't even know he was going until I got home and found the Post-it on the refrigerator. I… I get it. But it—"

"What a fucking coward!" Luca burst out, and Isaac whimpered again.

"No yelling," he begged.

"Not even at Todd," Luca soothed. "Baby, I promise. Look—you've seen me and Allegra in action, okay? We'll back you, I swear. You do all the cooking and planning 'cause you seem to like doing it, but let us do some, okay? You've got a housecleaning service—let us help keep up in between. I get it's going to be rough, Isaac. I may only have seen a taste of it in May, but you're not alone this time. Have some faith in us, okay?"

Isaac nodded against Luca's chest. "Okay," he whispered. "Okay."

They couldn't cling like that, not in the swelter of August, but later that night, after Roxy and the kids had gone home (to a grateful Brian, who had been working hard on a project and had happily met his deadline with everybody out of the house), and everybody had taken a cool shower, and the air conditioning had finally made a dent in the ambient eighty-five-degree outside temperature, Isaac stared at Luca in the moonlight as he slept.

"Whatcha thinking?" Luca mumbled, so not quite asleep. "Tell me so I can get some rest."

"I'm thinking if we make it through to October, I'll have to knit you something."

The corners of Luca's mouth turned up. "A watch cap," he said. "Something warm that doesn't itch. Any color that makes you happy."

"Even magenta?" Isaac teased.

"Especially magenta," Luca murmured. "Everyone will ask, 'Hey, did your boyfriend make you that?' and I'll say, 'How jealous are *you*?'"

Isaac chuffed out a breath of sleepy laughter. As he felt himself drop off, he heard his own voice say it, the words he'd held on to since July.

"I love you, Luca. Even if you're gone in October, I'll still love you. You're like a gift."

And he fell asleep, planning a green and magenta and blue hat more beautiful than stars.

September Mornings

THE THING about Sacramento, Luca thought, was that September could be as gawdawful hot as August.

Except it stayed dark longer, so he could stay in bed while Isaac ran around and tried to do all the things before he ran out of the house with wet hair, no lid on his travel cup of coffee, and at least one sheaf of papers he *really needed* still on the couch where he'd left it when he'd fallen asleep the night before.

Yeah, the first four weeks (so far) of school were everything Isaac had promised they'd be, but harder.

Poor Isaac.

Allegra had started cooking two days a week—no ask, just cooking. Sometimes it was something great and healthy. Sometimes it was frozen manicotti covered with sauce from a jar and big handfuls of shredded cheese. Isaac was always distractedly grateful, sometimes at ten o'clock at night because he'd been supervising a game or a club or something and then attended a PTA meeting before he came home to eat for the first time all day.

On the days he was going to be gone until late, Luca would hang in the house with Allegra, not only to keep her company, but also to help her pick up the living room and sort the junk mail off the kitchen table and generally do the big cleaning things that Isaac would spend all weekend doing if they didn't pick up the slack.

Luca could see what he'd been talking about, that hot, sticky day in August—but he could also see what he hadn't.

That Isaac hadn't needed to worry about his relationship—he'd needed his relationship to support him!

A little bit of work—picking up the living room, sorting the junk mail, making sure the trash got taken out, or even Allegra's most half-assed cooking—reaped big rewards.

The first week Luca had taken the trash out, Isaac had literally sunk to his knees in the bedroom and given him the best blow job of gratitude Luca could ever recall receiving. He hadn't even known such things existed, but apparently a teacher in the first six weeks of school had a lot more energy to expend toward sex if his partner and roommate didn't make him do all the other work. It was amazing—Luca needed to write *that* little bit of wisdom on the inside of his eyelids so he never forgot.

And this morning, Luca was going to *really* up his game.

He rolled out of bed while Isaac was in the shower, crept down the stairs, and tried to remember his list.

Okay—first thing, make coffee. He'd seen Isaac make it before for the two of them, special little French press and all—*voila*. Coffee was working.

Second thing, fix lunch. He'd seen Isaac do this sometimes by shoving a cup of noodles in his lunch bag, throwing a yogurt in afterward, and then running out the door.

Luca had shopped for this one. First he made a nice sandwich in two parts and used a sandwich container to separate the pickles, tomatoes, and lettuce from the slathered bread and lunchmeat. Then a yogurt, a container of sliced apples, two big bottles of soda (one for Roxy), a bag of cookies, and two bags of chips. He'd worry about Isaac actually eating all that, but he knew that often the things like the cookies or the chips or even the yogurt or cottage cheese got given to a student who had forgotten their lunch. Today was Chess Club during lunch and an IEP meeting after school, so that food was going somewhere, Luca was positive.

Then, while Isaac was running down the stairs, muttering to himself, Luca pulled the bagel out of the toaster and spread a smear over one side and avocado on the other, then handed it to Isaac to eat while Luca pulled his travel mug out of the dishwasher and added coffee to it, with an unhealthy dollop of cream and sugar.

Isaac stared at him, his mouth full of bagel, his eyes wide. "Wha' di' 'oo do?" he asked before swallowing. "What is all this?"

"You were looking a little ragged there," Luca said kindly. "I thought I'd, you know, help out this morning. Sorry it took me so long to figure out what you needed."

To his horror, Isaac's eyes got shiny. "I yelled at Allegra yesterday," he said in a small voice.

Luca snorted. "Yelling" had been an overstatement. Isaac had gone to sit down on the couch, and Allegra's yarn work wasn't only *on* the couch, it was *all over* the couch, and he'd said, "Allegra, can we just… you know!"

And Luca's sister had said, "Tell me to get my shit off the couch, Isaac. You gotta right to your own furniture." She'd been sitting in one of the armchairs, *facing* all the yarn on the couch, and she'd struggled to her feet, because her "emerging volleyball," as Isaac had called it in August, was now an "emerging beachball" in mid-September.

"No, no, no," Isaac had said, sounding horrified. "My bad. I'm sorry. Here, I can just, you know…." And he shooed her to sit back down while he bustled around the couch, reducing the area she was using to the corner so he could sit and pick up his own work, which he seemed to be keeping secret from Luca *and* Allegra, which was funny since he worked on it while they were both watching him, but he wouldn't tell them what it was going to be.

The blanket had been completed—and it was quite stunning, Luca thought. He'd wanted to hang it up in the nursery, but Isaac and Allegra had both said no, it would be sturdy enough to be loved to tatters, and that's how they thought a good yarn object should be treated. He'd taken pictures, though, and Isaac had shown them to his students, and there was interest in doing another blanket design in the spring, maybe this time giving the blanket to charity. Isaac and Roxy were already floating ideas, which was great, and Luca suddenly got that the tangle of September in school was like the tangle of yarn in Isaac's stash. It was all about the great potential everybody had to create something *better* with the materials at hand.

The fact that Isaac respected that for Luca's sister as she tried to create more of her own yarn things made Allegra absolutely adore him.

And not just Allegra.

Luca had heard that whispered confession of love that sticky night in August. He'd wanted *so badly* to respond, to tell Isaac that he wasn't alone, that Luca loved him too.

But he'd seen that night how these weeks—they were a test of the Isaac emotional support system. Isaac had been let down so badly before. He needed to make sure Luca wouldn't run, and Allegra wouldn't emotionally ghost him, and these people he'd let into his life—into his home—wouldn't simply disappear because Isaac was too damned much work.

Isaac's *job*, well, that was a lot of work. Luca could see how good teachers burned out in a minimal amount of time. But Isaac? Isaac had been *so* grateful for the smallest bits of support. The week before, he'd muttered about how he *knew* he had some more of the yarn he was working with—a really lovely purple—and how he'd have to go into the stash that weekend and search.

Allegra had found it while doing her own search of the stash (it was sort of a mutual stash, now that she kept adding to it) and set it on his knitting basket, and he'd been so happy he'd almost cried.

Such a small thing. Such huge dividends.

Between that and watching Isaac trying not to lose his temper with Allegra's mess (the yarn on the couch wasn't the only time all the seat space had been taken by her stuff by any means), Luca thought that he really needed to up his game.

He slept over most nights of the week. Most of his clothes were at Isaac's, his laptop was usually there, and the only food in his fridge in his apartment was beer, and even that had expired. He'd gotten a feel for Isaac's morning routine, and the night before, as Isaac had tried hard not to yell at Allegra, Luca had gotten an idea.

"I…," Isaac said, looking at the lunch, the coffee cup, the bagel that he seemed to regard as deepest magic, "I can't believe all of this."

"It's no big," Luca said with a shrug. "I should have started doing this in August, I just…." He gave a sheepish smile. "I'm a big doofus, and I didn't realize what your routine would be. But don't worry—I've got it sorted now."

"But…." Isaac swallowed. "But you didn't have to…." To Luca's horror, Isaac's eyes grew red-rimmed.

"It's okay, Isaac!" Luca said. "I swear, I'll get the hang of things. I told you I wanted to support you—this is, like, the least I can do. And if the lunch is too big or you don't like the coffee—"

"I yelled at your sister," he said again, and this time he finished with a wail, and before Luca knew what was happening, he had an armful of tearful teacher, brought to his knees by a bagel and smear, absolutely leveled by somebody else handing him his coffee and telling him to have a good day.

A FEW days later, Isaac got home shortly after Luca and Allegra, looking… well, beat, was the only way Luca could describe it. He got home, dropped his briefcase on the ground next to the door, and stumbled to the couch, where Euclid was sleeping. Isaac picked up the boneless cat and held him, just held him.

And cried.

Luca and Allegra stared at each other for a moment, and Luca took a few steps toward him, only to be put off by Allegra motioning to her phone. She disappeared down the hall to make a call, and after a moment of watching Isaac, Luca followed her.

"Oh," Allegra was saying, her voice subdued. "Oh. Oh no. Oh, Roxy—that's so awful. Okay. Okay. We… we just didn't know what to do."

There was a pause, and then Allegra nodded at Luca. "Okay," she said. "Okay, I'll tell him. I… he's devastated."

Another pause, and this time Luca could hear sobbing.

"I guess you both are," Allegra murmured. "Oh, honey. I'm so sorry."

After a few moments, she hung up the phone and looked at Luca helplessly. "A carload of kids was driven off the road by a police cruiser last night. They… they weren't doing anything wrong, but the cruiser tried to pass them and then swerved back into the lane. Two of the kids were"—her voice caught—"killed. One of them was someone Roxy and Isaac had both taught."

Luca's brain shorted out. "Marcelle?" he asked. "Sheryl?"

"No," Allegra said, shaking her head. "No—nobody we've met, but… but you've seen them. They *love* those kids and… and Roxy said something like this shakes up the whole *school*. Luca, what do we do?"

Luca gave a small smile. "Well, you go ahead and order pizza," he said, "because nobody here is cooking tonight."

"What are you going to do?" she asked, wiping her eyes with the back of her hand.

He stepped close enough to hug his sister and kiss her temple. "I'm going to go sit next to my boyfriend on the couch while he stares into space. I think it's my job."

She nodded and wiped her face on his shirt. She was his sister, but that didn't make her perfect.

"Two pizzas," she said, her voice choked. "It'll be easier to make his lunch tomorrow."

"There's the spirit."

Isaac was still holding the cat when Luca got back, but he'd stopped crying.

Luca sank his weight into the couch cushions, and Isaac leaned against him, just that simply, his head on Luca's shoulder.

"Roxy told you?" he asked, after the late afternoon shadows through the drapes had turned into early evening shadows.

"Yeah."

"Her name was Delilah. I had her as a freshman. I… I was looking forward to having her in my junior class next year."

Luca wrapped his arm around Isaac's shoulder. "Isaac, I'm so sorry."

Isaac nodded and turned his tearstained face up to Luca. "Do you… do you even have any clothes left in your apartment?" he asked.

Luca blinked at the change of subject. "Yeah, why?"

"Bring them over. We can put your bed or your desk or whatever in Todd's old office and the rest of your stuff in storage. Move in with me. Make it official."

Luca gaped. "Uhm…."

Isaac gave a fleeting smile. "I love you."

"I love you too." He shrugged sheepishly. "I, you know, wanted to wait until you were less stressed to say it. Maybe, uhm, a date with wine, a pricey dinner, all the romance stuff we haven't done yet."

"Save it for some day in March," Isaac said, obviously not caring about wine and dinner and romance. "After the Valentines Day bullshit has cleared the stores. I don't… I've had the proposal and the appropriate romance, and that led to a really unhappy marriage and a man I still get mad at for dropping dead because he thought he was smarter than his blood pressure medicine. My life would have been so much… so much *better* if I'd gotten a divorce instead. So I don't need to do the 'appropriate' thing. I love you. You sat next to me and stared out into space for an hour, just… just *being there*. That's more emotional support than I got from Todd in the last three years of our marriage. Tonight's going to suck. I'm going to cry again. I-I don't have any idea how to get through the next few hours, or tomorrow, or next week. But I know that you haven't left my side yet. Move in with me. We can be a family. Don't leave my side until you can't stand me anymore. Life's unpredictable. Fuck it. Let's be together."

Luca had never smiled through tears before. "That's some goddamned romance," he murmured and pulled Isaac even tighter to his side.

The night was awful, as predicted. They had a sitcom marathon, which Isaac cried through, and Allegra sat next to him when Luca was off doing things like dishing up pizza and cleaning up the kitchen.

But at the end of the night, Luca took Isaac upstairs and undressed him, slowly, with purpose, and then kissed him and touched all his skin until he wasn't thinking about sadness or grief anymore, but was pulled out of himself, pulled to a place where sadness couldn't touch him.

And then they were moving together, quietly, until Isaac's back arched, and he let out a soft cry and came.

Luca followed, and in the harsh breathing and roaring heartbeats that followed, Isaac murmured, "See that? That was some fucking romance."

Luca's eyes burned even as he laughed, and he held Isaac even closer. He thought they might make it through the six weeks after all.

One Day in October

Luca's move was so seamless a transition, Isaac only noticed it a week later, when he realized how glad he was that Luca didn't have to go back to the apartment to make sure the place was still there.

He'd already adapted to leaving his work boots on the porch, going around to the side door to undress, and putting his work clothes in the garage. He kept a robe there, so he could shower in the downstairs bathroom. He even kept clothes in the cupboard.

All the things Todd would have disdained about living with somebody who worked hard for a living, who used his hands and actually made things, Luca minimized with thoughtfulness and common courtesy.

And he was there for Isaac. There were more breakfasts shoved into Isaac's hand on his way out the door, more coffees made before Isaac got out of the shower, more giant lunches packed before Isaac could even think of what to make.

Isaac still shopped twice a week, and he usually had a meal plan, but Allegra helped, and Luca brought home takeout, and everybody cleaned up, and they were good—so good—at not letting the burden of caring for three people fall too heavily on any one person.

It was one of the most marvelous things Isaac had ever experienced.

And that night, that terrible, painful night after the school had been rocked by the tragedy, Luca had sat next to him, not saying anything, just holding him.

Being there.

Ordering pizza.

Making love to him.

Isaac didn't have words to explain how much Todd would *not* have cared about how hard that night was for him. Todd's basic understanding for those sorts of emotions seemed to have been broken somehow. Isaac had mistaken that brokenness for strength, right up until the first time he'd lost a student—that one to cancer. There are losses in every school. Every teacher has stories like the night Isaac came home to hold Euclid. It's part of being human. But until Isaac had come home after Christine

Flores's death, about three years into their marriage, and Todd had stared at his tearstained face like he was a two-headed frog, Isaac hadn't realized how broken Todd had been.

And how much of that emotional burden Isaac would be forced to carry.

To have Luca sit next to him and hold him, to say he was sorry, to *care* for Isaac's emotional health and his physical well-being when Isaac had needed somebody so badly—his lover in particular—that had *fixed* things in Isaac's heart that had crumbled over years of neglect.

He could *trust* a lover now, because a lover could be there for him. He could *enjoy* the company of a sister because his sister made his life better. Suddenly the things he gave to the relationship weren't things he had to worry about replenishing so he could keep up his strength; they were things that were replenished by the relationship itself.

The epiphany had been awe-inspiring. Amazing. Breathtaking.

And as quiet as looking Luca in those glorious brown eyes and asking him to live in the same house, sleep in the same bed, and be a part of his life.

The sweetness of Luca's reply, that he'd been waiting for a pricey dinner and a bottle of wine—well, that was the first time it had really hit Isaac that Luca was younger than he was. Thirty and not thirty-eight. But if you were going to be young, that was the way to do it, right? With a little bit of idealism, some romantic gestures, some stars in the eyes.

But no selfishness. No callow insistence on his own way. No pouting because everything in Isaac's life did *not* revolve around him. And the emotional openness to say, "I wanted to do something nice for you," as opposed to, "That's not appropriate, Isaac. We need to do it this way."

There was no talk of Allegra moving somewhere after she had the baby. There might be eventually. Isaac knew that someday Allegra might find a partner who would deserve her and love her baby like his own—but not now.

Between May and October, they had become a functional little family, with visits from grandparents Isaac had already loved and plans for a baby, *in his house*, that Isaac couldn't wait to love.

And a man in his bed that he loved with such sweetness, such purity, he was afraid every morning to wake up and find it was a dream.

So far it had been very, very real—right down to Luca and Allegra pitching in the money for the housekeeping and gardening services because they appreciated them too.

Isaac had only given in on that because *they'd* felt they should help, not because he wanted them to be one iota different than they were. After living for ten years in an emotional desert, he'd been gifted this amazing house. The transaction hadn't been his intention—when he'd first fallen in love with Todd, he would have lived with him in a shitty apartment or a hovel in the woods. But the things that had made Todd broken emotionally had also made him good with money, and Isaac found that sharing that with people he could laugh with, play with, *love* with, gave him a sort of balance, drew things full circle....

Made him no longer hate the memory of the first man he'd ever loved.

He was absolutely sure Todd wouldn't have approved of a thing Isaac had done since that evening in May when he'd refused to finish that damned brown sweater, but now Isaac could say, in all honesty, that what Todd approved of—or disapproved of—was no longer a driving force in his life.

That alone was like being freed from a prison in his own heart.

But that didn't mean he was sure about what to do that night in mid-October.

He and Allegra had spent one of their yarn Saturdays decorating the front yard for Halloween. (The neighbors two doors down kept trying to get him to call it "Jesusween," and not only did he refuse, he hadn't been able to tell Luca about it because he was afraid Luca *would* decorate for "Jesusween," and then they'd all be going to hell.) The giant fruitless mulberry tree in his front yard had turned mostly yellow but hadn't dropped its leaves yet, and the weather, which had been in the hundreds in late September, had dropped to the low eighties and was actually crisp in the mornings. Putting big monster masks on the front door and along the window sills had been incredibly joyful for the two of them, and hearing Luca's big laugh as he entered the house from the back had lightened the house every bit as much as the smell of the pumpkin spice candles that Isaac promised Allegra would be the first thing to go once her emerging beachball got legs and became mobile.

So that had been a happy moment—and so had the moment Allegra told him that her birthday was the week before Halloween. He'd been working on a bolero-style sweater—one that would warm her arms but leave her beachball uncovered and unfettered, and *also* would fit her next year. Something that would comfort against the overzealous air conditioning that Luca's office seemed to emit in the mornings but wouldn't be too hot as the day got warmer. It was in a bright magenta, because *Allegra* was so vibrant and happy (as well as dark-eyed and dark-haired, so the color would look *amazing* on her) and crocheted in a series of shells and flower-like stitches that just shouted joy.

But Allegra and Luca hadn't *seemed* happy. In fact, something had been looming over them, a sour cloud, and now that Isaac's schedule wasn't spinning like a roulette wheel and he had his feet under him again schoolwise, he felt like they needed to tell him what was going down.

He wanted to do his part of the emotional support, dammit—they'd both been pretty awesome at it for *him*.

So on Thursday, because school got out a little earlier that day and he didn't have any meetings to fill the time, he went shopping for some pork chops, which he threw in marinade as soon as he got home. By the time Luca and Allegra got home, both of them acting like they'd rather slog through bitter snows to an icy hovel in the heart of Minsk than take one more step into the kitchen, he had one of his best pork chop recipes simmering, along with rice and a tossed salad.

And a layered pudding dessert in the fridge.

Oh yeah. He knew their weaknesses by now. He had no compunction about using their love of good food against them.

Luca and Allegra tried really hard to keep things light and happy during dinner, but when Isaac broke out the pudding dessert, both of them looked like they were going to cry.

"Oh my God!" he said, setting down a whopping big dish of the stuff in front of each of them. "If you two don't tell me what's going on, I'm stealing the rest of this and putting it in the staff room!"

"Don't you dare!" Allegra ordered, her mouth full as she demolished her first bite. She, at least, looked like Snow White after she'd been revived by the prince's kiss or a magic potion or something. Her eyes were sparkling, and her posture straightened, but her brother was not that easy.

He sat slumped over his dessert, staring at it like it was water but he wasn't allowed to drink.

Isaac went to him and wrapped his arms around Luca's shoulders. "Come on, baby," he murmured. "You can tell me. It's what I'm *here* for."

Luca let out a sigh and seemed to grow a little smaller. "Allegra and I sort of—"

"We don't have to do it," Allegra said after swallowing another bite. "It was a stupid deadline. We don't have to—"

Luca straightened, leaned his cheek against Isaac's, and smiled sadly. "Baby, we have to. I mean… they might *not* talk to me. But what if you could have Mom in your life? What if you could have grandparents for the baby? You haven't said anything, not once, but…."

"But I have Roxy," she said with dignity. "And Grandma. And Isaac." She took another bite of pudding. "And this stuff, which may have spoiled me for all other desserts." She gave Isaac a watery smile. "Seriously, Isaac—I can't believe you haven't served this earlier."

"It's got so many calories," Isaac told her. "I save it for big deals. I was going to serve the banana kind for your birthday, but…." His smile went a little soggy. "You were both so, so stressed. Tell me what you're thinking about doing?"

"We were going to visit our parents," Luca said softly. "For closure. To know they weren't an option. And also to… to…."

"To say neener, neener, neener, we have lives and they're not in them," Allegra admitted, staring at the last bit of pudding in her bowl. "How many calories?" she asked wistfully.

"None," Isaac told her, taking the bowl and adding another piece of the layered dessert. "No calories. Absolutely guilt-free."

She gave him a grateful glance. "You're the second-best brother a girl could have," she said sincerely.

"I'm proud of that," Isaac said, and then he kissed Luca's cheek. "But you know Luca's a lot to live up to."

He sat down and stared at his own dessert, which was not looking nearly as tasty now. "When were you guys going to do this?"

"Well, my birthday's Saturday," Allegra said. "And according to Nonna, my parents don't do anything on Saturday nights, and we know they haven't moved…."

She shrugged, and Isaac got the picture.

"You're doing this on your birthday?" he said, almost horrified. "Baby—I feel like maybe, since, you know, you can't get shitfaced afterwards, maybe you should do it the day after your birthday. Like, have a great birthday—Sophia and Pop Pop are coming over on Saturday. Now that I'm out of the weeds, I have all sorts of plans for afternoon dinner and a cake and another dessert like this one and a whole celebration thing that revolves around *you* and not the stranger in your uterus, you know?"

Allegra turned dewy eyes to him. "Really? Like what?"

"Well, Roxy and Brian and the kids were coming over, and Marcelle and Sheryl wanted to come, and—"

"Your students?" Allegra asked wistfully. "They can come?"

"You're pregnant, honey. If we can keep Nonna and Pop Pop from serving wine—"

"Leave that to me," Luca said. "I know you can lose your job."

Isaac gave him a grateful glance. "And Jimmy Bob and his niece."

Luca and Allegra exchanged glances. "You planned all this already?" Luca asked, sounding a little blown away.

"Well, yes." Isaac gave him his most hopeful smile. "You guys, I'm so grateful for you. Both of you. And Luca, I know your birthday is in early March, but Allegra, this is a big birthday. I wanted you to know I appreciate you. You're a good roommate. I'm… I know I'm not an official *anything* in your life, but I'm looking forward to your baby *so much*. And the baby is going to be here in December, which is always a whirlwind, and I wanted a day to celebrate *you*."

Allegra mopped her face with one of Isaac's cloth napkins, but Isaac didn't care, not even when she blew her nose.

"I think that sounds awesome," she sobbed, and Luca shifted his chair next to her so he could wrap his arm around her shoulders.

"I think my boyfriend is kind of the best," Luca said, meeting his eyes. Luca's eyes were shiny, and he seemed to be having trouble swallowing. Isaac handed him another cloth napkin, and Luca wiped his eyes and blew his nose with it, the same way his sister had, and Isaac realized that he *truly* didn't care. Not even if he had to throw the napkins away. Love wasn't having cloth napkins that lasted a millennium. Love was giving something to people you cared about that meant so much it made them cry.

How had Isaac not known that before?

His parents had loved *him* like that. Unconditionally. Without blinking—not at his obsession with *The National* in high school, not at his unrequited love for Gavin Rossdale and Katy Perry. He had a sudden moment, a memory, of the last birthday he'd ever spent with them.

It had been his twenty-second, and he'd been about to graduate from college and start the teaching credential program, and they'd taken him and his college roommate to Disneyland, and they had eaten dinner in the restaurant that looked out over the bayou in the Pirates of the Caribbean ride. And as exciting as that had been….

His mother, holding his hand as they brought him his dessert with the sparklers in it. "Oh, honey—this went so fast. Thanks for letting us celebrate this with you."

"Mom…." Isaac had given his roommate—a sweet straight boy named Rob, who had stayed up late gaming with him through their entire senior year—an embarrassed glance.

"No," his father said, also looking surprisingly wobbly for a man who didn't get excited at much of anything except a new sports stadium in Sacramento. "She's right. You grew up so fast. Thanks so much for letting us celebrate with you."

He'd smiled then, and gotten a little wobbly himself, and the whole time he was thinking, This is stupid. I'm only twenty-two—hell, they're only forty-five. We'll be celebrating for a long, long time.

Except they'd had less than a year, and the year after they'd passed, he'd been with Todd, and Todd had "wanted Isaac all to himself."

And except for Roxy's kids, Isaac had given up on birthdays, until now. Now… now he knew that life went fast, and the people you *really* wanted to celebrate weren't always there to be loved.

It was amazing how much celebration you could throw into your world when you realized what was important.

That night, in bed, Luca had held Isaac close like he always did— *always*—not on birthdays or special occasions or when Isaac had done something nice or was sad.

Always.

But tonight, Luca told him haltingly, not only about how his parents had kicked him out, but *how his parents had kicked him out*. How he'd trusted in his childhood, trusted in their love, and they'd betrayed him, and then Allegra, in the worst way possible.

"Oh, baby," Isaac said softly. "Do you… you're not hoping for anything, are you?"

"No," Luca said quickly.

Too quickly.

Isaac just regarded him silently, because Luca wasn't a child. He knew when he was fooling himself.

"If nothing else," he said reluctantly, "I'm hoping they give Allegra a second chance." He shrugged, his heavily muscled shoulders rippling in Isaac's arms. "I'm pretty sure they're both homophobic as hell—the flag in front of their house hasn't changed in the last ten years—but Allegra… I mean, she's gonna be a *mom*, Isaac. Shouldn't they love her baby more than their stupid religion or patriotism or whatever?"

"You'd think," Isaac said. He was remembering that terrible moment with Angel sobbing in his classroom—in *the closet* in his room, actually, hidden by the lost-and-found coats—while Isaac got the shit beat out of him. The same sickness infecting Luca's parents had infected that mob, and they were both old enough to know that while a child's love, a child's *need* for love, should have been a cure, it was most obviously not.

Luca sighed. "I like your idea," he said. "We give Allegra a *wonderful* day, and then, on Sunday, we hit them after church, and we give them one last chance."

"And then we go out for pancakes," Isaac said happily. To his eternal gratitude, Luca laughed shortly.

"That's your cure? Pancakes?"

"Don't pancakes cure everything?" Isaac asked innocently. They both knew it wasn't true, but for this moment, this painful moment, Isaac wanted it so badly to be true.

"Absolutely," Luca said, grunting as Euclid jumped from the head of the bed to his chest. "So do kittens."

"Mmm…." Isaac stroked his cat's ears, loving more and more how the goofy orange thing made his home a better place. "I'm so lucky I have one."

"A kitten?" Luca asked.

"A hotcake," Isaac told him pertly.

Luca laughed—quietly, but it was a true, warm laugh, and Isaac felt like maybe he'd returned just a little to Luca and Allegra that they had given to him. That moment with his parents in the restaurant at Disneyland, with the friend who still sent him Christmas cards of his wife and adorable children and called him up six times a year, flowed behind his eyes like water. Family. Those sad, quiet years with Todd, how had he forgotten that this was what family was all about?

"Luca?" he said softly into the sleeping silence.

"Yeah?"

"I want to come with you and Allegra when you see your parents, even if I wait in the car to take you both to ice cream. I mean, pancakes."

"Aw… Isaac…."

"What?" Isaac rolled to his side, the better to meet Luca's eyes. "What are you afraid I'll see?"

Luca glanced away. "I'm…. Allegra and I, we're gonna be a mess."

"Luca, remember back in May when I trauma dumped all over you because my dead husband really messed me up?"

Luca huffed out a breath. "You didn't trauma dump—"

"I so totally fucking did."

Luca feathered a touch through Isaac's hair. "You were hurting."

"And you were practically a stranger, and you… you listened to me. You were kind. Let me be there. Let me hurt with you. Let me drive you both to ice cream—"

"Pancakes."

"Sure. You believe that. Let me drive you there while you cry in the back. Let me take care of you while you and your sister take care of each other. I-I won't think less of you for hoping, Luca, just like you didn't think less of me for being mad at the dead. What do you say?"

Luca breathed out and nuzzled his ear. "Sure," he murmured. "I always dreamed I'd have a guy who wanted to take care of me."

"Yeah?" Isaac wouldn't mind being Luca's dream guy. "Am I that guy?"

"Even better. We take care of each other."

Isaac's body relaxed a little as Luca continued to nuzzle. "Would you like me to take care of you?" he asked coyly.

"After that dessert tonight?" Luca asked, moving the kisses to Isaac's neck under his sleepshirt. "I think you're the one getting the gratitude blow job."

"Oooh…." Luca's lips under the shirt, grazing his nipples, were all he needed for the pulse of desire to wake him up.

"Good noise," Luca purred. "Let's see if we can make some more."

Isaac arched is hips so Luca could pull his pajama pants and briefs off, and the cool air, coupled with Luca's warm touch, made every brush of flesh shivery with sex.

The heat of Luca's mouth as he took Isaac inside was enough for Isaac to close his eyes and groan, and for a moment, Isaac was content to let Luca take care of him, his mouth hot and wet, his hand firm, his every touch purposeful and delirious.

And then Luca breached him with a spit-slick finger, and he knew what *real* delirium was all about.

When Isaac was shaking with arousal, and so, so close to coming, Luca slid up his body and shoved gently at his thighs. His cock at Isaac's entrance was—as usual—almost scary big, but it was also welcome, and Isaac pushed against the intrusion, knowing he was relaxed enough to open for it, to engage and grip it as it slid into his body.

Ah! Gods, this never got old.

Luca started to move, and Isaac let out a small groan, not too loud, and then a louder one as Luca thrust faster and harder, their passion building, *burning*, and his need opening like a black hole in his gut.

A hole Luca was already filling.

Their rhythm changed, grew faster, brutally fast, and Isaac cried out again, louder, as Luca's fucking took over his body, and for a moment he was lost in the chaos of sex, of cock and ass and come, until it erupted, blowing everything apart, Isaac's body, his psyche, his soul.

Until he came to himself, Luca still lodged in his ass, their harsh breathing filling the air, and Isaac wondered vaguely how he'd managed to survive his clubbing years and ten years of marriage and still not know what sex was.

As his breathing slowed, he caught Luca's soft laugh and smiled as he kissed the hollow of Luca's neck, which he knew was sensitive.

"What?" Isaac asked shyly.

"You gonna say the word?" Luca asked, tilting his head back and thrusting again hopefully.

Isaac smiled, feeling smug. "The word?"

"Yeah, Isaac—what were we just doing?"

Isaac laughed softly. "Fucking, Luca. You were fucking me."

"God yes." Luca thrust again, and to Isaac's surprise, he was growing harder. "And you fucked me back."

Isaac grunted, and some of his own desire flooded back, his entire body open to it now, one big exposed sexual nerve, his reserve stripped away by open communication—and glorious fucking.

"Yeah, I did," he said, moving against Luca, starting to crave their friction again in spite of his come-sloppy body.

Luca's grin in the dark was sweetly diabolical, and Isaac's cock started to harden even as their bodies resumed that thing, that thing, that glorious fucking thing that felt like their whole purpose right now.

"Wanna do it again?" Luca asked wickedly.

"Fuck away," Isaac told him, shivers of need gaining traction in his stomach, his ass, his spine.

"Oh yeah."

ISAAC DIDN'T say anything to Luca and Allegra, but Allegra's birthday party was one of the biggest things he'd ever done. He'd enlisted help—Jimmy Bob and his niece invited the friends from work and organized their food and drink, Roxy told him where he could call for a cake and delivery, Luca was responsible for setting Euclid up in Isaac's room, away from all the people, and Marcelle and Sheryl were put in charge of making sure Allegra's only job was to go to the bathroom and come back—and to relay to the other partygoers if things got too loud for Allegra and she had to nap in her room.

Allegra wasn't an introvert, though—pregnant and tired, yes, but she was energized by all the people and held court in her favorite chair with her feet up, her knitting in her lap like a queen. Sheryl and Marcelle brought her presents and sparkling cider, and her nonna sat on her left and entertained them all with charming stories of their senior home. Luca and his guys spent part of the time giving tours through the house next door, which, after a final coat of paint that they planned to put on after Halloween, was looking *more* than ready for a resale flip, which would keep his grandparents financially stable for a very long time.

And Pop Pop had quietly promised Luca a bonus for his crew, who had all pitched in to help at one time or another. He'd spent part of his life as an accountant, he'd told Luca solemnly while Isaac served him tea, but he remembered what working construction through school was like. He was very grateful for their help.

While the party commenced, Isaac manned the kitchen, making sure the food was staying covered if it wasn't being eaten (which was rarely) or the dishes were being replaced if they were empty (which happened a *lot*, because Luca's crew of construction guys and their wives ate a *lot*) and occasionally running back to the nursery to make sure Roxy or Brian was well-provided with food while they watched their children.

This time he found Brian sitting quietly in the rocking chair with Sparrow Anne on his shoulder, watching his younger two fondly while they played with giant Legos.

"You okay in here?" he asked softly, leaning against the door frame and taking in the scene.

"Yeah," Brian said. "It's almost nap time. I'll settle everybody down and come out." He glanced around and sighed. "I know it'll be busy for a couple months after she has the baby, but honestly, I can't wait until they all play together. Nobody tells you that kids are a blast, you know?"

Isaac nodded. "Yeah. I-I mean, Todd didn't want them, but I was always so happy to be Uncle Isaac for your kids. I'm excited to get another chance."

Brian gave him a sideways glance. "I'm going to butt into your business here, and you know I've stayed out of it the entire time you and Roxy have been friends."

Isaac grunted, remembering when Brian had run him cookies and ice cream and had *put it in his lap with a spoon* instead of putting it in the kitchen and expecting Todd to get it for him.

"Of course," he said blandly, and Brian's mouth pulled in at the corners as he tried not to laugh at that.

"Todd was a dick," Brian said. "Roxy doesn't want to say it because you're her friend and she wants to let you get all your feelings out on your own. I can say it because I'm just the husband and nobody expects me to have an opinion. But he was a dick. You're a good guy, Isaac. In fact, you're an *amazing* guy. This is the part where a hetero chest-thumper would say, 'If you weren't gay, I'd be jealous,' but you could be as hetero as I am—"

Isaac snorted, and Brian rolled his eyes but kept on talking.

"—and I'd still know you were too rock-solid to move in on somebody else's partner. You're a good uncle—and you'd be a great dad. And you and Luca are so nice. When you lived here with Todd, it was a really big house, but you came to visit us in our tiny one, and you looked happy. Now? We come to visit you, and it's a home. You've got a good family here. This party is really wonderful. I wish I'd thought to throw one for Roxy when she was pregnant with Falcon. And you probably would have thought of it—I *know* you would have—but Todd wouldn't have let you throw it here in spite of the fact that all your guys' friends are your own coworkers. So, uhm…." Brian petered to a stop. "That's all I wanted to say, really. Be happy. Enjoy the new baby. And the new sister. And the new guy. You deserve them all."

Isaac stared at him, eyes burning. "And now you made me cry!" he accused, and to his surprise, Brian pulled him into a one-armed, baby-holding dad hug.

"My family is grateful for you," Brian told him. "Be happy." He pulled away to set Sparrow Anne in the porta crib, where she proceeded to bat at the baby toys inside. "And watch my kids while I go to the can and pretend this never happened."

Brian scrammed, and Isaac looked down to see Justice standing in front of him, arms out.

"You want a hug, big guy?" Isaac asked, squatting to pull the boy up into his arms.

"Daddy gave you one," Falcon Justice said. "So you need one."

Isaac hugged the kid for a moment, and then he squirmed to be put down, and Patricia was in his place.

Isaac hugged her too, and then set her down, and she went to get one of the books from her mother's crap bag (as Roxy called the diaper bag) so she could read it quietly in the toddler bed.

Isaac watched as she lay back and closed her eyes to sleep without prompting, as did the baby, and with a grumpy little *"Humth"* and a gentle push toward the bed next to his sister, so did Justice, and he thought about kids. How when their parents were gentle, you could see it in their behavior. They still got loud, sure, but they cried when somebody nearby raised their voice in anger. They still hit, sure, but they stopped when asked nicely. Little kids were desperate to please—gentle parents were pleased by gentle behaviors, and Roxy and Brian had some of the sweetest.

For the first time, Isaac thought about getting to help with Allegra's baby, and how they could teach the baby kindness and joy and fun and gentleness

And that quickly he wondered how parents could turn their backs on kids after taking that much care in their raising. What did it take in a person's heart to simply turn their back on a lovingly cared-for child?

What poison did somebody have to have nurtured to let a relationship that special be killed with just a word?

Isaac leaned against the door frame of what was, even now, a happy nursery, and wondered at the empty place in Luca's and Allegra's hearts to have that relationship yanked away.

He understood their anguish now, their willingness to risk rejection this one last time before they gave up on their parents completely. Isaac would give so very much—*so* very much—to be able to see his parents again, to tell them they were the best, and that he loved them, and to tell them what his life was like right now, and how much he loved and was loved.

But he wouldn't give *this*, this moment with the family he'd found in his heart. He knew his parents would never ask him to.

And he knew that for Luca and Allegra, that sacrifice was the one they'd be asked to make.

"Whatcha thinking?"

Isaac startled and then closed the door on the nursery and turned to smile sadly into Luca's eyes.

"I'm thinking about parenthood," he said. "And the past, and the present, and sacrifices we'd make, and sacrifices we shouldn't."

Luca grunted. "That is some incredibly deep shit. Come on. Allegra's cutting the cake as soon as Romper Room in there wakes up, and I haven't seen you sit down once."

Isaac felt a pleasant, giddy sort of tiredness in his legs and back. "Once would be nice," he admitted.

"I know it. Come on. Let me make you a plate, and you can say hi to Nonna and Pop Pop, and everybody can tell you how awesome your party is." He paused. "Including my sister, who has never—and I mean not even as a kid—had something this awesome."

"She didn't get a princess party as a kid?" Isaac asked, surprised.

"Our parents believed in small family parties," Luca said with a shrug. "You may not know it, baby, but you just set the bar for every party our little tadpole has."

Isaac thought of that, of a baby with birthday parties, many of which would be held in this very house. Suddenly the house, which had seemed like a giant, echoing monstrosity in May, was *very* useful, and *very* important, for a busy social family of four.

"That's the best present ever," he said happily. "I can't wait."

Luca paused then, to place a sweet, lingering kiss on his forehead, and then they were in the front room, and Isaac was being introduced as the party host, and new friends and old friends and his new sister and his new lover were all applauding, and for a moment it was Isaac's birthday too.

THE NEXT day they were all dressed and ready by ten in the morning.

"My God," Luca said, staring at his own khakis and button-down. "It looks like *we're* going to church."

There was enough chill in the air for Isaac to have put on his Halloween vest. He'd made it years ago, but Todd had only let him wear it on Halloween. This year he'd been wearing it at school at least twice a week in October and had made plans to start a new one in January, that one with more DayGlo orange, green, and yellow, with a purple background instead of one in flat black.

He'd forgotten how much fun Halloween could be when you didn't care how silly you were or whether you were wearing the appropriate colors at the appropriate time.

In this case he wanted to wear the vest because it made Luca smile. Three nights ago, he'd spent an entire television show tracking the different motifs—black cat, skull, dancing skeleton, witch's hat, spider—knitted into the vest in fine wool.

Isaac would have worn anything to make Luca smile, which he was only now starting to realize was a whole different level of actualization than wearing something just to avoid your lover's steely-eyed censure.

"We'd better do something after this," Allegra said, frowning at the high-waisted autumn-green-and-gold blouse she was wearing unhappily. Roxy had given her a boxload of maternity clothes, this dress (or shirt meant to be worn with leggings) being on top, and while Allegra was grateful—and loved Roxy's taste—Isaac could tell she was getting to that part of pregnancy where every article of clothing felt like a circus tent. Even a rainbow was disheartening when you were swathed in acres of it and the bottom of your stomach still showed. "Wait," she added, reaching for the cardigan Isaac had given her the day before. Isaac raised his eyebrows because the magenta and the gold and green went nowhere near together, but Allegra gave him a flounce of her head to indicate she was wearing it whether it clashed or not.

"Of course we are," Isaac said, kissing her on the cheek, loving her more for all the raucous color she was willing to endure. "This thing, it's just a stop on our way to pancakes and the yarn shop."

"Really?" Allegra perked up.

"Really," Isaac said. "The specialty yarn shop, where the owner has her own line of yarn, dyed in small batches, and kits and such. Where you can buy some really glorious lace-weight yarn and make a scarf for you and nobody else."

Allegra's shining smile was all he needed to see, but as Luca stood back to usher them out of the house, he got a solid kiss on the lips.

"Isaac?"

"Yeah?"

"I love you. You're perfect. I don't say it enough. Let's go."

The day was already better than he'd hoped for, because he was aware that it could get so much worse.

WHEN THEY got to the house—one of the gracious older homes off Winding Way in Fair Oaks, Isaac glanced around the perfectly sculpted yard and the precision-trimmed hedges and got an icy tingle in his stomach. The house itself had two stories, a peaked roof, and dark brown trim on a beige exterior. Halloween was in a week, and in deference to the holiday, Isaac saw one tasteful wreath of autumn leaves on the door. No spiderwebs, no flags, no colorful scarecrows. No flowers, seasonal or otherwise.

Todd would have loved this.

He hadn't seen a house like this in Luca and Allegra's past. He'd seen Luca's work boots, his kindness, his easy way of moving about the house when he was cleaning it. He'd seen Allegra's cheerfully messy room, her enthusiasm, all of the ideas she had spinning in her head.

He hadn't realized the same lockstep thinking that had squeezed Isaac into a box for ten years had been the box they'd burst out of when they'd turned eighteen.

Maybe they hadn't realized it either. Like Isaac, they'd felt safe and cared for in that box, until Luca, whose heart was so pure in all the ways that counted, had told them one thing about himself that didn't fit.

"Hey," Luca said, a note of forced joviality in his voice that Isaac hated. "At least Dad let her put up a wreath this year. She always wanted to do Halloween decorations."

Allegra snorted. "Next year, me and Isaac are gonna hit the sales, and we'll *show* you Halloween decorations."

Luca grabbed her hand as they approached the door. "Can't wait," he said.

Isaac was torn, watching Luca and Allegra approach that forbiddingly perfect doorway. Out of respect for their privacy, he thought he should hang back and let them take care of their own business. Out of support and protectiveness, he thought he should knock and negotiate terms.

Even as he moved up to Luca's side, he heard Todd in his head, telling him stay out of it because it wasn't his family.

They're my family, he told Todd. *They're my family, and I love them more than you could ever understand.*

As the door started to creak open, he bumped Luca's hand with his own, squeezing when Luca laced their fingers together. Okay. Yes. This was where he belonged.

The woman who opened the door was thin and elegant, with high cheekbones and thick, dark, glossy hair swept back from an expressionless face. She wore a rose-colored twinset, which made her golden complexion sallow and a little sickly, but Isaac got it. Somebody had told her to wear muted colors to church.

In contrast, Allegra's bright gold and green (and magenta!) was wild and whimsical and exciting. Even at almost eight months pregnant, Allegra's brilliance could not be dimmed.

"Allegra?" For a moment, Isaac saw an unfettered joy cross the woman's severe features, and his heart fluttered with hope. Wouldn't it be wonderful if this strictly limited box could expand, grow bountiful, with a little bit of love?

How can you not love them? He wanted to scream it, but he squeezed Luca's fingers instead.

"Hi, Mom," Allegra said, giving a small smile. "Can we come in?"

The woman's lipsticked mouth opened, and Isaac thought, *Yes, yes, yes!* And then her eyes flickered to Isaac and Luca, and the emerging light shut down, and the bar between her dark eyes said *NO!*

"Only you, Allegra," the woman said, a note of hesitation in her voice. "Your grandmother told us of your condition, and your father will allow you to come stay with us if you wish, to raise your baby." Her eyes flickered to Luca again, and Isaac didn't imagine it—for a moment, there was a maternal hunger as she took him in, looked to see how he'd grown.

And then she shuttered down on it, and what was left was only a blank coldness, a frozen piece of a human soul stuck in her eyes.

But Allegra was back on her words. "Allow me?" she asked, her voice rising. "*Allow* me inside? To stay with you while I raise my baby? That's real generous of you, Mom, but I was here to *allow* you into my baby's life. To *allow* you to get to know your grandchild. I guess that's not so important to you, is it?"

And those frozen eyes blinked again, a little bit of soul seeping back in. "We understand that you need help, Allegra. We're willing to give it to you—what more do you want?"

"*I don't need help*!" Allegra shouted. "I *would like* my mother to be in my life when I become a mother, but believe me, I don't need to be 'allowed' in the house. I've *got* a home. I've got a nursery. I've got a job with my brother, and we have a *blast* working together, Mom. He's got his own business—you didn't even fucking *ask*—"

"Don't swear," her mother said automatically. "And I know your… *situation*. Your grandmother keeps me informed." Again, that terrible split-personality eye-flicker to Luca. "We're both glad to hear your brother—"

"*He's right here*!" Allegra *and* Isaac shouted it. Luca's hand in Isaac's had grown icy, and Isaac heard Luca's breath growing shorter, and knew the suppressed tears were there in his chest.

"I'm right here, Mom," he said softly.

And that prompted her to look at him, full-on, her face older, worn down by pain and denial. Her eyes full of pity, her face still cold.

"But you're obviously still choosing a lifestyle your father and I cannot condone," she said softly.

"I'm in love," he said, a smile touching his pale features. His full mouth was drawn now, his lips pressed together, probably in an effort not to scream. "I know you don't care. You'd rather I was dead than in love. But I'm in love. And me and Isaac and Allegra, we're a *family*. We had a birthday party for Allegra that would put a queen to shame. Her nursery is adorable. She and Isaac and Nonna, they made this blanket that could welcome an *emperor* into the world. And my business is in the black, and I got jobs booked for years. Years, Mom. I don't even have to work a site. But you don't care about that. You just care that the person I'm in love with isn't who you think I should love." His lower lip wobbled. "But I'm not going to change that for you. We came here...." He glanced at Allegra, who nodded.

"We came here," she echoed.

"To ask you if you wanted to be part of our lives. 'Cause we're having a great time, and we wanted to share. If you don't want to share, well...."

"You don't have to," Allegra said firmly. She took Luca's hand and kissed it. "'Allow me' to come in, my fat ass, Mom. Like I'd leave these guys behind for that sort of ice-cold comfort in a million years."

With that she spun on her heel and headed back to the car, calling over her shoulder, "C'mon, fellas. I was promised *pancakes*."

Luca turned to follow her, but Isaac stayed behind.

For a moment, Mrs. Giordano stared at him. "What?" she asked, her voice gratifyingly wobbly.

"My parents died when I was younger than Allegra," he said. "They knew who I was and loved me, and would have loved Luca and Allegra and that baby so much. I just wanted to tell you that. That the best people I've ever known would have loved us and embraced us as a family, and you're missing out on that. That could be you celebrating your grandbaby. Your son's business. Your son's relationship. But it's not. And that's all your fault, because it's right there. How's it feel to have everything in the world right there at your fingertips and be too blind to see?"

She stared at him, her mouth open, and he turned to take Luca's hand as they made their way back to the Kia.

"I'm sorry," he mumbled. "That probably wasn't my place."

"It's fine," Luca said, wrapping his arm around Isaac's shoulders. "It's fine," he repeated, leaning over to kiss Isaac's temple. "I love you so much for standing up for us."

Isaac paused as they neared the Kia and hugged Luca, leaning his head on his chest and just standing there, breathing him in.

"My parents would have loved you," he said softly. "They would have *loathed* Todd, but they would have *loved* you. I'm so mad your parents can't see that. It's so unfair."

Luca wrapped his arms tight around Isaac's shoulders, and for three breaths—one, two, three—they breathed all the things that should have been.

And then Isaac did the grown-up thing and held his hand out for his keys.

"You two sit in the back and cry," he said. "I'll get us to pancakes."

They found a local place that served fluffy pancakes and savory crepes. While Luca and Allegra stopped every so often and wiped their eyes, they still kept chatting about the food, about Halloween decorations, about Christmas, and how they were going to handle the baby in the middle of Christmas.

Isaac listened to them happily, his brain buzzing away with his own plans.

"Whatcha thinkin'?" Luca asked when he and Allegra finally wound down. Casually, he snuck his fork across the table to pick up a whipped-cream-covered banana Isaac had left behind. Isaac laughed at him while he stuck it in his mouth and then answered.

"I should just start my Christmas kid-knitting," he said, and while that was part of what he'd been thinking about, it wasn't all of it. "I've got my people stuff planned and mostly executed, but I usually spend November and December knitting for the kids."

"Every kid?" Allegra asked, wiping the last of the whipped cream off her plate with her finger before popping her finger in her mouth. "That's a *lot* of kids!"

Isaac shook his head. "No. I make them work for it. There's always skills to master or a contest to win. My fifth period is going to create their own word problems and figure them out and justify their answers, and the best ones get put on the test. I give away four hats there—two for the best grades on the test, and two for what the kids vote as the best word problems, the ones that are challenging but a good test of their skills." He snorted. "It's a great exercise, and the contest keeps everybody focused until the test. Anyway, the other classes have something similar. Plus I've got three TA's, and *they* all get something, and I owe a couple of teachers knitwear. It's time."

"Wow," Luca said, shaking his head. "That's a whole lot of work. What made you decide to do all that?"

Isaac sort of chuckled. "It grew," he said, thinking about it. "I started knitting and bringing it to school because it calmed my nerves, and—"

"Wait," Allegra said. "How did you start knitting? You never told us that!"

It was like the question, innocently asked, dropped him through a wormhole in time.

"Can we go to the movies?" Isaac asked, looking outside at the glorious day around them.

"No," Todd mumbled, doing his crossword puzzle at the breakfast table.

"Maybe visit the park—there's wind, we could fly kites." They were getting married in a few months—they had to have more adventures in them than this, right?

"We're grown men," Todd said, not glancing up. "No."

"Maybe I could call that one woman from school—Roxy—and we could go shopping—"

"Oh my God," Todd muttered. "Isaac, could you sit still for one goddamned minute? My God, get a hobby. Do a jigsaw puzzle, arrange flowers, learn to knit or something!"

Isaac tried to mask his hurt. "Don't you want to spend time with me?" he asked.

Todd spared him a glance and then rubbed the back of his neck as though trying to calm a fractious child. "I do," he said, obviously striving for patience. "I do. But my brain is all busy from the workweek and I... I really need some quiet today. Seriously, Isaac, can we just spend some quiet time together?"

Isaac sighed, deflated, and started to straighten the Sunday supplements, because he knew Todd would get frustrated at the mess if he didn't. "Fine," he muttered, and then he spotted the ad flier for a sale on yarn at the craft store, along with needles, hooks, and how-to books. "You know—let me run to the store, though. I'll be back in an hour. Knitting isn't really a bad idea."

"Isaac?" Luca prompted. "How *did* you learn to knit?"

"I taught myself," he said, the memory so clear. "Todd was... well, I was driving him batshit because I wanted to go out and do something and he wanted a quiet day at home. So I ran out and got some yarn and some how-to books, and I sat down and read and fiddled and studied and then made this really awful scarf that not even Todd would claim, and I just… just kept doing it. Reading, studying, fiddling. Trying new things. Getting better. Pretty soon, it became an obsession," he said, smiling.

"Wow," Luca said, and there was something warm in his eyes. Something forgiving.

"What?" Isaac asked, but he could feel it too.

"Todd's the one who gave you knitting. And yarn. That's…."

"That's the nicest fucking thing I've ever heard you say about him," Allegra said, and Isaac had to laugh.

"He wasn't a monster," he said, fingering the Cthulhu on his vest and smiling. "I… I need to remember that."

"No," Luca said softly. "You wouldn't have loved him if he'd been a monster. He was simply not…."

"Not a good time," Isaac said with a small laugh. "But for a little while, I thought he was what I needed."

"And now?" Luca asked.

Isaac smiled into his eyes. "And now I've met someone who's not only a *great* time, but who is also *exactly* what I need."

"Ooh," Allegra teased her brother. "Did you hear that? I think he said he loves you more than yarn."

Luca chuckled. "Now I wouldn't go *that* far—"

"I would," Isaac said, and that warm moment, that piece of his soul that hadn't sat right for years and years and years finally clicked into place. "I *do* love you more than yarn."

Luca's attention was completely on him, their eyes saying these things that their hearts heard.

"Oh stop that," Allegra ordered. "I was promised pancakes and yarn, and after this morning, somebody had better pony up!"

THAT AFTERNOON—AFTER a giddy and expensive trip to the yarn store— Isaac volunteered to put the new purchases in the stash boxes, keeping things vaguely organized. He was moving boxes around when he spotted it—that linen tote with the many skeins of ugly brown alpaca yarn.

Except it wasn't ugly, he thought, pulling the canvas bag of it out of the box and touching it with gentle fingers. It was, in fact, amazingly soft, and it wasn't *really* crap brown. It was spun through with other colors, surprising hints of orange or purple or blue or red saving it from being boring, suggesting all sorts of things that it could be that *didn't* include a plain sweater, no cables, no lace, no colorwork.

Hats, for example. Hats with Christmas lights dancing around them. Or maybe reindeer prancing. Maybe a thick scarf with purple and orange and red and blue stripes. Maybe a headband with an intricate pattern in cream or white worked into it in contrast.

Maybe all the things that would keep his students and his teacher friends warm in the winter and spread the love and the joy of the hobby while purging this yarn of the bitterness of what had felt like a betrayed heart.

Todd had never betrayed him, Isaac thought sadly. Todd was who he'd always been, but that person was not who Isaac had needed. That didn't make him a monster—or even a mistake.

It made him a person Isaac had loved once, someone who'd had moments of kindness, moments of passion. Even, Isaac thought, remembering their wedding day and Todd's simple, almost embarrassed kiss at the end of the justice of the peace ceremony, moments of sweetness.

Isaac would probably have moved on from that relationship if given a little more time. Thinking back on it now, he'd been making plans to leave, to move out, in the quietest part of his mind. But they hadn't had the time to say goodbye, to part amicably, to be friends who were no longer meant to be lovers.

Luca, he thought, pulling out the balls of contrasting yarn for the brown, *Luca* had been meant to be his lover. Isaac might not have made it to meet Luca if he hadn't spent that time with Todd.

When he had the project bag full of yarn and needles, of ideas and plans, he stepped back from his stash and looked at the brown alpaca/wool blend in the tote hanging from his wrist.

Todd didn't need to be erased from his memory. He didn't need to be hidden in the back of Isaac's mind like unwanted worsted. Memories of Todd could be woven throughout Isaac's other memories of that time, and he would be sturdy and necessary—and yes, loved.

But he wasn't who Isaac wanted to be with *now*.

With a happy little sigh, Isaac took his kid-knitting projects into the living room and sat down, determined to put his life into order like perfect little loops on a shaft of wood, ready for all its potential to be released into the world.

Thanks and Giving

Luca had spent Thanksgiving at Nonna and Pop Pop's since he'd been kicked out of the house. In fact he'd lived there for the first two years after his parents had disowned him, but they'd kept that fact hidden so Allegra would be allowed to visit. It was one of the reasons he'd been so dedicated to remodeling their house for resale—after those years of fixing leaky faucets and tripping over soft subflooring, he knew where the fixes were needed, and he was itching to repair them.

After Allegra had her own showdown with their parents, she'd done the same—right down to the two years of living with them before she found roommates and then her useless boyfriend.

But this year, Nonna and Pop Pop were coming to Isaac's house, which more and more each day felt like Luca and Allegra's house too. Allegra had asked permission (at first) to hang up more framed pictures—in the hallways, in the guest rooms. Then Isaac had told her she didn't need permission, but she did need to let him in on the decision-making, because they had too much fun picking stuff out.

Lots of hours of poring over catalogues came after that.

They'd even repainted the guest rooms and made lists of furniture they'd like to buy. Luca had gotten in on that action and had started thinking about light fixtures, backsplashes in the bathrooms, window treatments, new tile. The house, which had loomed behind Isaac like an unfulfilled promise, was suddenly sheltering them, *caring* for them, as they returned the favor. Isaac had added to the art in his bedroom with something that looked like an impressionist jungle, and they'd spent a giddy morning in bed trying to find different animals. Was that a cheetah? Or a mandrill? Was that a tiger or a snake? The painting was beautiful, and even the ambiguity was part of that beauty.

Luca couldn't imagine Isaac's late husband loving that painting, but he couldn't imagine a world in which Isaac hadn't found it. Luca had started a quiet monologue in his head, talking to Todd Dupree, telling him all the things he hadn't known about Isaac, the things he'd been missing out on.

He loves the color blue. Blue. It's so easy. I don't see one single item of blue anywhere but the yarn room. You couldn't have filled his life with blue the way he tried to fill your life with tan?

The tea set is lovely. I can't lie. I'm a little jealous I won't be able to get him one of those. You couldn't have sat down with Nonna once in a while? She barely remembers you.

How could you have not gotten excited over that vest? The Halloween one? I love that thing. I want him to make one for Christmas and Valentines Day and Pride. What were you doing in your life that you couldn't have celebrated something he did so well?

And finally, *I wish you'd had more time so you could have known the Isaac you were missing. He's practically luminous right now. Did you know what you had? Who you loved? Or did you just want a stabilizer, somebody in your home to balance out the beige deadweight of your own damage?*

That last one was uncharitable, and Luca tried to regret it, but he thought of the wonder Isaac had shown in the last six months, the blossoming of his heart, of his personal confidence. It had been so easy to nurture that bloom. Coffee and a bagel in the morning, earnest conversation at night. Laughing at jokes. Cuddling during movies. Bantering with Allegra and holding her hand when she was worried or scared. Liking Isaac's friends. Being interested in his students. Every day, Luca wondered how anyone could have somebody as amazing as Isaac in their life and not celebrate it.

Celebrate being the keyword, he thought, particularly when Isaac had tentatively suggested Thanksgiving at their place (*their* place—he'd said *their* place) while inviting Nonna and Pop Pop.

It was going to be small—Roxy and her family were going to Roxy's in-laws' house, but Jimmy Bob and his niece were on their own, since most of their family lived in Bakersfield, so they were coming over around three and bringing a pie to go with the other three on the counter.

Seven people—a large turkey for leftovers (Isaac had planned), along with the basics: mashed potatoes, green beans, stuffing, salad, homemade bread, sweet potato casserole, and balsamic fried brussels sprouts.

The sheer length of the list had made Luca and Allegra gasp and then try to talk Isaac down a little. Nonna could bring green beans,

Allegra had said. Who the hell ate brussels sprouts for Thanksgiving? Luca said.

But Isaac had insisted that most of it could be made the day before and then heated up on Thanksgiving.

Luca said one man could not possibly do that, and since his sister was about to pop and needed to sit and knit and look glowy (and exhausted and weepy, but he wasn't going to say that while she was in the kitchen during this discussion), Isaac absolutely *had* to let Luca help him.

Isaac had stared at him, a little bewildered. "Help?" he asked. "You're raising this ruckus because you want to *help*?"

Luca stared back. "Well, it's not because I'm going to watch football on TV and listen to you cook, Isaac. That was a helluva lot of work you outlined there. You can either cook all that and let me help, or cook less of it and let me help less, but one way or another, I'm not sending you into the kitchen like that's what you do!"

Isaac's smile had gotten a little wobbly. "Okay," he said. "Okay. I forgot, you know, I'd have help. Todd had—we both had—a lot of expectations for Thanksgiving, you know. There was always a list. He'd clean the day before. I'd cook for two days, just for the two of us, but I'd cook enough for leftovers and give them to Roxy and her family, and he'd yell…. But this is for lots of us. It'll be fine." He nodded.

Luca swallowed, and glanced helplessly at Allegra, who was swallowing too, her eyes shiny and bright, and he opened his mouth to say, "Of course I'll help, Isaac," but what came out was… less than optimal.

"Oh my God, Isaac. *Fuck* that guy. Fuck him. I hate him. I—Jesus Christ, baby—you're so much more than unpaid labor!"

And then he realized he'd said it. He'd said what he'd been thinking. Six months of trying so hard not to badmouth Isaac's late husband, and he'd just told the dead to fuck off.

Isaac and Allegra were both staring at him, and Isaac's eyes were watery, and Luca had made his boyfriend cry five days before Thanksgiving, when even he could see they needed to go shopping so they could get this circus on the hay.

"Oh hell," he said, the shocked silence in the room more than he could bear. "I'm going to go mow the lawn."

Isaac's backyard was as large as the front, and though Isaac had a garden service in place to keep the lawn green and the shrubs watered,

Luca had taken over some of those duties. Isaac had protested at first, but since moving out of Nonna and Pop Pop's, Luca had been in one crappy apartment after another. He'd always dreamed of having a nice landscaped yard of his own to take care of, and while the yard service did a nice job keeping all the plants pretty and healthy and weeded, mowing the lawn once a week just *felt* right.

And it saved Isaac twenty bucks a week for yarn, which had sort of been the selling point for Isaac letting him do it.

The mower was electric, and not as loud and obnoxious as some. By the time Luca was done—and it took a good hour to do, because the backyard was pretty big—Isaac was outside on the little concrete apron, sitting on a painted wicker patio chair, wrapped in a blanket, and knitting. The patio chair had been dragged out into the sun, because after October, they'd pulled everything back under a protective overhang to shield the patio set from all but the fiercest rain.

Luca killed the lawnmower and walked up to the table, taking the full glass of iced tea and gulping it down. It was only around sixty-five degrees, but he was thirsty and grateful for the care.

He set the glass down with an unintentional clatter and sighed.

"I'm sorry," he said.

"Don't be," Isaac said, keeping his eyes on his knitting. It was something… complicated, a hat with a motif on it of some sort. The hat itself was a deep blue, but there were other colors—yellow, red, brown— that went into the making of the thing. Pretty. Isaac always made pretty.

"I shouldn't say that," Luca continued doggedly. "I… it's not my business—"

"Of course it's your business," Isaac said, finally setting the yarn in his lap and glancing up. "You've been cleaning up his mess for the last six months, Luca—you think you don't have a right to be mad when something he did years ago suddenly trips you up like a spoke in a bike wheel?"

Luca stared up at that perfectly blue sky—Isaac blue, he would think of it forever ever after.

"Yeah, but it's not fair I should yell at *you* about it. That's like making you suffer *twice*. Once through it and once through me. It was dumb. I'm sorry."

Isaac gave him a rather gamine smile. Under the blanket, there was a… disquieting movement, and the cat stuck his head over the edge of Isaac's lap and meowed loudly before burrowing back in.

"You brought the cat outside?" Luca asked, suddenly concerned.

"He's in my knitting bag," Isaac said, obviously baffled. "He kept getting back in every time I lifted him out. We got out here, and he was suddenly terrified. I tucked him under the blanket, and he was happy to be there. I don't know. You explain it to me. Did somebody put a catnip mouse in the bottom?"

Luca thought about it. "Yeah," he said, remembering the last time he and Allegra had thrown a new batch of the things around the house. "*Euclid* did. *He* put the catnip mice in the bottom of the knitting bag."

"Luca, I hate to say anything, but I think my cat has a drug problem."

"Hey—you brought him home half-baked and drooling. Remember that? It's not our fault he's been searching for the ultimate high ever since."

Isaac's laugh was low and sweet. "Luca," he said, when he was done chuckling.

"Yeah?" Luca came closer, squatting next to the chair so he could be near Isaac, take in this moment under the chill November sun.

"It's okay if you're a little mad. Don't be mad at *yourself.* You offered to help when all I saw was a big list of stuff only *I* could do. That's huge. Suddenly Thanksgiving's fun again. We gotta come up with some stuff your sister can do or she's going to feel left out."

"Make the centerpiece," Luca said. "Even if she's buying one from the craft store." He paused. "You have no idea—none—what this means to her. Decorating for Halloween. For Thanksgiving. For Christmas— you *are* decorating for Christmas, right?"

Isaac grimaced. "We have really boring ornaments," he said. "Plain silver balls, red bows, white lights. I'm tempted to tell her they all fell down and got smashed in the garage so she can go to town at craft fairs and on Etsy."

Luca chuckled. "Maybe like the house. Move out the old stuff a little at a time. When did you want to get the tree?"

"The week after Thanksgiving," Isaac said. "But I wanted to hit a sale at a nearby hardware store for some multicolored lights. At the very least we can have those."

Luca's heart, which had been shivering and a little cold since he'd run out of the kitchen, grew warm again. He pushed up and took Isaac's mouth, pulling back to rest their foreheads together.

"Isaac, you should *always* have color in your life. Let me know if I ever let you down in that department, okay?"

Isaac let out a little sigh and a hum. "You *are* color in my life," he said softly.

Then Euclid meowed loudly again, and Isaac shivered in spite of the blanket, and they took their show back inside.

LUCA DIDN'T mind getting sucked into the entire holiday. He and Isaac had fun in the grocery store, bouncing ideas off each other, changing plans at the last minute. They went from a pumpkin pie to a pumpkin cheesecake with a few keyboard strokes on their phones, and bought accordingly. Luca sorely overestimated how many sweet potatoes they would need, and Isaac told him dryly they needed to buy an extra box of cornflakes and five extra pounds of butter to make that happen. So Luca did, because the way Isaac described sweet potato casserole, that was the only reasonable answer. And both of them were quite surprised when they ended up with a whole extra turkey because of grocery store points.

"But what are we going to do with it?" Isaac asked as they pushed the incredibly overloaded cart to the car.

"Cook it the next day, then freeze everything and have turkey casserole and turkey sandwiches and turkey hash for the next three weeks!" Luca said, incredibly excited about *all* of that. "Can you imagine? For three weeks, we don't have to answer the question, 'What's for dinner?' It's *always* going to be turkey!"

Isaac whimpered. "How about we stop by the soup kitchen on the way home and drop off the extra there?" he said. "And maybe a couple pounds of sweet potatoes too."

Luca sighed. "Killjoy."

Which made Isaac laugh, loudly and roundly, as they loaded the back of the car up—before he looked up directions to the nearest donation place that would be super excited for a whole turkey.

The night before Thanksgiving, during which Luca had spent half the day cleaning with Allegra and half the day cooking with Isaac,

Allegra sat at the table and tried to put together a silk flower bouquet in autumn colors—dark orange, brown, purple, mauve, and gold.

Luca was busy peeling and cubing potatoes—both sweet and otherwise—and he barely noticed his sister's even breathing as she stood, stretched out her back, and then leaned over the table, bracing her weight on her arms, and tried to do the same thing.

Isaac was the one who looked up from pressing garlic into the stuffing broth and said, "Allegra, that's the third time you've done that in the last hour. Is there something we should know?"

Allegra stared back at them blankly, and like a freight train, Luca was hit with what she'd been told at her last doctor's appointment.

She was close—her due date was in three weeks. But that didn't mean the baby wouldn't come at any time.

Labor can be anything from the classic breaking of waters to breathlessness after leaning over doing a task. Watch out for small signs. A tightness in the back, lower abdomen cramping, even a violent mood swing or moodiness—all of it could mean labor is coming.

Like a one-two punch, it hit him that Allegra had been quiet, turned inward and thoughtful all day. She hadn't had any commentary to offer after Luca's Todd blowup four days before. Not that Luca expected his sister to weigh in on his love life, but, well, that had never stopped her before.

She swallowed. "No?" she said. "No," she said, a little more firmly. "No. Isaac, I refuse. You and Luca promised, right? You were going to come with me to the hospital. I—" She took a deep breath and said, "I should maybe just find another position while I finish up with this. It's stressing my back out, is all."

Luca met Isaac's eyes, and Isaac shook his head.

Fifteen minutes later, Allegra had stood up from her spot and was doing the same stretching routine.

Fifteen minutes after that, she was done with her project—and stretching again.

Fifteen minutes after that, she'd set the table completely, with napkins and coffee cups and a table runner and the centerpiece.

And this time, when she stretched, her breathing caught a little more tightly.

They started keeping silent track of when her restlessness would start and when she'd subside into her chair—even after she declared herself tired and done and had moved into the living room to knit and watch *It's a Wonderful Life* on TV.

"Fourteen minutes," Luca murmured softly to Isaac. "It's happening every fourteen minutes."

Isaac glanced over at her, pausing while grating cheese for the potatoes. Luca knew what he'd see. She'd fallen asleep, her knitting on top of her stomach, a line drawn over her brows even as she breathed softly in rest.

"Are they waking her up?" he asked.

"Yeah," Luca murmured. "But she doesn't realize that's what's doing it." The last time, he'd watched her grunt, wake up, and yoga stretch some more from her chair, her breath quickening as what she probably thought of as a back cramp caught up with her, before she fell back asleep.

"Okay, then." Isaac pursed his lips. "We've got a lot of it done," he said. "We've got the turkey prepped and ready to go into the oven tomorrow morning. We've got the stuffing and sweet potatoes ready to pop in while the turkey's resting, and the mashed potatoes ready to boil and beat while the turkey's in. We've got everything *prepped*, Luca— we just need people to do the right things at the right times tomorrow! Including go to get Sophia and Geordie."

Luca grunted. "Let's text everybody tonight and tell them it may happen—maybe we can come up with a plan."

Isaac nodded. "I mean, Jimmy Bob and Trixie met your grandparents at Allegra's birthday party. How awkward would it be, throwing them together for a day and saying, 'Hey, cook this when we say so'?"

Luca chuckled. "Either way, you finish up what you're doing, and I'll go upstairs and start calling." He pointed to the pad of paper where he'd been keeping track of Allegra's contractions. "She's due for one in about seven minutes. If it's significantly shorter than that, let me know."

"She doesn't even have a name picked out," Isaac said softly. "We don't even know the *gender* yet."

Luca grinned at him, trying to mask his own anxiety. "Sure you don't want to go back to the days of beige and perfect planning?"

"That was cruel and unwarranted." Isaac sniffed. "I was only panicking like a perfectly normal uncle-in-law."

And the fact that he was playing—*playing*—with the idea was enough to lighten Luca's heart. They had two major projects going in the next twenty-four hours. The one thing they didn't have to worry about was each other.

Luca went upstairs to make the requisite calls, but as he sank down onto the bed, Euclid hopped up (*oolf*—their kitten was now about ten pounds!) and started kneading his thigh. Rubbing the purring monster orange boi gave him a moment to pause, to think, and he placed his first call to Roxy. While Isaac had kept trying to explain the plan to him, he was still hazy on this "How to cook five thousand dishes at the same time" idea. Like any student, he didn't want to bother the teacher when they were in the middle of a thing.

Also, Roxy had become Allegra's big sister, and while Allegra had asked for Isaac and Luca to be there when she had the baby, he had the feeling Roxy's voice, at any stage she could make it, would be helpful.

"Oh!" Roxy said, and the sound of her voice told him she was in the middle of something too. "So now? So I'm elbows-deep in sausage stuffing, and Brian's up to his eyeballs in pie, and your sister's going into labor now?"

"They're still about fourteen minutes apart," he said. "I don't think *she* even knows it yet."

Roxy huffed out a breath. "Okay. So, yeah. You guys are doing good not to panic—and good to plan ahead. Brian's mom's thing is at three. Let me putter along here and get my shit done, maybe cop a few hours of sleep. Call me around eight to let me know how she's doing. Unless, of course, the whole thing blows up and you're heading to the hospital at two in the morning—also a possibility, but it happens less often than you think, okay?"

Luca glanced at the clock, saw it was nine, and got almost physically sick at the thought. "You're terrifying me," he said on a whimper.

"Cool your jets, big fella. You guys are doing good just clocking the restlessness, keeping it all calm. Now I'm going to suggest you have her do two things—one is pack a bag, and the other is take a long, luxurious shower."

"Will it help with the labor?" he asked, thinking about all those back stretches.

"Sure," she said. "It will also be the last time she gets a long, luxurious shower to herself for a while. Nobody tells you, but what's coming is sweaty, uncomfortable, and exhausting, and the shower facilities at the hospital are very, very small."

"So noted." Luca tried to keep the panic out of his voice. In spite of the prepped nursery and the copious shopping trips, the drawers stuffed with onesies and tiny footie pajamas in seasonal colors, in spite of seeing his sister double in size and rest swollen ankles the size of grapefruits on the ottoman day after day, the actual reality of what was about to happen hadn't hit Luca until *right now*. He'd been excited about the *baby*—but the *labor* had barely been on his radar.

"Don't panic, honey," Roxy said, her voice throbbing in sympathy. "It's going to overwhelm her too. If you and Isaac are panicked, she's going to feel like something's wrong. Your job is to keep everything calm and to stand up for her in the labor room."

That brought Luca up short. "Stand up for her?"

"Hopefully you'll get a good doctor and staff—but you don't always. If she's in pain and *you* know she's in pain, it's your job to let everybody know that she doesn't act this way for a hangnail. If she's hooked up to a baby monitor and the monitor is going bananashit, don't assume anybody else will notice. It's your job to make people pay attention. If they put her on her back and her labor stalls, it's *your* job to have them roll her to her side so it can start up again. You and Isaac took the classes with her?"

"Yeah," Luca said, although they'd both been tired and distracted and not really on their game.

"All the shit they tell you not to do in Lamaze, I swear to God, some medical professional has tried to do to me when I was on my back and vulnerable as fuck. Make sure it doesn't happen to your sister. As far as I'm concerned, it validated Brian's entire entrance into parenthood, because he may not have *been* in labor, but by God he was present for me when I was."

Luca nodded, trying to imprint everything on his brain. "Okay," he said, feeling a little weak about the whole thing. "Uhm, one more thing."

"Yeah?"

"Should we tell her she's in labor?"

Roxy grunted. "You're *sure* she hasn't figured it out yet?"

"No. We started timing her getting up and stretching because her back was cramping. It seemed really... regular."

Roxy's laugh was relieved. "Yeah. No. Don't tell her. She'll figure it out when she's ready. Remember, most women can't sleep when labor gets close—the contractions wake us up because they're super strong. Right now, she's relaxed, she's moving, she's excited about tomorrow. You call me as soon as you're ready to go to the hospital, and I'll come over to take over the kitchen thing. That sweet kid—Jimmy Bob's niece—whatwazername?"

"Trixie," Luca supplied.

"Yeah—between Trixie and Nonna and probably Jimmy Bob himself, we can get the dinner ready and on the table. You, Isaac, and Allegra go do the hard part, okay?"

"But Roxy, what about your own Thanksgiving?" he asked, feeling terrible.

"Oh, honey—I literally went into labor with Falcon during my sister's wedding. I was the maid of honor. Someone stepped in to pick up her train, Brian helped me to the car, everybody made jokes at my expense during the toasts, and the other bridesmaids made up the slack. I tried to apologize to Joanie the next day, and she told me to go away, she was bonding with the baby. They're part of life, Luca. Babies are *never* when or where you expect, even when they're asleep in their cribs. I guarantee you, one night you're going to wake up, and it's going to hit you that there's a whole other human being in your house that you were not planning on knowing. It'll freak you out, but take deep breaths. It's worth it."

Luca laughed softly. "You're really something," he said. "Thank you for this. For everything. Allegra—" He swallowed. He didn't doubt, not even for a moment, that Allegra and probably Isaac had dumped the entire sorry visit to his parents' house on her. "Allegra really needed a big sister, and you're like a gift from God."

Roxy cackled. "You know I'm only doing this so I can get a playmate for Sparrow Anne, right? Which reminds me—Brian and I have a betting pool on the name and gender of the little tadpole. Winner gets a foot rub. There's a fiver in it if you tell him it's a boy until after he pays up, even if it's not."

Luca was still laughing when he signed off. Calling Nonna and Jimmy Bob was a lot easier then. Somehow, Roxy's "We got this" was infectious. He knew normally that was *his* job—it had been his job since he'd gotten kicked out of the house.

I got this, Allegra—I'll move in with Nonna and Pop Pop. It'll be okay.

Don't worry about a job, Allegra—I got this. I really need help at the shop.

Oh, baby—I'm sorry your boyfriend's a douchenugget. We got this, right? You move in to my place, and it'll be okay.

And he'd been good at it. He knew that when he went downstairs and talked to Allegra and Isaac, *he'd have this*. But somehow, Isaac's support system was his now too. And the enormity of what he and Isaac were about to help his little sister do was not as frightening.

Don't worry, Allegra—we got this.

BY THE time he got downstairs, Isaac had covered all the dishes, put them in the refrigerator, and put instructions on each dish with a Post-it. He was in the middle of stacking dishes in the dishwasher when Luca came up behind him and gratefully pulled his slender body up against Luca's chest.

"Mmm…," Isaac murmured, turning to lean his head on Luca's shoulder. "This is nice. What's news?"

"Well, I'm going to talk my sister into taking a long shower, and *you're* going to go pack her and the baby a go bag. Roxy says she'll figure it out for herself when it's time."

Isaac grunted. "I think we need to come down while she's sleeping and clock her contractions, don't you?"

"That's really creepy, Isaac."

"Look at her!" Isaac muttered. "I don't think it's occurred to her yet that this is happening!"

Luca glanced over at his sister, who was watching TV, crocheting a baby sweater that would probably fit next year, and doing that yoga stretch with her back again.

"Fourteen minutes?" he asked.

"Thirteen," Isaac said grimly.

"According to Roxy, if it's the real thing, it'll wake her out of a sound sleep."

"I sort of remember that from Lamaze," Isaac mumbled, sagging in Luca's arms.

"Here, baby. Let me finish this while you dish up some ice cream. We can sit, finish the movie, and have a nice quiet night at home. From what I understand, we don't get a lot of those in the future."

Isaac suddenly jerked in his arms. "Oh my God," he said.

"What?"

"Luca, in as little as two nights, there is going to be a *whole other human being* in our house! What are we going to do with *that*?"

It was so close to Roxy's words that Luca found himself laughing. A little bit hysterical, sure, but it was cleansing and glorious to hold Isaac in his arms and pour out his muffled laughter into the hollow of his lover's neck.

Isaac clung to him and laughed too, maybe not understanding *Luca's* laughter but, and Luca could feel it, secure in his arms, knowing his fears, his giddy panic, his excitement, all of it was absolutely fucking fine, totally acceptable, and extremely valid.

After a shaky moment, they parted, and Luca took another long, deep breath as he started to stack dishes. Worrying about Allegra was fine, as long as they kept it to themselves—but he and Isaac were going to be okay.

AN HOUR later, after ice cream and knitting, and the tranquility of a quiet evening, Luca said, "Hey, honey—your back is really bothering you tonight. How about you go take a long shower, pamper yourself a little, and get some rest for tomorrow, okay?"

"Oh God, yeah," Allegra murmured, standing up and stretching, then morphing into a warrior pose as she tried to alleviate the discomfort. "Yeah. I think that's a *really* good idea. Thanks, Luca!"

"I've got some laundry to put away," Isaac called as she moved down the hallway. "I'll just set it on your dresser, okay?"

"You're a peach!" she called back.

They heard her door click closed—not locked, so Isaac could get in—and met eyes with equally grim determination.

"I'll get her bag from the closet," Luca said.

"I'll pack her essentials," Isaac said. "But I need you to get your ragged old sleep sweatshirt from your drawers. The one she steals at every opportunity."

"Why?" Luca asked, puzzled.

"Because she's spending at least one night in the hospital, sweetie. She's going to want something that reminds her of home."

And with that they skedaddled. By the time Allegra poked her head out of the bedroom, her blow-dried hair back in a soft ponytail, to say she was going to bed, there were two packed bags next to the doorway. One was a baby bag covered with rosebuds, because girl or boy, Allegra had fallen in love with it, and the other was a soft duffel, with a pair of maternity pajamas as well as Luca's sweatshirt and some maternity sweats to wear home—with lots of maternity underwear for accidents. Apparently Isaac *had* been paying more attention than Luca, because when Luca asked about the larger clothes, Isaac had explained patiently that Allegra wasn't going to be anywhere *close* to her old sizes for at least six weeks.

"Oh God," Luca muttered. "Where was *I* when the nurse was telling us those things?"

"Asleep," Isaac told him, amused. "Baby, we've *both* been going balls-out to get ready for this, you know?"

They were sitting on the couch, leaning back exhaustedly. The TV was off, and Isaac wasn't even *fondling* his knitting, although he *had* packed what Luca thought of as his "knitting go bag" and had set it next to Allegra's bags by the door.

Luca smiled and then turned his head toward the nice man who *still* liked to knit out on the porch in the evenings, only now with Luca's sister next to him, and sometimes, when Luca got home early from work, with Luca sitting on the Adirondack chair Isaac had quietly set out after Luca had spent a couple of sweet September evenings leaning against the porch railing so they could all talk.

"What?" Isaac asked, his eyes half closed.

"Six months ago," Luca murmured. "Six months ago, I never would have guessed this would be us. That we'd be a team. That we'd be a family. That you and me would be helping Allegra do this huge, important thing. That we'd be welcoming a whole new human being into *our* home—not *your* house, but *our* home. God, Isaac. I'm so lucky to have you in my life. I mean, Allegra *and* I are lucky, but… but you are *such* a good partner. You are *so* good at just *being there* for people. It's your superpower. I don't know how you've gone about unworshipped for so long, but you deserve *all* the big noise and celebration, you know that?"

Isaac's eyes were no longer half closed—but they were a little damp.

"Has it only been six months?" he mused. "It feels like…." He frowned a little, like he was trying to do math. "That's so odd," he said. "That time I spent with Todd feels so… small. Like a footnote. This time with you and Allegra, being your family, having a noisy, happy home—it feels like my real life. Isn't that odd?"

Luca felt the hugeness of having an Isaac in his heart. "No," he murmured. "Not strange at all."

Isaac reached for his hand and squeezed. "We'll go to bed in a minute," he murmured as Euclid hopped up on the couch and spread out between them, purring. The warmth and vibration of the cat only added to the somnolence of the moment.

"Just as soon—" Luca yawned. "—as you're ready."

They were still there, on the couch, Isaac leaning on Luca, Luca leaning on the arm of the couch, the cat asleep between them, three hours later when Allegra came down the hallway, leaning on the wall.

"Hey, guys?" she said, and Luca choked on his own snore and tried to focus.

"'Llegra?" he slurred, while Isaac grunted and rubbed his eyes. Painfully, Luca tried to twist his body so he could see his sister.

"Those back pains… they're… they're getting really strong. They're waking me up, like, every eight minutes or so. Is that… is that bad?"

"No," Isaac said on a yawn. "But it *is* getting close. You got any other signs of labor?"

"Labor?" Allegra repeated, sounding stunned. "Is this… is this *labor*?"

Luca untangled himself from the cat and his boyfriend, stood up, and balanced one hand on the arm of the couch so he could collect himself. "Yeah. Sorry, sweetheart. Don't worry about it. We packed your bags and everything. When you get to, like, five, six minutes apart, we'll go to the hospital."

"But…." To his horror, he watched her lower lip wobble. "But tomorrow's *Thanksgiving*! We *planned*! You and Isaac cooked, and we've got company, and—"

"Shh, shh, shh…." Luca hugged her close, standing a little to the side to make room for her tummy. Even as he held her, he felt her stiffen, watched in fascination as her stomach, pushing tight against her sleepshirt, rippled in hard, dramatic waves. When it was done, he saw a tiny little "pop" of an agitated foot against a home that had gotten far too small.

"Whoa," he said, voice hushed in awe. They'd *all* seen the baby moving under her skin, but that was the first time he'd seen it done with that sort of controlled violence. "This kid is getting *pissed*. Yeah, I think it's definitely coming today."

"But I'm not ready!" Allegra wailed, and Luca had to hold her some more, trying to calm her down, until the next contraction—seven and a half minutes, Isaac told them—rippled over her where she stood and almost brought her to her knees.

"Isaac!" she cried, after Luca helped her to her chair. "Isaac, make it stop! You can do anything—make it stop! Make the contractions stop! I'm not ready!"

"Allegra!" Isaac said sternly, in what Luca had come to recognize was his teacher voice. "Allegra, stop this. No—no, don't argue. Stop this. You are grown, sweetheart. You are strong. You knew this was coming. You've got—" He checked his Fitbit. "You've got *five minutes* to prepare for the next contraction. You need to breathe, just like the class taught you, and find that calm space inside yourself. You remember that space?"

"Isaac…," she whimpered.

"You know we love you, honey," he said, still stern, "but you are going to help nobody if you freak the fuck out. Now look at you. You've decorated your room and the nursery. You've trained someone at work so you don't have to go back for three months. You've already gone out and found day care for when you need it. That was a lot of grown-up shit you did to get ready for this baby, and you know we're here to help. But the next part of this is *all you*. Luca and I can hold your hand and tell you you're pretty, but you need to look in your heart and remember who you're doing this for."

"My baby," she whispered, her breathing much quieter.

"Who?" Isaac demanded.

"My baby!" she said, and she sounded stronger this time.

"That's right. Now breathe. Get all the oxygen you can. Calm yourself down. Wait for the next one. Okay?"

"Okay." They locked eyes, and she nodded with Isaac, and for a few minutes, there was only the sound of them breathing.

All too soon, her breathing quickened, and Isaac was checking his Fitbit, and the next contraction was on.

By eight in the morning, it was time to call the hospital and take their show on the road.

By eleven, with Luca on one side and Isaac on the other, Allegra grabbed her thighs, spread her legs and *heaved*, and the new baby emerged into the world, squalling and healthy and red and wrinkled and perfect.

Allegra wept, giving her hands to Luca and Isaac, and whispered, "How is she?"

"How'd you know it was a she?" Luca asked, smoothing her hair from her brow.

"Don't know," she laughed tiredly. "Maybe it was 'cause I thought Brian deserved the foot rub."

Luca chuckled and kissed his sister's cheek. "I promised Roxy I'd lie. First person on the phone wins."

"Later," Isaac said, watching the baby's progress from the cleanup station to the eyedrop station to the swaddling station. "Let's meet her first."

For a moment there was more pain and more panting as Allegra finished the messiness of delivering a child, and then she was washed up and blanketed, and the swaddled little creature was placed in her arms.

Allegra held the baby to her chest, and the tiny thing scowled back, and Luca was enchanted.

"Does she eat now?" he asked.

"You really did sleep through Lamaze, didn't you?" Allegra shot back.

"All she has to do now is exist," Isaac told him. "She's doing great, aren't you, sweetheart?"

Tentatively, Isaac reached out a gentle finger to soothe a wrinkled red cheek, and the baby closed its eyes and seemed to lean into the touch.

"Oh, see," Allegra murmured. "Uncle Isaac's the favorite already."

"It's a family requirement," Luca said, taking the three of them in. Unexpectedly, he felt his eyes grow hot. "Oh my God, Allegra. Our family—look at it."

"It's so beautiful," she murmured, although her eyes seemed to be exclusively on her daughter. Fair enough, Luca thought, but as Isaac leaned in, as in love with their new member as Allegra was, Luca remembered their dreamy, exhausted conversation on the couch.

Their family. It was as miraculous as he'd always imagined.

Two hours later, Luca left Isaac knitting by Allegra's bed so he could go settle everybody in for Thanksgiving, as well as tell them all the good news. He'd been torn as to whether to stay by Allegra and have Isaac do that, or go himself, but in the end he had to concede that it was *his* grandparents and *his* friend and coworker, and he should probably be the one to go give details and tell stories and, in the end, put together care packages of Thanksgiving dinner to bring so Allegra didn't have to settle for hospital food on Thanksgiving.

His grandmother insisted on serving him while he regaled everybody at the table with the gory details. This included Roxy, who was getting picked up by her husband shortly, since she'd arrived to start putting things in the oven.

"So?" Roxy said, waiting while he finished a heavenly mouthful of stuffing and gravy. "Isaac already blabbed that it was a girl—and way to drop the ball on getting me the foot rub, by the way."

Luca gave her an unrepentant grin. "Your husband will give you a foot rub anytime you want one and you know it," he teased fondly.

"Yeah, but stolen foot rubs feel better," she retorted. "And you're dodging out on the question. What did she name the baby?"

Luca's smile stretched his cheeks as he remembered Isaac holding the baby while his sister slept. "Blessing," he said. "Blessing Noelle, because, you know, so close to Christmas."

Sophia clapped her hands, and Geordie hugged his wife in excitement. "Perfecto!"

"Blessing Noelle," Roxy said, staring. "'Cause that won't get the little darling beat up on the playground *ever*."

Luca cocked his head. "Your husband named your children after *birds*."

Roxy chuckled. "Yeah. Falcon Justice will protect her. It'll be fine." She yawned—as she should, since she'd pretty much worked on *two* Thanksgiving meals that day. "So, how's *Isaac* in all of this?"

Luca closed his eyes, the contentment on Isaac's face suffusing him with joy. "Thrilled," he said, struggling to open his eyes for the people in front of him. "Happier than I've ever seen him."

"Good," Roxy said, reaching out to take Luca's hand. "You guys, hold on to each other as long as this lasts. Family, *good* family, is exactly like that baby. A blessing. A true, real blessing."

Luca's arms ached to hold his lover, to feel the truth of that, but today, in the midst of this hectic, magical maelstrom, he knew that he had to hold it all in his heart.

"Truth," he said happily. "So much truth."

ROXY AND his grandparents sent him up to his room for a two-hour nap before he got to bring food back to the hospital. When he arrived, Allegra was nursing the baby—who was eating like a champion now—and Isaac was practically sleep-knitting in the corner of the room.

After thanking him for the food and catching up on how Thanksgiving was going, the conversation lulled, falling into exhausted patterns of comfort topics while the three of them recovered from a quite unrestful night.

It was Allegra who drew attention to what Isaac was knitting.

"Wait a minute," she said. "Isn't that the yarn? The brown stuff—pretty for brown, but you kept shoving it into the back of the stash."

Isaac smiled a little and held up what was obviously a hat. "Yeah," he said. "I'm using it in my student hats this year. It's got so many hidden colors in it—it really works well as the background for colorful designs. And this way I can get rid of it without…." He shuddered.

"Having to make a crap-brown sweater with nothing but plain stitching," Luca filled in, remembering that one fateful day.

Isaac gazed sleepily into his eyes. "Not all brown is bad," he said. "This yarn has some good properties. It's time it found a place where it can be used and loved. I think the kids are really going to like these hats."

Luca stared at the fanciful colorwork and had no doubt.

And then he took in his lover's pleased expression as his fingers worked nimbly on what Luca knew wasn't a simple project at *all*, and he realized that, much like it hadn't been a sweater that Isaac hadn't wanted to make, this wasn't merely a hat that he *did* want to finish.

Isaac's love was all in the present now, Luca realized. The ghost of his ex, while perhaps always a flicker of light and shadow in Isaac's heart, was now a ghost of the past, and not of the here and now.

The baby at Allegra's breast broke off feeding and emitted a tiny cry as Allegra put her little body against her shoulder and started to pat. That teeny little person emitted the most amazing burp, and the adults in the room laughed.

"Blessings," Luca said softly, "come in all forms."

THE FIRST NOELLE

"HEY, MR. B!" Marcelle's voice cut urgently into Isaac's dream.

"Hmm?" Isaac mumbled.

"Dude, that teacher is coming—the one who let you take the cat! She's about to come in. Isn't she your boss or something?"

"Oh shit," Isaac muttered, blinking hard. "Did I fall asleep?"

"Yeah, dude. You put in the movie for fifth period, and this is *sixth!*"

That made Isaac sit up. "Oh my God—*Marcelle!* You let me sleep through fifth period? I had grades and hats and—"

"All given," Marcelle said promptly. "You had me set up the gifts, right? Well, they all saw you sleeping, and since I had the grades, I called them up just like you would and gave them their gifts and their grades. It was fine. But it's the middle of sixth period now, and you need to wake up!"

Isaac wiped drool off his face, took a swig of the soda Luca had packed for him that morning, and tried to get his shit together. Marcelle was one of three TAs this year, and Isaac was grateful, because the last three weeks since Thanksgiving—when Noelle had come into their lives—had been *hard.* Nobody was getting any sleep. Not Allegra, not Luca, and not Isaac.

Colic was a *beast*, and everybody had taken their turn walking the baby across the floor, but even with three people, sleep was a rare commodity. Isaac had managed to finish his Christmas knitting (and had bought adorable tchotchkes and candy bars for the kids who weren't getting hats or fingerless gloves), but this was the last day before Christmas vacation, and he couldn't remember the past hour of teaching. His respect for Roxy and Brian had gone up a thousand percent, and he was starting to *dream* about knitting since he got so little time to *actually* knit.

But one of the things he'd finished—and was damned proud of it— had pretty much wiped out the last of the brown yarn, as well as the scraps of contrasting yarn he'd had left after doing the student projects.

And it would, hopefully, buy him some goodwill from the woman who had been his nemesis, but who had, as the new semester progressed, worked her way more and more into his good graces by asking after his cat.

Euclid the stoner kitten had continued to be a force of good in Isaac's home. In spite of the many, *many* huge changes that had rocked Isaac's life since May, walking into the house to be greeted by that insistent orange force of tranquility and evil was still a furry miracle that Isaac didn't take for granted.

Opening his home for Euclid meant opening his home for Allegra.

It meant opening his heart for Luca, and opening his life for family.

Having this coworker, who used to seem disdainful of everything Isaac *was*, greet him with a smile and ask him about his *cat* was along the same miraculous lines of… well, of being able to say, "My late husband used to love sunsets."

Todd *had* loved sunsets. It was why he'd made sure the porch had a swing, where Isaac had gotten into the habit of sitting and knitting. Todd had sat with him, and they'd quietly watched the sunset for years of their marriage.

Those moments, quiet, accepting, meditative, had been some of the best moments of Isaac's life at the time.

But… at the time, he hadn't spent twenty minutes crocheting garlands with pom-poms out of scrap yarn to soak in catnip so his cat could have an amazingly sparkly afternoon. At the time, he hadn't come home to Luca, doing his best cooking with spaghetti and meat sauce and garlic bread because it was Friday and he'd gotten home early and wanted Isaac to start his weekend off doing something besides cooking. At the time, he hadn't fallen asleep on the couch with a suddenly somnolent baby on his shoulder, tired to his bones, only to wake up and find that his boyfriend had fallen asleep next to him and the baby's mother was taking a picture of the three of them because "you look like adorable hell."

Todd had loved sunsets. Isaac could love that about his late husband. He could also love Euclid and Allegra and Noelle.

And Luca.

Especially Luca, who had brought all of them into his life. Well, Euclid had sort of brought himself, but Luca loved Isaac's idiot cat as much as Isaac did, so it *felt* like they'd arrived together.

So Isaac had come to all sorts of peace in the last six months, and part of that peace meant forgiving Paula for being a passive-aggressive twat when he'd first started teaching. He had no idea where she came from. Had she been raised religious and spent the last ten years getting over it? Had she simply not realized he was gay and hadn't realized how she sounded? Or had *he* been bitter and defensive and unaware of how much that affected the people around him who *weren't* Roxy? However she had been *then*, she was becoming a friend *now*, and the contrast between *then* and *now* in his life was so severe that he thought a little bit of knitting forgiveness was a small price to pay for improvement.

But he couldn't very well give her the gift he'd planned while he was still rumpled and drooling after falling asleep at his desk and letting his student TA do all his adulting for him.

"How do I look?" he asked Marcelle, wiping the last of the sleep from his eyes.

"Like a new parent who just fell asleep on his desk," Marcelle said astutely. "But she might not see it."

Still, he was standing up behind his supply table and "observing" his class when she poked her head in, so that was something. He smiled gamely at her and snagged one of the last gifts from the table, moving to the open door while the students sat immersed in the last ten minutes of *Hidden Figures*, the happy math teacher's best movie friend in the world.

"Happy holidays, Isaac," Paula said with a shy smile. "I added you to my baking list this year." She handed him a Christmas tin that he understood was full of cookies, mostly because he'd never been on the list before and had been envious as hell of the other people who had.

"Thank you!" Oh wow. His surprise and excitement were *genuine*— but so was his relief, because he didn't have to accept the gift empty-handed. "And you've been added to the knitting list." He held out her package but didn't quite relinquish it. "And you get the same talk that Roxy got—don't expect something big at every holiday. Some days it's a pom-pom for the end of your pencil, some days it's a blanket—it all depends on what I feel like yarning."

Paula chuckled and nodded her head. "Understood," she said. Her gaze went sideways and got quietly sad. "I'm grateful to be on the list," she said. Then, "It… it wasn't because you were gay," she added. "I know you thought that was why I didn't like you, but that wasn't it. It was… you and Roxy had your own secret club. You were funny and made all these exciting plans and… and I felt excluded." She managed to meet his eyes. "We're the same age, Isaac—it hurt that you guys thought of me as the Wicked Witch of the Math Department."

He knew his mouth had fallen open, and he was stunned—not just by how much she had revealed, but by how much he had misunderstood. And how much she'd overheard—he and Roxy had apparently not been as adult in their immaturity as they'd thought. And he felt compelled to make the same sort of confession.

"My late husband," he said, "was… was *really* controlling. Those Wicked Witch comments you heard—one more person, even my boss, telling me what to do was… was going to make me hostile. It wasn't your fault." He gave her a small smile. "I'm so sorry we hurt your feelings."

"I'm sorry your husband was shitty," she said softly. "We had no idea. We thought you were in mourning, until this semester when…." She gave a little shrug. "You've been *really* happy this year. *Tired*, this last month, but happy."

His lips quirked. "Want to see a picture?" he asked, and as she unwrapped her gift, he produced pictures on his phone. Blessing Noelle, of course, and Allegra holding her infant daughter, and finally, with a burst of trust, the picture Allegra had forwarded to *everybody* of Isaac and Luca asleep on the couch, the baby tucked up against Isaac's shoulder.

"Aw," Paula murmured. "Uncle Isaac." And then she unwrapped the cardigan, brown with autumn-purple-and-orange trim, that he'd created using a pattern based on the sweaters Paula usually wore when the weather got chilly. Suddenly all talk of the baby disappeared as she wiped her red-rimmed eyes and said, "Oh, Isaac—I *really* love this color. How did you know?"

THE REST of the day was a blur—although he did remember Marcelle's grateful hug when he opened his own gift and got a brown knit hat with Christmas lights dancing all over it, Isaac's second-favorite item from the batch of repurposed alpaca that had changed his life that day in early May. In the end, he'd left his cleaned, orderly room with an empty briefcase, because he'd gotten his grades in, and a clean conscience, because everybody who'd tried had passed.

He and Roxy had plans to get their families together on Christmas Eve, which was in three days, and Isaac, Allegra, and Luca would be all about Christmas prep between Saturday morning and that ring on the doorbell.

He arrived home to find Allegra facedown on the couch, her hand draped over the end to rest on the baby's stomach, while lights from the Christmas tree twinkled in the background. The original glass ornaments had all been destroyed in the first week—Euclid had been *unmerciful* in his takedown of the shiny silver things. In their place was a sparce peppering of emergency wooden and stuffed ornaments that could be knocked off (and some of them were on the ground already) but not defeated. The baby, awake in her infant carrier, was facing the twinkling lights, but her actual focus was up, into the face of Isaac's contented, drooling cat, who kept licking her downy little head like she was the bald kitten of his dreams.

"Uhm…," Isaac started, but Allegra raised her hand to shush him.

"Don't jinx it," she mumbled. "They've been staring at each other for an hour. It's been blissful."

Okay, then.

Isaac quietly set his briefcase down by the entryway and slid off his loafers. Then he hit the head, grabbed a handful of grapes from the fridge, and came back into the living room, silent as a, well, cat.

"Okay, honey," he murmured. "You go to bed now. It's Uncle Isaac's turn."

Allegra didn't argue, just shuffled off to get some uninterrupted sleep. Isaac peered at the baby again, who was now blowing bubbles at the cat, who purred back.

Well, alrighty. With a burst of optimism, Isaac picked up his knitting and grabbed the remote, turning on Christmas music while he worked.

While it was much too early for real smiles or actual laughing from a creature that was basically a boiled potato for another few weeks, Isaac watched as Blessing Noelle's eyes fluttered shut and she began to sleep, right there, in the middle of the living room, under the cat's watchful eye.

It was literally a Christmas miracle.

AND IT lasted. When Luca got home that night, Isaac was in the kitchen, cooking, while Blessing sat in her car carrier on the kitchen island and Euclid stared at her some more.

"Oh my God!" Luca said, taking in the scene. "And seriously— what are we having for dinner? It smells amazing!"

"Baked chicken," Isaac told him promptly. "With a butternut squash soup."

"Oh wow, what's the occasion?"

"This," Isaac said, giving him a happy buss on the cheek. "My boyfriend, a happy baby, a sleeping mom, and my idiot karma kitten, who apparently has magic baby powers that I'm not going to question."

Luca put his hands on Isaac's hips and stopped him for a better kiss, which Isaac didn't object to at all.

"Mmm...," Luca murmured. "I missed those. We need more of those. When does that happen?"

Isaac chuckled. "I seem to recall that Christmas vacation was like a sex oasis in the desert of the school year. Since we did pretty good in that department before the baby came, I'm going to hope we get a little bit of that mojo back."

"Ooh...." Luca waggled his eyebrows. "Sometimes it's just knowing you want it as much as I do that makes the wait worth it."

Isaac felt his face—hell, his entire *body*—light up. "You have no idea," he said seriously. "I-I mean, not to speak ill of the dead, but I swear his cock's stiffer now that he's a corpse than it ever was when he was a living human."

Luca's jaw dropped open in amused horror, and Isaac clapped his hand over his own mouth.

"I can't believe I...."

"Oh my God, did you really...?"

And then, whether it was the exhaustion (which probably prompted the comment in the first place!), or the end-of-the-semester celebration, or that giddy, brilliant happiness that came with Christmas and a baby and a stoned miracle in orange-boi fur, but the two of them burst into muffled giggles.

They couldn't howl with laughter—they *couldn't*—because the baby was happy and content and adorable, and the cat was still buzzing off whatever high he was riding that had prompted this glorious little reprieve from the colic gods, and it was *absolutely imperative* that nobody wake the baby.

But they couldn't hold it in either. Luca buried his face against Isaac's shoulder, and Isaac bit his own fist as they giggled, snorted, and sputtered as quietly as possible.

Which of course made the giggles last longer.

Finally, they slid exhaustedly down to the floor, their backs to the kitchen island, their breath still coming in bursts as the wave that had crashed so hard receded, leaving them tired and happy and the teensiest bit high from the endorphin burst of a really good laugh.

"I'm sorry," Isaac said in all sincerity. "That was unforgivable of me. I just… I had a really good day today, and I've, you know, put some of the bad stuff in my heart away in the appropriate cupboard. It'll still come out sometimes, because it's *there*, but it'll also get dusty and forgotten a lot because… time." He turned to smile at this glorious gift of a man. "And better memories blocking the cupboard."

Luca took his hand, lying limply on his own thigh, and kissed the back of it.

"Isaac," he said, "I know this is sort of a weird question, but what was your wedding like? I've only seen one picture of the two of you—it's on the tchotchke shelf by the TV."

"That's the wedding photo," Isaac said, thinking about the two of them, looking sober and awkward in their best suits. Isaac only wore that suit for other people's weddings and funerals. Todd wore them all the time, since he worked in banking. For Todd, it had been another Tuesday. "We made an appointment with the justice of the peace, and he brought his friend from work as a witness. Roxy and I weren't tight yet—friends, you know, but not 'Hey, come witness my wedding' level tight, so that was it. We had a wedding, went out to lunch, and then he went to work, and I came home because it was summer vacation."

Luca was frowning, his eyes a little glossy. "I want ours to be big," he said simply. "Not formal—not suits—but I want everybody. Like Allegra's birthday."

"It should be in early June," Isaac said dreamily. "And Allegra and I can learn to sew. We can make you and me matching Hawaiian shirts, and the kids, Roxy's too, can wear the same thing. Summer dresses for the little girls—"

"Hell, summer dresses for Allegra and Roxy!" Luca said, getting excited too.

"And we can have some sort of kiddie pool in the back so Roxy's kids can splash and get wet when it's over."

"I'll get us a barbecue as a gift," Luca said, "and we can roast dogs and burgers—"

"And guests can bring salads and potluck stuff instead of gifts!" Isaac added.

"And the guys from the shop—"

"And other teachers. I can invite Paula, because she's a friend now—"

"And we can have a party," Luca finished, nodding. "And we can celebrate it like we've been celebrating birthdays and babies and cats and people, like, from the beginning."

Isaac smiled, feeling boneless and hollowed out and filled with light. "It will be amazing," he said simply. "God, Luca. I love you."

"You'll marry me, right?" Luca said softly, like there was any doubt.

"In the sunshine with the kids and the sprinklers and the babies—"

"And a dog," Luca said.

"A dog?" Isaac asked, surprised.

"That cat is way too sure of himself," Luca said, nodding. "We need to get a dog."

And Isaac could see it, a big ugly brute of a dog with sweet eyes and a heart of mush and gold. "Of course we do," he said. "A big good dog."

"Yeah." Luca smiled and kissed the back of his hand again. "And you and me and cats and babies and dogs. It'll be a good life, Isaac. I swear. We'll have fun, and we'll have family, and we'll laugh and smile and make love. I promise. We'll put a whole lot of boxes in front of that cupboard, because I want to fill us both up with memories."

"Oh, honey." Isaac leaned his head against Luca's shoulder. "You already have."

At that moment, the stove timer beeped, and Isaac hurried to his feet to finish dinner while Luca set the table and roused his sister so her days and nights didn't get all topsy-turvy. But when they all sat around the table and chatted about their day, he didn't mention the wedding to his sister.

Isaac thought maybe he was waiting until they could start planning for it, or until Allegra looked a little more awake and the new-baby exhaustion was a little less weighty in everybody's bones. That was okay, though, because Luca hadn't broken any promises to Isaac, not in six months, not even when they weren't dating and were just… hopeful friends.

Isaac would trust that he would bring it up, and he had no doubts they would be happy.

Noelle ate after Allegra ate, and then her nightly fuss began. It was Luca's turn on the walking the baby up and down the floor, and Isaac was somewhat surprised when Luca climbed into bed next to him after a mere hour. He set the baby monitor up next to their bed, and Isaac asked, "What happened? Please tell me you didn't abandon the kid at a fire station."

"Naw," Luca murmured, running his hand over Isaac's stomach under his sleep T-shirt. "Kid fell asleep after an hour. I put her in the crib and came up here."

"To molest me," Isaac said, arching his back and asking for more touching.

"Wanted to prove your future husband has his priorities straight," Luca told him, and then they were kissing and sliding their clothes off and falling into each other's arms, but Isaac had heard the part about the "future husband," and he knew he'd been right not to panic.

Trusting Luca was so very easy to do.

THE COLIC gods had apparently smiled at them—or Allegra had figured out what to eat and what not to eat—because the next four days were a rather blissful period of the baby sleeping for four hours at a stretch, then waking up to be fed and sleeping for four hours again. Allegra started sleeping with the baby in the bassinet in her room full-time, because it was just as easy to wake up, nurse her, and go back to sleep that way, and they all got some much-needed rest.

It sure did make prepping for Christmas easier. There was fudge-making and cookie-baking and preparing for a simple meal of fried chicken and mashed potatoes on Christmas Eve. Roxy brought two salads, Nonna and Pop Pop brought a side, and everybody had cookies and sweets on hand for dessert.

The children got to open their presents from Isaac's family, and Roxy and Isaac exchanged gifts. Roxy gave him a gift certificate to his favorite yarn store. Isaac had been working on a lace-weight sweater for her on and off all year. There were other gifts—Allegra and Luca and Brian got into the act, and for a frantic, *joyous* time, the living room was full of ripped paper and happy exclamations and gratitude.

Then Roxy said, "Hey, guys, what about you? When are you opening your gifts to each other?"

"Tomorrow morning," Isaac said promptly, giving Luca a sideways look. He'd made Luca the requested watch cap—but he'd done some of the best colorwork of his life. The hat featured a delicate herd of reindeer on a snowy field of midnight blue. The pattern hadn't been easy, and Isaac had used scraps of the brown alpaca to emboss the deer in duplicate stitch across the background, but it had come out almost ethereally beautiful.

Like Isaac thought of his strong, kind, amazing lover. Perfect, and perfectly sweet.

Isaac wanted Luca to open it when they were alone together, because he knew—*trusted*—that Luca would know what an act of faith that hat was. Isaac was hopeful, so hopeful, that Luca would understand that every stitch was an act of love.

"Well, yeah," Luca said. "We got gifts for each other for tomorrow, but I got one I wanted to give Isaac tonight. When we're surrounded by family."

Isaac froze. Not in horror, but in hope. Really?

"Really?" he asked. "You're going to do this now?"

"Yeah," Luca said, going to the tree and coming back with a small box. Suddenly the once-chaotic living room grew absolutely still. Even the cat stopped battling paper in the pile, and little Noelle gave a hiccup in the middle of a fuss and was abruptly silent in Allegra's arms.

"Isaac?" Roxy asked, her eyes wide.

He held a finger to his lips. "Don't jinx it," he whispered. He was sitting in his usual chair, the one where he sat to knit, holding Patricia on his lap as she played with the doll Isaac and Allegra had picked especially for her. Roxy held her arms out for her daughter, and Isaac silently nudged the little girl until she ran across the room to where Roxy was sitting on a kitchen chair.

And then Luca was simply *there*, like he'd appeared in Isaac's life, except he was on one knee, holding the box out for Isaac to take.

"Really?" Isaac asked, wondering if astronauts could see his glow from space.

"Yeah," Luca said. "I… did you think that conversation disappeared into the ether?"

"No," Isaac told him truthfully as he began to rip little pieces of paper off the box. "I… but… you got them in four days?"

"Naw. I've had them since October," Luca said, ignoring Isaac's little gasp of shock. "I wasn't sure you were ready. But, you know. We talked, and I knew."

"Oh, you guys," Allegra breathed. "Stop telling each other secret stuff and let Isaac open that box!"

Isaac smiled up at her and got to the diminutive black velvet package of dynamite in the center. Too excited to build suspense, he popped open the lid, and there they were. Two rings in stressed multicolored gold. Isaac lifted one out, and it had a heart with Isaac's name on the inside, and Luca lifted the other out, showing Isaac a heart with Luca's name.

Luca held his ring for Isaac to slide on. "Yeah?" he asked.

"Yeah," Isaac whispered, and it wasn't until a hot tear splashed on the back of his hand that he realized he was crying.

His finger slid right in, a perfect fit, and he wondered if Luca had seen the other ring, plain gold, that he kept back with his cufflinks, because he hadn't wanted to wear it anymore.

Like a memory in a cupboard, brought out sometimes when it was needed, but collecting dust in the meantime.

Not this ring, Isaac thought, staring at it as it rested on his finger. This ring wasn't a memory in the cupboard. This ring was a living, breathing person who was now the other half of Isaac's heart.

"Good tears?" Luca asked, his voice thick.

"Good tears," Isaac confirmed, wiping his face with the back of his hand. "Kiss me now, when everybody can see, and it'll be official."

Luca leaned forward, eyes closed, the perfect prince.

And the cat leapt on top of his head, bounded off, and landed in the middle of the giant pile of paper again.

In the midst of shrieks of laughter, Luca finished the kiss, and Isaac fell into it.

This—*this*—was what happy ever after must feel like.

He couldn't imagine anything more.

Keep Reading for an Excerpt from
Bowling for Turkeys
by Amy Lane

A "Get Out of Bed" Surprise

"Get up."

"Mariana, no…." Milo knew he shouldn't have answered the phone—he *knew* it. Sure, Mariana Roberts was his forever bestie, the keeper of his secrets, and the sister of his heart, but… but… but *oh my God*, she was *so* much a lot!

"Mariana, *yes*!" she retorted with her usual terrifying determination. Mariana had been forced to drop out of college in her third year so she could help support her mentally ill sister. She'd taken a job on a hospital phone line and now made way more money than Milo did with his degree in graphic communications, and she often claimed that her major was in fixing people's lives.

She'd managed to fix her sister's; Serena now lived in an assisted care facility, where Mariana visited at least twice a week, and she apparently had friends and hobbies and was happy.

Since Mari was often cheerfully single—and Milo was *not* cheerfully *anything*—that left *Milo's* life to fix, and sadly, he was giving her a *lot* to work with.

"But Mari, it's *Saturday*," he whined, and knew it for a whine. "It's my day to lounge around and—"

"And skip out on lunch with your bestie, you bastard," she snapped.

He winced. "I'm sorry. You're right, I shouldn't have bailed on you—"

"Twice. You bailed on me *twice* since the breakup, and I get that I had to work overtime in September, but it's *October* now, and we haven't seen each other since your vodka-and-ice-cream pity party and… and *dammit*, Milo, I'm worried about you!"

Milo glanced around his duplex in a daze, noting the dead plants he'd meant to water, the laundry he'd meant to do, the dirty dishes he'd meant to wash. Hell, he was probably out of coffee, and he wasn't sure if there was anything in his refrigerator to eat. How was he supposed to "lie in" when there wasn't enough here to keep him alive? "Two months?" he asked, feeling stupid. Did Stuart break up with him two months ago? "It hasn't been two months, has it?"

Her sigh was eloquent. "Yes, baby. It's been two months. Now wake up and get out of bed!"

He did what she told him to because that was the pattern they'd established in high school. Mari made the plans, Milo carried them out. She was good at it, he thought wretchedly, trying to find a bare place on the carpet to place his feet.

"I'm awake," he told her crossly. "I'm out of bed. Now what?"

"Come answer your door, asshole. I've been here for ten minutes."

Milo's eyes went wide, and he cast desperate glances around his once-neat little duplex in panic.

"No," he almost whimpered, seeing the piles of dirty laundry draped on every surface of his bedroom. He was wearing his last pair of boxers, and his T-shirt was getting a little ripe. He knew without looking that the sink was piled high with dishes, his living room awash in a sea of takeout, and his kitchen table piled high with bills.

He was pretty sure his power was about to be turned off.

"Oh yes," she said grimly. "You thought you could curl up and die that easy? You've got another goddamned thing coming. Now come open your door. We're coming in."

"Wait," he said desperately, although the long habit of following Mari's orders seemed to have morphed into an actual magical compulsion. He was walking. Wow, had his laundry actually spilled into the hallway? And what the hell was that smell coming from the bathroom? Holy jebus, when had he last eaten? The food on the dishes in the sink was… well, uncomplimentary colors.

The only clean thing in the place was Chrysanthemum's food and water bowl on its little placemat in the corner of the kitchen, waiting for Stuart to bring him back. Milo almost paused there, but Mari squawked from the front door.

"Get out here, you coward! I'm not going anywhere!"

Which was how, through the wreckage of a life he'd once been proud of, he slogged, hating himself more with every step.

What kind of loser let his life get this disgusting in so short a time?

By the time he opened the door for Mari and hung up his phone, he was almost in tears, ready to confess to the sin of giving up completely and beg for her help to clean up his mess.

But Mari was not alone.

"Here," she said, shoving a leash into his hand. "Go sit on the couch while I go get shit from the car." She stood on her tiptoes and peered past his shoulder, her bright brown eyes inquisitive and judgy. "And it's exactly as bad as I knew it would be. Jesus, Milo, you couldn't have called me before it got this bad?"

"I didn't know it had gotten this bad," he said muzzily, staring at the creature on the end of the leash. Lean and muscular, with the head of a pit bull and the body of a… kind of stocky Chiweenie? The dog had short white-yellow hair with flat pit-bull eyes and Chihuahua ears.

She was staring at him quizzically from under a cat-eared headband.

"Mari?" he called to her as she hustled out to her sedan, which sat right behind his in the driveway. "What in the hell is this?"

"Your dog, Milo," she called back. "She's here to replace Chrysanthemum."

Milo glanced down at the unimpressed dog wearing the cat ears. "I don't remember asking for a dog," he told the dog. "I don't remember putting in an order."

The dog nuzzlcd his shin, and he bent down and fondled her ears. She gave him a tentative look of "like," and he fondled them some more, which is what he was doing when Mari hustled past him, her arms full of grocery bags—one of which was emanating a very… promising smell.

"Now sit down, Milo," she commanded. "I've got your breakfast—or lunch or last night's dinner…." She peered at the mess in the sink with a practiced eye and then squinted at the takeout containers in the living room. "Oh, Milo," she said with a sigh, "you haven't eaten in *days*, have you."

"Maybe three," he hazarded. He had a distant memory of somebody putting a sandwich in his hand as he sat at his desk during his one mandatory in-person appearance at work that week.

"Yeah," she sighed. "I'm sorry I was so late. Now sit down on the couch. I'll give you some food—you too, Julia—and we'll have a talk before we tackle this place."

Milo opened his mouth, and she said, "But in return you have to take a shower and brush your teeth."

"Okay," he said, cowed. He glanced down at the dog. "Julia?" he asked, and the dog didn't twitch a whisker.

"That's what the shelter named her," Mari said cheerfully, setting the bags down before getting to work doing something bustling and organizational. "My sister's roommate's brother called me up to ask me if I could adopt an animal, but, as you know—"

"You have the county allotment of cats," he said dutifully.

"I have *over* the county allotment of cats," she agreed. "Mostly because Georgie has snuck me a couple of extras." A ginormous breakfast burrito, with chorizo and hot sauce and about a dozen scrambled eggs wrapped inside with tater tots, appeared in his hand, and he doggedly munched while she went back to the kitchen.

Mari worked from home too, which gave her lots of time to clean cats and feed cats and make rugs and beds for cats and generally pour all the love in her formidable soul into the apparently *more* than five cats that had taken over her small house.

"Georgie?" he asked, lost already.

"Serena's roommate's brother, who is sort of a derpy hottie, and we may end up sleeping together," she told him bluntly. It was a trait that had cost her more than one boyfriend, but then, Milo knew none of those guys were good enough anyway.

"You have two more cats—" Oh Lord, this burrito was everything that was right with the world. Every word he said was through a mouthful of eggs.

"Three," she said. "He's got a thing for cats with one leg or no eyes or tails that have been chewed off. I'm telling you, if you can resist a cat with a chewed-off tail, you're a monster, and I want nothing to do with you."

"And yet," he said, watching as Julia—freed of her leash—was currently rolling in a pile of blankets that were possibly the only clean things in the duplex, "you didn't bring me a cat, which I know how to care for—"

"A"—she said, still bustling. He couldn't look at her anymore. She seemed to be simultaneously putting dishes in the dishwasher, cleaning up takeout containers, and stacking mail on his table—"cats need very little in the way of care. If I gave you a cat, you would feed the cat and let it crap on all your stuff and forget to feed yourself, and then when you died you'd be glad the cat survived on your eyeballs. No. A cat is not high enough maintenance for you right now."

"And B?" he asked, watching as Julia found one of Chrysanthemum's toys under the pile of blankets. Tentatively she shook it and was rewarded when it squeaked. Her eyes opened in joy, and she shook her head, squeaking it some more.

"Julia was found two weeks ago," Mari said, her voice getting a little lost among a clatter of kibble in a stainless-steel bowl.

Julia stopped her assault on the squeaky toy enough to trot into the kitchen, searching for the source of that familiar noise.

"So…?" He sounded dubious—and he was—but he still watched the creature to see if she would eat and drink from Chrysanthemum's bowls.

"See her tummy?" Mari said patiently, bending to fondle Julia's ears as she came to eat. "See the elongated nipples?"

Milo grimaced. "I didn't want to say anything in case it made her self-conscious."

"How very kind," Mari told him, and she may have rolled her eyes at him, but she was continuing to pet the dog, so Milo couldn't see. "But yeah. She'd had a litter, and she *mourned* her litter for her first week and a half, and Georgie said she was getting depressed, because maybe she got dumped because the puppies were cuter and everything she loved had just gotten, you know…."

"Yanked away," Milo said, suddenly desolate. Because that's what it had felt like when he'd gotten home that first week in August to find that Stuart had taken all his stuff, including his ugly table lamps and his weird art on the walls and the half-grown cat Milo had gotten them to celebrate their first anniversary three months earlier.

"Yeah," Mari told him, suddenly bending over the back of the couch to hug him. She dropped a kiss in his greasy hair, and his eyes were blurry for a whole other reason besides hunger. "Just like you," she said softly. "And that's why I brought her."

Milo took a gulp of air, hoping he could maybe not cry. "Why the cat ears?" he asked.

"Because you've never had a dog before," she told him. "I thought maybe they'd make it easier to adapt."

Milo nodded and felt another sob coming on. "Oh Jesus. Mari, can I go cry in the shower?" Because he *really* needed the shower.

"No," she said softly. "You acted so together in August. I should have known you weren't. You cry right here."

And he did, Mari's arms around his shoulders, until Julia, still crunching on kibble, jumped onto the couch and rested her chin on his knee.

EVENTUALLY MILO stilled, wiped his face on his filthy shirt, and managed to struggle up to excuse himself to the bathroom.

When he got there, he flushed the toilet (which helped with that awful smell) and scrounged up a towel that wasn't mildewy before jumping in the shower.

He had to wash his hair with hand soap because he was out of shampoo, but at least he still had toothpaste when he got out. His beard tended to be scraggly and patchy anyway, so the electric razor took care of that, but unfortunately all that self-care forced him to *look* in the mirror.

Ugh. No. His face was thin to the point of gauntness, his cheeks sunken, his eyes—which were usually an attractive almond-shaped brown—also sunken, his skin practically green.

Yeah, he wouldn't want to shag himself either.

Out in his kitchen he heard Mari, still clattering, and thought of how busy her life was, and how she'd taken a special day here to wade through his trash and do a wellness check on her jerk of a friend who had blown her off for a month.

At his door he heard a tentative scratching sound, and surprised, he opened it.

Julia was sitting there, staring up at him with those oddly shaped flat eyes, her cat ears still firmly in place. He couldn't tell if she was reproachful because he'd locked her out or irritated that he'd gone somewhere she hadn't, but something told him the two of them were now bound inextricably in the mutual endeavor to make sure Mari hadn't wasted her time.

"Well, old girl," he said softly, bending to scratch her behind the ears, "I think we're about to become a thing."

She snorted and walked toward his bedroom in a slow, stately gate unlike any Chihuahua or Chiweenie he'd ever met. He didn't even want to look to see what he had clean.

"Oh my God," Mari said when he emerged, carrying a load of laundry. "I can't… I can't even…."

"Bella Vista Broncos," Milo said grimly. "I swear to Christ, they're the only clean things in my drawers."

"Who keeps their gym clothes from high school?" she demanded. "Milo, you're *twenty-eight years old.*"

"They were almost the last things in the drawer," he said. "Everything else was from before my growth spurt in eleventh grade." He glanced down at his bright blue sweats, grimaced, and in a conspiratorial whisper, added, "I'm going commando."

Mari put her yellow-rubber-gloved hand over her eyes. "Oh my God."

He scowled defensively. "Remember those times in college when I carried you over my shoulder to your dorms?" he asked. "You've puked on my ass, Mari. *Puked on my ass.*"

She took her hand off her eyes and grinned at him. "That's my Milo," she said, and he could swear she had hearts in her eyes. "I knew you were here somewhere. Good. Now I've already got a load of your bathroom stuff in, so set that down on the washer and go through your bills. Jesus God, I can't even believe you held down a job in this mess."

Milo tried not to groan. "Well, God bless working from home," he said frankly before going through the connecting door to the garage and doing what she'd suggested with the laundry. When he'd climbed back up into the kitchen, he surveyed the mess again and let out a breath. "Believe it or not, I think I've gotten a few promotions."

"Aw, my poor little graphic artist," she chided. "Did you get all lost in your head to avoid your broken heart?"

"I'd tell you to go to hell," he said, although they both knew he wouldn't, not in a thousand years, "but…." He glanced around his duplex, thinking about the carefully chosen area rug and the leather furniture, the bright contrasting tiles on the floor, and the big holes in the wall where Stuart's hideous "art investments" had been.

"I don't know, baby," she said with a sniff. "You've been here for two months. How's the view from hell?"

"Boring," he said, thinking about the artwork. He had his own in the garage. He should put that on the walls tomorrow. He resolved to do that. By himself. "Lonely," he admitted, sitting at the table with a sigh. She shoved his empty recycling bin next to him in a helpful manner.

"You want some music?" she asked. "Or a movie for background noise?"

"The *Star Trek* reboots," he said promptly.

"Three comfort movies coming up," she said.

They knew the dialog by heart.

MARI COULDN'T stay over on his couch that night because, in her words, she had eight furry food-vacuums she had to care for. Apparently two of the new ones needed medication too.

But by the end of the day, he had clean clothes for a week and more in the laundry, a clean kitchen, a bedroom he could walk through, and groceries.

And a dog.

Julia had followed them both throughout the day, watching them with interested, calculating eyes, and accepting their shows of affection with a sort of genteel grace.

It wasn't until they sat down in the evening, both physically tired from cleaning and emotionally exhausted from hauling Milo inch by inch from the quagmire of his depression, that she showed any real personality at all.

"I'm sorry, Mari," Milo said as she leaned on him and they watched the sun set through his newly fluffed and aired curtains. "I didn't mean to suck up your time. You barely have enough as it is."

"Shut up," she mumbled, digging in. She wasn't tall or wide, but she had a sort of weight about her that was, he suspected, entirely muscle and determination. It probably didn't show up on a scale, but when she nestled, she *nestled*. "I should have seen it in August. I was busy, and God, Milo. You're such an easy-care friend most of the time. *I'm* the one who needed the trip to rehab in college. *I'm* the one who needed her hand held at the abortion clinic when Calvin the creep bailed on me. This isn't a sorry. It's not a you-owe-me. It's me being your Mari and you being my Milo, okay?"

He swallowed. "You'll always be my Mari," he whispered.

Stuart hated her. Milo remembered all the times he and Mari had met for lunch or gone to the movies, and Stuart hadn't known he'd been with his bestie. Had never suspected either. One or two cutting remarks about, "Your little phone-clerk friend," had made Milo simply… not involve Stuart in his life outside of Stuart. Thinking about it now, about how Stuart *hadn't* liked Mari, *hadn't* understood the two of them, their bond through high school and into college, through life changes and beyond—that should have clued him in, shouldn't it?

It wasn't even that Milo had lied, it was that Stuart had made him. Milo had *told* Stuart that he and Mari had come as a matched set, and Stuart had laughed and said sure, any friend of Milo's was a friend of his.

And then Stuart hadn't approved of her, had asked Milo to blow her off, had made whiny punkass bitch noises when Milo had said, "Okay, I'll hang out with her. You don't need to."

And Milo had found it very easy to not involve Stuart with this part of his life.

Which was ironic seeing that Milo's relationship with Mari had gotten so tight because that's exactly what Milo's parents had done to *Milo*. Just… just *not involved* themselves with Milo's life.

"We understand you feel compelled to live this lifestyle, Milo, but don't expect us to be involved in it."

So they hadn't met Stuart, hadn't approved of Mari either—something about her father working as a garage mechanic—and had mostly sent him birthday cards and invited him to Christmas dinners they'd been relieved he hadn't attended.

"Milo?" Mari said softly. "Why did Stuart leave? You never told me."

He sighed, remembering their last terrible fight when Stuart found out Milo had been giving money to help her keep her sister in a good care home for mentally ill adults since she'd first found the place.

"And I never will," he said now, holding her tighter. "It's not nearly as important as you coming here today."

She might have pressed the matter then—he knew it—but they both heard the noise at the same time.

"What the…?" Mari said, peering into the kitchen and frowning. "Julia, quit that with the dog bed. What are you…? Oh."

Milo looked too and was surprised.

"What does she have?"

Julia trotted back to the couch where they sat, very pleased with herself, and Mari started laughing.

"Oh," she said, clearly surprised. "It's… see, I got sort of a new-dog bundle? You've got a plastic container of food and a list of vet's appointments and a bed and blanket for her, and I put that cat toy she liked and a few other dog toys in the bed, and it was *under* some stuff, and she dug it out. Wow."

"Wow what?" he asked as Julia began to gnaw at the bright yellow, soft-plastic thing in her mouth, her movements getting more and more gleeful as it made more and more noise.

"I've never seen a dog that into the squeaky toy. I mean… *look* at her!"

Shake-shake-shake-shake-shake! She was growling and shaking, and then to Milo's delight, she rolled over to her back and pawed the air, the squeaky still squeaking as she indulged in an ecstasy of "kill the squeaky!"

"Julia," Milo said with authority. He'd never owned a dog, but he assumed they responded to their names. "Julia, come here. Give me the squeaky!"

She did.

Mari burst out laughing, holding her hand to her mouth. "Oh my God! Lookit her! Throw it!"

The living room had a little bit of length on it, but with a turn, he could get the thing down the hallway from where they were sitting. He put a bit of spin on the thing, and it bounced off the hardwood floor in erratic loops as Julia—

Vroom!

"Wow!" he laughed. "*Wow*. Julia, *wow!*"

She was *so* fast and muscular and happy and excited to chase that wobbly, oddly shaped squeaky piece of rubberized plastic. She brought it back to him, and he went to take it, but she growled playfully and shook her head. He tugged on it, and she tugged back, and in a moment they were wrestling over the squeaky toy like they'd been wrestling buddies their entire lives.

"C'mon," he begged. "C'mon, girl. Give it back. Give it—"

"Drop it!" Mari commanded with authority, and Julia let go immediately, then sat back on her haunches, gazing hungrily from the squeaky to Milo's face and back again.

Milo turned for the windup, Julia got into position like a race car, and he threw it again.

Their sad, tired conversation forgotten, Milo and Mari threw the squeaky toy to the joyful dog for the next hour, until she didn't bring the thing *back* but simply dropped it in the middle of the living room and stretched out at their feet.

"Wow," Milo said, staring at her.

"I'm saying," Mari echoed. "I-I mean, I had dogs all my life, but I've never seen one so… so *dedicated* to the squeaky toy."

Milo stared at her and smiled. "She's got a one-track mind," he admitted, but that was fine. He felt like he already knew this dog.

He felt like they could be friends.

MARI HAD to leave shortly thereafter, but not before they both ate leftovers and she wrote out a schedule for him so he could take care of the dog and then come back and work and then take care of the dog and himself some more.

"She's going to ruin your stuff," she warned. "She's going to chew on your coffee table, your shoes, your rugs, your furniture. You are going to have to figure out when to put her outside to poop in the backyard, but go out with her first or she might escape."

He held his hands to his heart. "Escape," he breathed. "But she just got here! I *want* her here. How do I stop that from happening?"

"Take her out on the leash at first," Mari said patiently, "then take her around and look for hazards. Where can she get out? Where's the dirt soft? Where are there gaps? She'll probably tell you where the worst ones are, but use your imagination. Pretend you're a dog whose sole obsession is a squeaky toy, and that uses up your walnut-sized brain."

"Oh…," he said uneasily. "Mari, my brain isn't much bigger."

She smacked him. "Oh my God, Milo. You are *so* much smarter than that. That's your problem. You could never *see* why you were better than Stuart on any given day. He never deserved you."

"He was rich, he was handsome, he was—"

"A fucking putz," she said viciously. "Stuart was a fucking putz. Screw him." She scowled. "He was your first big relationship postcollege, and I get it. He was your Calvin."

Milo scowled back. "I still maintain that man would have looked a lot better with a price on his head."

She nodded, her short black curls dancing around strong features and snapping brown eyes. "*Now* you're seeing my side of the Stuart equation." She stood on tiptoes to kiss him on the cheek, and because she was Mari, she didn't bother to wipe her lipstick. That was her claim to Milo right there. He was hers for life.

Then she was gone, leaving him alone with Julia, who stared at him with the same sort of interest he was showing her.

"You ready to explore the backyard?" he asked dubiously, but when he picked her leash up from the kitchen chair, she trotted right to his feet, ready to do just that. He grabbed a roll of poop bags and headed for the sliding glass door, ready to embark on his new adventure.

Stuart, he thought grimly, would have *hated* this dog.

He was pretty sure he loved her already.

A week later, he knew he did—although he was also sure she was trying to kill him.

Following Mari's carefully made schedule, he'd been taking her walking at the nearby park in the morning. The first day he'd had to stop every ten feet because apparently your body didn't forgive you for going to bed for two months and not getting up. The second day he'd hurt even more, but by the third he'd figured out that Julia had a… glitch.

She was fine, sort of. She didn't mind the leash, but she didn't understand it. She'd race behind him to sniff from the retaining wall to the grass or to scope out what was on the side of the walkway that looped around the park. Once she'd almost castrated him when she'd been behind him—and he'd had his arm behind his shoulder to accommodate that—and she'd seen a squirrel cross his path on the walk.

And then right when he thought he had a handle on how to get her to walk by his side, the leash would fall gently across her posterior, and she'd stop. Just stop, like a game of freeze tag with rules only she knew.

Milo tripped on her once and went sprawling, and she'd huddled abjectly under the leash, looking like she expected him to *whip* her with it.

He'd sat in the middle of the sidewalk and pet her until she stopped shaking, and then, unmindful of the blood on his palms or the holes in his old high school sweats, he'd picked her up and carried her the rest of the way.

So he was a little desperate the next day. For one thing, he wouldn't be able to take her walking the day after. It was the in-house day at his ad firm, and while he'd bought a sort of dog box and put a dog bed in it, which she seemed to take comfort in when he was home and could leave the door open, he wasn't sure she'd be so comfortable locked in the thing for an eight-hour day. He was contemplating barricading her in the kitchen with the dog-box cage thingy so she could maybe do less damage to the couch and the coffee table, but he still didn't like the idea of leaving her alone. Should he maybe leave the television on?

So whatever he was going to do, he needed to make sure *today* was a good day. Which was why, as he walked around the completely empty park, he had an idea. He took her to the middle of one of the soccer fields first, hoping that if this went horribly wrong, he'd be able to get a head of steam on her and body tackle her if he needed to.

Then he unhooked her lead.

She sat there untroubled and gazed at him, waiting for further instructions.

Then he wandered down toward the walkway, and she… well, wandered with him. She was fine. She'd run up ahead a little, then stop and smell the flowers or the sticks or the other dog's pee, and then wait for him to catch up. It was… *pleasant*. It was *blissful*. She was *so good*.

And then the most magnificent thing happened. The park had several sections, all of which were looped by the walking/riding path. He and Julia wandered the whole of the loop, from a rise on which picnic tables and bathrooms and a child's play area were set up, down past the soccer field, around a little wooded area, and around and back up the rise. On the other side of the rise was another soccer field, bracketed by a tennis/pickleball area way down the parking lot.

On this day as the sun leveled itself on the misty October field, Milo topped the rise by the picnic area and was confronted with, of all things, *turkeys*. A good two dozen of them!

At first he was amused. Oh my God, lookit the lot of them! Then he was horrified. Oh no, Julia!

Frantically he grabbed for her collar as she buzzed past his shins and onto that calm, strangely bucolic field of oblivious wild birds.

"Julia!" he called frantically, charging after her. Oh no! She'd eat them! Or they'd eat her! Or—oh God, oh—

"Oh my stars," he breathed. "Lookit you *go!*"

She never caught one. She wasn't even trying. She just raced from turkey to turkey, barking until the birds scattered, running from one end of the field to the other. She was so *happy*!

Milo stood, helpless to stop her, and watched a creature absolutely in her element, and while he *should* have felt bad for the turkeys, all he could think was that his dog was happy. *So* happy.

Without warning, a laugh snuck up his body, shaking his stomach until it ached, and he *howled* with it, feeling as happy and as free as his idiot dog—and for all he knew, as the turkeys, who once they stopped running, didn't seem particularly bothered by her.

He laughed until she slowed down and trotted to his side, panting happily. He put the lead back on her, a day late and a dollar short, perhaps. But still….

He'd forgotten how drunk you could get, how intoxicated, how shitfaced silly and oblivious, all by another creature's joy.

Writer, knitter, mother, wife, award-winning author Amy Lane shows her love in knitwear, is frequently seen in the company of tiny homicidal dogs, and can't believe all the kids haven't left the house yet. She lives in a crumbling crapmansion in the least romantic area of California, has a long-winded explanation for everything, and writes to silence the voices in her head. There are a lot of voices—she's written over 120 books.

Website: www.greenshill.com
Blog: www.writerslane.blogspot.com
Email: amylane@greenshill.com
Facebook: www.facebook.com/amy.lane.167
Twitter: @amymaclane
Patreon: https://www.patreon.com/AmyHEALane

THE 12 KITTENS of CHRISTMAS

AMY LANE

Killian Thornton likes his downtown life, tending bar, and enjoying time with his friends and community. He'd given up on passion long ago—he wasn't cut out for grand romance or dramatic gestures. Then one night, in a characteristic act of kindness, Killian offers his couch to help a friend's little brother find his feet in a new city, and everything Killian thought he knew about himself and his little life gets turned upside down.

Lewis Bernard, the funny, quirky guy happy to find a spot on Killian's couch, can't believe his luck. After being forced to flee his parents' house, he was afraid of what came next, but Sacramento seems to be treating him just fine. The stunningly handsome bartender who lives downstairs from his brother offers Lewis his couch and doesn't even balk when Lewis discovers two abandoned kittens in a vacant lot as they walk home.

Vet bills, cat food bills, litter boxes—none of it was on Killian's Christmas agenda, but he jumps in gamely to help because all the shelters seem to be full, and that's just the kind of guy Killian is. But kittens can multiply faster than rabbits, and Killian and Lewis accidentally rescue more and more cats.

Lewis starts to panic. He really wants to know Killian better, but with each act of kindness, Lewis falls further in love while ruining Killian's life. How can Killian find time to fall in love with Lewis and ask him to stay if they're inundated with destructive furry poop-machines who all seem to need a home before Christmas?

FOR MORE
OF THE BEST GAY ROMANCE